BARBARA NADEL

DEADLINE

An **INSPECTOR İKMEN** mystery

headline

First published in 2013
by HEADLINE PUBLISHING GROUP

First published in paperback in 2013
by HEADLINE PUBLISHING GROUP

1

Cataloguing in Publication Data is
available from the British Library

ISBN 978 0 7553 8890 5

Typeset in Times New Roman by Palimpsest Book Production Limited,
Falkirk, Stirlingshire
Printed and bound in Great Britain by
Clays Ltd, St Ives plc

HEADLINE PUBLISHING GROUP
An Hachette UK Company
338 Euston Road
London NW1 3BH

www.headline.co.uk
www.hachette.co.uk

Trained as an actress, Barbara Nadel used to work in mental health services. Born in the East End of London, she now lives in Lancashire and writes full time. She received the Crime Writers' Association Silver Dagger for her novel DEADLY WEB.

Praise for Barbara Nadel:

'Nadel's evocation of the shady underbelly of modern Turkey is one of the perennial joys of crime fiction'

Mail on Sunday

'The delight of Nadel's books is the sense of being taken beneath the surface of an ancient city which most visitors see for a few days at most. We look into the alleyways and curious dark quarters of Istanbul, full of complex characters and louche atmosphere'

Independent

'A colourful and persuasive portrait of contemporary Istanbul'

Literary Review

'Nadel's novels take in all of Istanbul – the mysterious, the beautiful, the hidden and the banal. Her characters are vivid. A fascinating view of contemporary Turkey'

Scotland on Sunday

'Nadel makes full use of the rich variety of possibilities offered by modern Istanbul and its inhabitants. Crime fiction can do many things, and here it offers both a well crafted mystery and a form of armchair tourism, with Nadel as an expert guide'

Spectator

'The strands of Barbara Nadel's novels are woven as deftly as the carpet at the centre of the tale…a wonderful setting…a dizzying ride'

Guardian

By Barbara Nadel

The Inspector İkmen series:
Belshazzar's Daughter
A Chemical Prison
Arabesk
Deep Waters
Harem
Petrified
Deadly Web
Dance with Death
A Passion for Killing
Pretty Dead Things
River of the Dead
Death by Design
A Noble Killing
Dead of Night
Deadline

The Hancock series:
Last Rights
After the Mourning
Ashes to Ashes
Sure and Certain Death
A Private Business

This book is dedicated to my
wonderful 'other family' in Turkey.
You're brilliant and I love you.

Cast List

Police

Inspector Çetin İkmen – middle-aged İstanbul police detective

Inspector Mehmet Süleyman – İkmen's protégé

Sergeant Ayşe Farsakoğlu – İkmen's sergeant

Sergeant İzzet Melik – Süleyman's sergeant

Commissioner Ardiç – İkmen and Süleyman's superior

Dr Arto Sarkissian – police pathologist

Commander İpek – Special Forces

Bowstrings Theatre Group

Alp İlhan/İzzedin Effendi – founder of theatre group

Ceyda Ümit/Nuray Hanımefendi – Alp's girlfriend

Söner Erkan/Yusuf Effendi – theatre group member

Kenan Oz/Avram Bey – theatre group member

Metin Martini/Dr Enzo Garibaldi – theatre group member

Nicos Bey – theatre group member

Esma/Sarah – theatre group member
Deniz/Sofia Hanım – theatre group member

Other Characters

Lale Aktar – crime writer
Dr Krikor Sarkissian – Arto's brother, an addiction specialist
Caroun Sarkissian – Krikor's wife
Burak Fisekçi – Krikor's assistant
Hovsep Pars – an elderly Armenian
Samsun Bajraktar – İkmen's cousin
Ersu Nadir – maître d'hôtel at the Pera Palas
Saffet Güler – concierge at the Pera Palas
Ali Farsakoğlu – Ayşe Farsakoğlu's brother
Nar Sözen – a transsexual
David Bonomo – official at the office of the Chief Rabbi
Nurettin Akdeniz – ex-convict
Muhammed Ersoy – inmate of Silivri Prison, İstanbul
Kemal Aslanlı – Muhammed Ersoy's cousin

In spite of the pain, Çetin İkmen found his surroundings fascinating. Lying on a narrow, metal beam, he had one arm and one leg one side, one arm and one leg the other. Underneath him and illuminated from below, somehow, was a dome. Studded with star-shaped holes and jewelled with exquisite stained glass, it looked like the sort of dome one sometimes saw in a hamam.

However, lack of steam and/or the smell of soap, shampoo and cologne seemed to suggest that he wasn't hanging over the roof of a Turkish bath. In fact he wasn't actually outside in the open air at all. He was inside a building, a vast one, and his ribs and his lungs hurt as he tried to hold his position on the beam without crashing through the dome below. It wasn't easy.

In spite of a certain woolliness about the brain, a single thought did keep on presenting itself to him and that was the one about what would happen if there was an earthquake. The city of İstanbul was certainly due another large quake, everyone, including geologists, said so. The last really big one had happened back in 1999. İkmen tried to recall, without at first any success, what today's date was. The year 2010 was in there, but when in 2010?

He looked at the dome, lit from below, underneath him and tried to breathe as normally as he could, but without much success. His chest was being crushed by the beam; slowly but surely he felt it killing him. If a quake came, it could be a mercy, in a way.

How had he come to be in such a position? He was in mortal danger and, as far as he could tell, he was entirely alone in, if he strained his neck from side to side to look around, some sort of big, luxurious palace. What was someone like him doing in such a place? And then he remembered. Oh, yes, it was 12 December. It was his birthday. Nothing good ever really came of those, in İkmen's experience. And true to form, someone had just tried to kill him.

Chapter 1

Thirteen Days Before

'You know I can't stomach that sort of thing, why do you insist on putting me through it?' Çetin İkmen asked his friend Arto Sarkissian.

The light was fading quickly over the Bosphorus and the two men were the last customers remaining outside on the İstanbul Modern Café terrace. But then İkmen, at least, nearly always took his food and drink al fresco these days. Since 2009 it had been illegal to smoke in enclosed public spaces anywhere in Turkey. It was a law that, even as a serving police inspector, he hated.

His friend, a small, round Armenian, like İkmen of a 'certain age', smiled. 'It's all for charity,' he said. 'Think of it as a duty, if that helps.'

'Yes, but it's "fun" too, isn't it?' İkmen growled. He put his cigarette out in the ashtray in front of him and lit up another.

'You make it sound like abdominal surgery,' Arto said. 'Fun is supposed to be a good thing.'

'Huh!'

One of the waiters appeared and automatically gave Arto the bill for their coffee and glasses of wine. İkmen wasn't surprised that he didn't so much as give him a second look. His suit was crumpled and he reeked of tobacco. He was an old-fashioned Turk, an anachronism amid a race of people who were rapidly, at least in İstanbul, becoming very glossy. Even Arto, his oldest and dearest friend, had a sort of groomed patina. But then he was a doctor, albeit a pathologist, and so maybe he was taking something to make himself look that way. Some wonder drug.

'I don't like organised fun,' İkmen continued. 'It makes me anxious.'

'It's supposed to relax you,' Arto said. Then looking at him narrowly, he said, 'Would it help if I said it would be good if we had a representative from the police department at the event?'

'Mehmet Süleyman's going, he can do that.'

Arto looked at the bill and then placed a 50 Turkish lire note down on the table to cover it. The waiter, who had been hovering, whipped it away immediately.

'I know for a fact that Fatma is going to stay with her aunt in Bursa that week,' the Armenian said. 'She goes away that week every year.'

'For which I am always grateful. My wife is a very understanding woman.'

'You'll be alone, you can't cook . . .'

'I'll be alone as I always am!' İkmen said. 'I like it like that, you—'

'You invite Krikor and myself to some dreary bar in Sultanahmet – if you remember,' Arto interjected. 'If it crosses your mind to invite your own brother it's a miracle and I'm not sure that any of your more recent friends even know when your birthday is. As far as they're concerned you age in one long, unregarded and continuous stream of time.'

'Which is how I like it.'

'It isn't normal.'

'Whoever said that normal equals good?'

'You should at least allow your children to celebrate your birthday,' Arto said. 'They're your children! They love you. I'm sure they'd like to, at the very least, take you out for a meal.' Then he looked at the skinny, smoking figure across the table from him and added, 'Not that eating is really what you do.'

İkmen smiled. They'd spent a happy day together until the subject of Arto's brother Krikor's latest fund-raising event had arisen. Ambling around the İstanbul Modern gallery had been exhilarating for İkmen. Not that he understood what all the pictures, photographs and installations were really about. But in a country that in recent years had been ruled by a government with Islamic roots, an avowed secularist like İkmen felt cheered by the sight of artworks depicting things like sex, sexuality and dissent.

'If Krikor's project is to provide facilities to immigrant as well as Turkish addicts then it needs more money,' Arto said.

'Five thousand Turkish lire each, at least,' İkmen said. 'That's what this "fun" of yours will cost.' Then he shook his head.

Arto leaned across the table. Out on the Bosphorus the sound of a single ferry foghorn signalled that the night was destined to be one of dampness, mist and coughs. 'I said I'd pay for you and I will!' Arto snapped. 'It is my birthday and Christmas present to you!'

'But Arto, I'm not a Christian, I don't—'

'Oh, yes, and I'm in church all the time myself!' Arto leaned back in his chair and crossed his arms over his chest. 'Christians give presents to each other and to non-Christian friends because it is one of our traditions,' he said. 'As well you know.'

'Yes, well . . .'

'Çetin, it will be amazing,' Arto said. 'Krikor and his staff have engaged a professional acting troupe. Lale Aktar will be there. Lale Aktar!'

'So if Lale Aktar is there, I won't need to be,' İkmen said. 'Let the great novelist do her stuff.'

'Oh, Çetin, don't be childish!'

'Arto, why would I want to go to some play about murder? On my birthday? I deal with the real thing.'

Arto Sarkissian looked across at the Asian shore of the Bosphorus, now just very gently softened by sea mist. Both he and Çetin had been born over there, a long time ago. He turned back to his friend and said, 'It's for all the people who walk around this city with untreated sores from infected needles. For the kids from Romanian orphanages who sniff glue, for the girls who sell themselves for the price of a fix. Krikor never turns anyone away from his clinic. All they have to do is want to get clean. Money isn't an issue.'

'Except that it is.'

'If he's to carry on helping people with their addictions, yes, it is for Krikor,' Arto said. 'He doesn't have any more capital.' His brother, an addiction specialist, had already ploughed most of his own considerable fortune into his substance abuse clinic in the İstanbul district of Beyazıt. 'This city's population grows every day and so, unfortunately, do the number of addicts on the streets. Çetin?'

İkmen looked up and breathed in the dank, moisture-soaked air deeply. He believed in everything that Krikor Sarkissian was doing. Of course he did! He just didn't want to go to his extravagant fund-raising event. As well as being really not at all his kind of thing, the last time he had attended one of Krikor's fund-raisers it had led him, albeit coincidentally, into the life of a murderer whose crimes still, sometimes, haunted his sleep. But that had been nothing at all to do with Krikor Sarkissian or his very worthy project.

İkmen pulled a grumpy face (mainly because he knew that Arto would expect it of him) and said, 'OK, I'll come.'

Arto Sarkissian smiled as the evening call to prayer wound itself around them from every part of the city.

Inspector Mehmet Süleyman looked through the open door into Çetin İkmen's office and stared at the elegant woman looking intently at her computer screen. She appeared completely calm, absorbed and at peace with herself.

It stunned him. How could she be like that? In just over three weeks' time she, Sergeant Ayşe Farsakoğlu, was going to marry a man who looked like a 1970s Arabesk crooner – all moustache, jutting stomach and machismo. Why?

'Er, Sergeant Farsakoğlu . . .'

She turned round and smiled. 'Sir?'

Why he'd spoken at all, Süleyman didn't know. Maybe it was just to see her face. But that was ridiculous. He'd got over his brief affair with Ayşe Farsakoğlu years ago. But now he'd caught her attention, he had to find something to say.

'Where is Inspector İkmen?' he asked. He could just as easily have called or emailed and he knew she knew that.

'It's the first of December, sir,' she replied.

'Ah.' He felt stupid. If he could, Çetin İkmen always took 1 December as leave. Everyone knew that. It was World Aids Day and he liked to spend time with one of his cousins who had apparently lost someone or other to the disease. Nobody, including İkmen, ever really spoke about it.

'Can I help you with anything, Mehmet Bey?' Ayşe asked.

For a moment he'd almost forgotten she was there. Slightly flustered, he said, 'Er, no. No thank you.'

She turned her beautiful face back to her computer screen and resumed whatever it was she had been doing.

The reason behind his agitation over her fiancé was, Süleyman acknowledged, a source of shame. Since the collapse of his second marriage, Süleyman himself had been single and he had harboured some idle fantasies that Ayşe Farsakoğlu might throw herself at him again as she had years before. Not that he actually wanted a *relationship* with her. But she hadn't come anywhere near him. She'd gone to his sergeant, İzzet Melik, who was ugly and poor – and kind. Much as he tried to convince himself otherwise, Mehmet Süleyman knew that İzzet, in spite of his unappealing outward appearance, was also educated and had a deep appreciation of culture, especially Italian culture. Originally from the coastal city of İzmir, İzzet had been tutored in all things Latin by an elderly Italian Jew.

When they'd had their brief relationship, over a decade ago, Ayşe had been the one who had mourned its demise, not him. But now Süleyman wondered. He wondered what life would have been like had he stayed with Ayşe instead of marrying the volatile half-Irish psychiatrist, Zelfa Halman. But if he'd done that, his son, Yusuf, would never have been born and there was no way he would wish that boy away. He, if nothing else, was the light of his existence.

But his pride was still bruised. If Ayşe Farsakoğlu had wanted a man, why had she not come to him? He was good-looking, successful and he came from a well-connected if admittedly impoverished Ottoman family. But then he remembered how his Ottoman roots had frightened Ayşe all those years ago. Whether she had felt unworthy of him or just alarmed by his noble pedigree, he could no longer recall. But he'd been with his first wife back then, his cousin, Zuleika, who very shortly afterwards had divorced him. At the time there had also been an awful case involving a man who had been to his school. A lot had been going on. His recollections of that time were hazy. None of that, however, shed any light on why Ayşe was choosing to marry a man who looked like a particularly unkempt rural taxi driver. Could it possibly be that, even after all these years, it was to spite him?

There was a march down İstiklal Street and then a rally in Taksim Square, but Samsun Bajraktar didn't want to go.

'Why should I share my grief with a load of young people and politicos?' she said bitterly as she sat down on her tattered leather sofa and lit a cigarette. 'Anyway, I can't walk any sort of distance in my new boots.'

'World Aids Day is a time you should get out there, Samsun,' İkmen said.

'And get beaten up by the police?' she sneered.

İkmen drew hard on his cigarette and smiled. 'You think I'd let that happen?'

'It happens all the time to people like me! Even now! Even in lovely, fluffy democratising Turkey!' She threw him a look that could probably have severely wounded a lesser man. 'If we're lucky we just get laughed at!'

A long time ago, pre some very expensive Italian surgery, Samsun had been a man called Mustafa. The son of Çetin İkmen's maternal uncle Ahmet, like the rest of that family she was originally Albanian. Now in her early sixties and living just opposite the Grand

Bazaar in a small, lately rather down-at-heel flat, Samsun existed as a lone transsexual without her deceased lover, the leather merchant, Abdurrahman. He had died of an Aids-related illness five years before. Every 1 December, World Aids Day, Çetin İkmen spent time with Samsun, drinking, smoking and remembering her one true love, who had ultimately betrayed her.

'I'd walk with you,' İkmen said.

Samsun ignored him. The first of December was difficult because of what Abdurrahman had brought into their lives. The Aids virus had been hard for her. That she had not contracted it from him had seemed like a miracle for a long time – until she had read more about the disease and come to realise just how difficult it could be to catch. How Abdurrahman had caught it and from whom was still a mystery and that was a big part of Samsun's problem.

'How could he have done that to me, Çetin?' she said as she raised a large glass of brandy to her lips and then drank.

İkmen, who heard the same thing from Samsun every December, shook his head. He didn't know any more than she did. But Abdurrahman had been a big, good-looking and well-off man – many years Samsun's junior – and so temptation would have been put in his way. A popular leather merchant and former grease wrestler, he had never been shy about either his bisexuality or his legendary prowess in bed. But he'd made a commitment to Samsun, which he had broken even if he had left her all his worldly goods, which included this small flat. But then she, and only she, had nursed him through his final illness. İkmen hardly dared to imagine what she had seen and experienced. It was part of the reason why he always made time to see her on this day. He admired her courage and he loved her.

As usual, he said, 'I don't know.' And as usual she didn't listen.

'We were in love! Why did he need anyone else? I didn't.'

There was no answer. Samsun began to ramble on about how she had tried to stop Abdurrahman straying with spells and charms. Like İkmen's late mother, she practised witchcraft even though, a lot of the time and especially with Abdurrahman, it had appeared to be useless. Now, at least in her own mind, she was old and past her best and faced a future of unwanted singledom, alone in her little flat opposite the Grand Bazaar.

İkmen, as he always did, attempted to nod his head and shake it in all the right places. She was set to get roaring drunk and go on for hours and he'd support her through that. But İkmen actually had other things on his mind. This coming birthday took him up to fifty-nine. Just one year before sixty when, according to his brother Halıl, he would no longer be able to claim to be middle-aged any more. He'd be old. He'd qualified for his pension years before but had chosen to carry on working. How would his employment play out when he was sixty? He didn't know and so he thought about other things. Then his actual birthday and what it was going to consist of this year crashed back into his consciousness again and he felt himself begin to get angry.

In the normal course of events he would have spent his birthday alone, or with friends, getting quietly drunk while Fatma and their youngest child, Kemal, visited Fatma's ancient aunt in Bursa. Revelling in lonely misery was something that İkmen actively looked forward to. But not this year. This year his best friend had paid for him to have a treat. A gourmet meal and a night in one of İstanbul's most prestigious hotels. Oh, and something called a 'murder mystery' was going to happen too – all under the gaze of Turkey's youngest and most sensational crime writer, Lale Aktar. He'd seen her on TV a few times and she came across quite well, if rather flirtatiously. All he could hope for was that the great and the good who went to the event gave generously to Krikor Sarkissian's free drug and alcohol clinic in nearby Beyazıt. That, after all, was the point of the whole sorry affair.

He looked up at Samsun who was still drinking, smoking and going on about Abdurrahman. The last time Krikor had organised a fund-raising event of this magnitude, Samsun had only just met her now dead beau. Then the event had been held in a palace on the Bosphorus. This time another type of palace was involved.

Chapter 2

Eleven Hours Before

Getting out of the taxi, she tried to look cool – as if she had been going to such places all her life – and she achieved her aim. But try as she might, when she looked up at the historic and magnificent façade, she knew that this hotel was just about as far as anyone could get from her old village back home in Anatolia. This was the Pera Palas, where people arriving in İstanbul via the Orient Express would stay back in the first half of the twentieth century. It was the hotel where Mustafa Kemal Atatürk, founder of the Republic, liked to stay, where King Edward VIII of England had slept, as well as Greta Garbo, Ernest Hemingway, Mata Hari and Jackie Onassis. But most importantly for crime novelist Lale Aktar, the great English crime fiction writer, Agatha Christie had stayed here too. And she, Lale Aktar, a woman from the back end of nowhere, was going to spend a night in what had been her room.

As Lale walked underneath the brightly lit canopy towards the gleaming, art nouveau entrance, the door into the hotel quietly and seemingly automatically opened in front of her. A young man, wearing the smart grey Pera Palas uniform, said, 'Good morning, madam. Welcome to the Pera Palas. May I take your bag?'

Lale gave her small, lightweight suitcase to him without a word. She looked at her surroundings – exquisite marble flooring, doors and fittings of highly polished oak and mahogany, even a brightly decorated Christmas tree – and she thought, *I've arrived*. Even though she was Turkey's bestselling crime author and she was married to one of the country's most wealthy men, only now, here, did she feel she had *actually* arrived. It was just a pity her stay at the hotel was going to be so short.

A woman called Canan from the hotel's publicity department was waiting for her in the lobby and, together with the young porter, they all got into the creaking wood and wrought-iron lift. An original artefact from way before the recent hotel refit, it dated back to 1895 and had been used by everyone who had ever stayed here. Canan urged Lale to sit on the velvet seat at the back of the lift and then the porter closed the wrought-iron gates and they began to ascend.

After a moment, unable to contain her excitement any longer, Lale said, 'I never thought I'd stay in the Pera Palas. Not me.'

Canan smiled. Was it an indulgent smile? Lale couldn't tell. All she knew was that for a girl from her village to be able to read, much less write a book, was totally miraculous. But then if she hadn't run away from that hot, baked nowhere to İstanbul, would she have even thought about writing a book? Probably not.

The lift passed beyond the first floor and made its way towards the second. What she could see of the hotel was big, opulent and bright. Two years ago, Faruk, her husband, had taken her to Paris for a weekend. The Pera Palas reminded her of that city.

The lift stopped at the fourth floor. The porter opened the doors for her and Lale stepped out on to a sweeping oval concourse lined with guest rooms and decorated with furniture and artefacts from the hotel's illustrious past. In the middle, a great open space was cordoned off by an ornate, metal scrollwork banister. Lale looked up and saw that the roof of the hotel was made of glass. The sun was shining and it lit up everything it touched. They walked along the right-hand side of the gallery until the porter stopped in front of room 411. As he opened it with a key card, Canan turned to Lale and said, 'I hope you find the room inspiring, Mrs Aktar.'

'I'm sure I will.'

As the porter pushed the door open to reveal the antique furniture and modern fittings inside, Lale began to shake. Only very vaguely did she later recall Canan saying, 'Dr Sarkissian sends his greetings and says that he will meet you for tea in the Kubbeli Saloon at three o'clock, provided that is convenient.'

'It is.'

Lale moved into the room and came to a halt in front of a large, backlit photograph of a rather motherly looking woman in late middle age. Canan, smiling, said, 'I will leave you alone now, Mrs Aktar. Enjoy the room and if you need anything, please do not hesitate to call.'

'Thank you.'

The porter left, followed by Canan who, just before she closed the door behind her, said, 'You know, Mrs Aktar, Agatha Christie's room is supposed to be haunted. I hope you're not afraid of ghosts.'

Lale looked away from Agatha Christie's portrait for a moment and said, 'No. Ghosts don't bother me at all.'

'Happy birthday, Dad!'

Ever since he'd gone to live and work in England, Çetin İkmen's eldest son, Sınan, had always celebrated his father's birthday by phoning up and joyfully shouting his good wishes at him. It was touching, if annoying, especially if it happened when he was in his office.

'Yes, thank you, Sınan,' he said. 'It's very good of you to remember.'

Ayşe Farsakoğlu, who was fully aware that it was İkmen's birthday but knew better than to allude to it, looked up at her superior's disgruntled face and suppressed a smile. As far back as she could remember he had been a lugubrious man. Devoted to his wife Fatma and their children, a loyal and generous friend, he was nevertheless not one for outward displays of joy or big celebrations. Ayşe smiled in his direction.

İkmen ended his call from his son and looked at her. 'Yes?' he inquired.

'Oh, I was just feeling jealous about your stay at the Pera Palas,' she said.

'Were you?' İkmen sniffed disconsolately. 'If it's any help, if I could give my ticket to you, I would. I fail to see what all the fuss is about. My daughter Hulya got married at the Pera Palas.'

'But, sir, it's had a total refit since then,' Ayşe said. 'It's really fabulous now.'

'You've been there?'

'With Sergeant Melik,' she said. 'We looked at the ballroom as a venue for our wedding but . . . But it was too expensive.'

'Huh!' İkmen grunted. 'These sorts of places are always the same. They'll give a prominent man like Krikor Sarkissian the whole place for a night free of charge—'

'But, sir, it's for his charity, not for Dr Sarkissian personally,' she said. 'I think it's very generous, especially so close to New Year when they must have so many requests for accommodation.'

'Mmm.' İkmen was unconvinced. 'Anyway, no one needs their wedding to be wildly elaborate.' His certainly hadn't been. 'I think the venue you have chosen is very nice. I'm looking forward to it enormously.'

He wasn't and she knew it. But she was grateful and honoured that he and his wife had agreed to come. The small boutique hotel in Sultanahmet she and İzzet had chosen was pretty and had wonderful views of the Bosphorus and the Sea of Marmara from its terrace. But it wasn't *grand*. It didn't make a statement and it wouldn't impress Inspector Mehmet Süleyman even though he wasn't coming. Although why *that* bothered her . . . But it did and she knew full well why it did.

'What time are you leaving to go to the hotel?' Ayşe asked to distract herself from issues she didn't want to think about.

'Six,' İkmen said. The whole horrible social thing

started with a champagne reception in the Orient Bar at seven thirty. Before that he had to check into his room and climb into the awful tuxedo that Arto had made him hire. Mehmet Süleyman was going to look like a god in his tux, of course. He was handsome. İkmen knew that he would look like a skinny, rumpled old peasant wearing his 'best' suit for his son's wedding. But then he was a peasant, albeit a very well-educated urban one.

'I won't be happy until I'm back at this desk tomorrow morning,' İkmen continued.

'After a wonderful hotel breakfast, I hope, sir,' Ayşe said. 'When I went to look at the ballroom, one of the catering managers showed us the breakfast menu. They have everything. Nut preserve, can you imagine it? Things you've never heard of! Circassian smoked cheese . . .'

'Oh, well, I must make a point not to miss that under any circumstances,' İkmen said.

Ayşe knew he was being sarcastic.

'But at least the Pera Palas has one advantage,' İkmen said.

'What's that?'

'On certain floors you are still allowed to smoke in the rooms,' he said. 'I'm on the fourth floor where smoking is permitted.' Then he smiled. 'Now that is worth, in my opinion, many, many smoked Circassian cheeses.'

* * *

Dr Krikor Sarkissian was much thinner and had a lot more hair than his younger brother Arto. Unlike the pathologist, his patients were the living, if only just. Drug addicts and alcoholics. In spite of the hike in alcohol prices introduced by the current, Islamically influenced government, people still routinely used drink or drugs or both to escape their troubles. Life in the big city was fast and tough and could be stressful, especially if one was poor, even more so if one was an immigrant – Roma kids from Bulgaria and Romania, Russian and Czech prostitutes, and now also refugees from places like Iraq and Syria which, some said, was only just managing to keep a lid on internal dissent. They came, they stayed, they worked – or not – and sometimes, often, they resorted to alcohol or heroin just to keep themselves together.

Krikor had started his charitable foundation, in the form of a free addiction clinic, back in 1998. He'd obtained government support as well as gifts, stipends and the proceeds from numerous fund-raising activities from companies and wealthy individuals. But in the past twelve years, the problems as well as the numbers that the clinic had to deal with had increased. Now more money was needed and so he had used his own and his friends' considerable influence to organise what should be his most valuable fund-raiser yet. He'd started negotiations with the owners of the Pera Palas a whole year in advance of the refit which had finally been completed in September. Eventually a date, 12 December, had been selected and the hotel had agreed to host the event free of charge. Drinks and a meal would be served, which would be paid for by the guests. Certain key members of Pera Palas staff would work the event for free (casual labour would make up the rest of the staffing), as would Turkey's principal crime writer, Lale Aktar. The young company of actors would be paid.

Blonde and slim and groomed, Lale Aktar walked towards Krikor across the parquet floor of the Kubbeli Saloon and he stood up to shake her hand.

'Lale, it's so nice to see you again,' he said. 'I really do appreciate you taking the time to do this.'

She smiled. 'It's my pleasure,' she said. They both sat down.

'Would you like afternoon tea?' he asked.

She looked at the vast display of French patisserie, macaroons, Turkish pastries and sandwiches on display and then said, 'No, I'd just like a cup of tea, thank you, Krikor.'

'Are you sure?' He was too embarrassed to order the full Pera Palas afternoon tea experience just for himself but he knew she would not change her mind. When Lale Kanlı, as she had been then, had first come to İstanbul she had been a rather overweight girl with very bad teeth. But Krikor's old friend, the music promoter Faruk Aktar, Lale's husband, had taken care of both those issues. There was no way Lale would jeopardise her sleek new look.

Krikor ordered just tea for both of them and then Lale said, 'Faruk sends his best wishes.'

'It's a shame he can't be here too.'

She shrugged. 'He's looking for the next big club act. Somewhere down in the Hatay.'

'Young people make music everywhere,' Krikor said.

'And so here we are,' Lale said. 'I Googled that theatre company we're having tonight.'

He smiled. 'The Bowstrings.'

'Yes. How gruesome to name yourself after an Ottoman instrument of execution.'

'Ah, but the bowstring was only used on princes,' Krikor said. 'Not for the likes of you or me. I think the name is great for a company that specialises in murder mystery evenings.'

'Their literature says that they put on a sort of play, where a murder or murders are committed, and then the audience have to try and solve it.'

'Yes.'

The waiter arrived with their tea, which came in a silver teapot with bone china cups. When he'd finished serving them, he took a vast plate of chocolate pastries over to a large table of Russians who, between them, took the lot. Krikor envied them.

'The way we're going to do it is we'll split our guests up into investigative teams,' Krikor said. 'One team will be led by an İstanbul police inspector called Mehmet Süleyman and the other one will be led by you.'

Lale laughed. 'Eek! Up against a real policeman.'

'It's just a bit of fun,' Krikor said, knowing full well that if Mehmet Süleyman's team lost to one led by a crime writer, it would drive him insane. 'It doesn't matter who solves the crime as long as it is solved. You know Burak Fisekçi?'

'Your assistant. Yes.'

'Well, the murder mystery element of the evening is actually his baby and so he will speak to you before we begin later this evening. He's much more au fait with it all than I am.'

'But the play or whatever you call it will happen after the meal?'

'Most of it, yes,' Krikor said. 'I didn't want one of those stupid little murder mystery dinner things where someone just drops apparently "dead" beside the cheeseboard. This is a proper puzzle that you and the other guests will have to think about. People are donating large sums of money to the clinic, I have to give them something decent in return.'

'So, no pressure, as the Americans say,' Lale said.

Krikor laughed. 'Not on you, I hope, Lale,' he said. 'It is, like I said, meant to be fun.'

'Oh, I'm sure it will be, Krikor,' she said. 'I'm really looking forward to it. I do hope that we manage to raise the money you need and more too.'

Krikor sipped his tea. 'Well, your time, and I know you have so little of it these days, is appreciated, as is Faruk's considerable contribution.'

'We both like to do what we can.'

A waiter went by with a tray of cakes so heartbreakingly beautiful, Krikor had to actively stop his mouth from watering.

'You do such a lot for the disadvantaged in this city,' he said.

She lowered her eyes, her face suddenly grave. 'Only because I've been where they are,' she said. 'I've been poor and homeless and I know only too well about the temptations that can lead such people astray. If it hadn't been for Faruk . . .'

'Your talent would have shone through anyway!'

But she didn't respond to Krikor's jolliness with a smile. Instead, she said, 'I don't think that's really true.

You know, Krikor, my father was sent to prison when I was ten and he's still there. People like me do not get anywhere without people like Faruk and you. It just doesn't happen. We have to claw our way out.'

He was on the same floor as Çetin İkmen although not, thankfully, in the same room. Mehmet Süleyman looked around his elegant magnolia and grey deluxe hotel room and lit a cigarette. He opened the French windows on to his balcony and the sound of the early evening traffic swept in at him like a noisy wind. The sun was just setting over the Golden Horn and the city looked both exciting and comforting to him. He'd never lived anywhere except İstanbul and for all its massive increase in size and population, it was still essentially the same city he had been born into back in the 1960s. And the Pera Palas Hotel had been part of that. As a child, his mother had brought himself and his brother Murad to the hotel with her when she met her friends for afternoon tea. Back then it had been a neglected, slightly dusty place populated by rather odd foreign tourists and members of İstanbul's faded Ottoman remnants – like his family. He and Murad had usually amused themselves going up and down in the antique lift. The lift attendant, an elderly man, as Mehmet recalled him, had been both very patient with them and appalled.

Mehmet finished his cigarette out on the balcony and then went back into his room. There was a fabulous shower in the white marble bathroom and so, once he'd hung his suit up in the wardrobe, he took his clothes off and washed. The pressure of the hot water on his face and body was so much more vigorous than that of the one he had at home. His parents' bathroom was ancient and scruffy and neither he nor they could afford to do anything about it. Quite apart from the maintenance he paid to his ex-wife for his son Yusuf, Mehmet had to run a car, pay rent to his parents and try to have some sort of life in what was becoming an expensive city. There was no money left over for bathrooms.

He washed his hair, which he noticed by the very strong lights in the bathroom had become even more grey of late. Soon he'd have to decide whether or not he was going to dye it. But if he did that he knew that Çetin İkmen, if no one else, would laugh at him. The older man was just letting age happen to him. İkmen was really getting quite old now and Mehmet wondered, not for the first time, how much longer he could or would carry on working. It wasn't a thought that he found pleasing in any way and so he pushed it out of his mind. He had to stay focused. The main thing about this upcoming event was to solve the 'crime' that the theatre

company were going to stage and win the admiration
of Lale Aktar. Now there, according to her publicity
photographs, was a good-looking woman. And
married to a man who was not only old enough to be
her father, he was old enough to be Mehmet Süleyman's
father too.

Chapter 3

The Event

The late shift was going to consist of a largely casual skeleton staff who would come on at 11 p.m. when the meal was over and the murder mystery show was in full swing. Then the fun would really begin. The guests didn't have a clue what sort of spectacle they were in for. Or how much physical activity. The dinner menu included an extensive meze, lobster, lamb shank in pomegranate molasses, a range of desserts and cheeses, not to mention different wines with each course, which would mean that most of the guests wouldn't be in any shape to run about much. But then that was all part of the fun.

People were going to be talking about Krikor Sarkissian's fund-raising event at the Pera Palas Hotel for ever. It was going to be one of those occasions when individuals would ask each other, 'Where were you when you first heard the news about that nightmare that took place at the Pera Palas Hotel?'

'Can I get an Efes?'

Arto Sarkissian raised his eyes to the ceiling in despair. Warm and comfortable in the convivial surroundings of the Orient Bar, cushioned by soft, velvet-covered furniture and mingling with some of the most glamorous and interesting people in the city, he was being, to his mind, unnecessarily hassled by his oldest friend.

'You want beer?' he asked.

'I don't like champagne,' Çetin İkmen said. 'It gives me hiccups.'

Arto shook his head. 'Just go up to the bar and ask for whatever you want,' he said. 'They have Efes Pilsen, they have everything; drinks both lavish and plebeian.'

'OK.' İkmen eased past a very influential media couple and made for the bar. As soon as he'd got his beer, Arto knew that Çetin would take it outside into the cold so that he could smoke. He was fifty-nine years old this very day and he was still behaving like some sort of intellectual working-class snob. He wouldn't drink champagne, especially not with the glitterati, because he didn't approve – of either the drink or those who drank it. But they were the ones, at the present time, who made the world go round and Çetin, Arto felt, really needed to get used to it. It was all about celebrity now.

'Doctor?'

He looked round and saw a very smartly dressed Mehmet Süleyman standing next to him. Champagne glass in hand, he represented the type of person the Pera Palas had been built for. In a way no less of an anachronism than Çetin İkmen, the easy grace and lack of glitz of a true Ottoman gave the Orient Bar a touch of regal class.

Arto Sarkissian smiled. 'Inspector.'

'Is that Hovsep Pars?' Süleyman asked, pointing to a very small man sitting alone in one of the distant corners of the bar.

'Yes.' Arto looked down.

'I thought he didn't go anywhere since . . .'

Arto shrugged. 'Family tragedies happen,' he said. 'One must carry on and live one's life.'

'Yes, but he—'

'What Hovsep's sister and her husband did was nothing to do with him,' the doctor cut in. 'It's just tragic that it has taken him such a long time to come to terms with it. If indeed he has.'

They both looked at the small, lonely man, his head down, concentratedly drinking his champagne.

'He came for Krikor,' Arto said. 'Not as a fellow Armenian or even as a man of wealth, but because he loves my brother. Everybody does.'

Çetin İkmen, now furnished with a glass of Efes Pilsen, caught Süleyman's eye and nodded his head towards the back of the room as he made for the exit.

'I think Çetin wants me to go outside and have a cigarette with him,' Süleyman said to the doctor.

'Are you going? I'd deem it a favour if you did. He's so uncomfortable here.'

Süleyman smiled. 'What a strange world we live in, Doctor, where Turks must smoke in the cold.'

He started to make his way out of the bar but then suddenly he stopped. In common with everyone else in the Orient Bar, Süleyman stared at the tall, elegant figure of a woman dressed in a full-length golden evening gown. Slim and beautiful, her shining blonde hair, which came down to her shoulders, was swept dramatically to one side in a Veronica Lake style, hiding her left eye almost completely. For a moment nobody spoke. Then conversation started again and the woman glided up to Krikor Sarkissian and kissed him. Süleyman walked back to Arto and said, 'Is that Lale Aktar?'

'Yes,' Arto said. 'Beautiful, isn't she?'

'Even more beautiful than in her photographs!'

'And married too, Inspector,' Arto said with a smile. 'Faruk Aktar is a personal friend of Krikor's.'

The warning duly noted, Süleyman went to the back of the bar and followed İkmen out into the cold.

* * *

She knew how to work a room.

'So here he is, the person behind the murder mystery theme,' Krikor heard Lale Aktar say to Burak Fisekçi, his assistant. She gave him her hand which Burak gallantly kissed. An ugly lump of a man, Burak seemed both flattered and appalled by her attention, probably because it made people look at him. Krikor saw his usually sallow complexion turn bright red.

'Dr Sarkissian did most of the work,' Burak said.

'He doesn't give himself enough credit,' Krikor said to Lale. 'If it hadn't been for him, this evening would just have been a simple dinner party. He is my right hand.' Krikor patted his assistant on the shoulder. Then he turned away and introduced Lale to some of his other guests. He watched her charm them all. It was as if she'd been doing this sort of thing all her life. Sometimes it was quite difficult to remember that Lale Aktar's first book had only been published five years before.

Written using her unmarried name of Lale Kanlı, *The Çukorova Mystery* had been a minor literary event. Some critics likened her work, which was exciting but conventional, to that of Agatha Christie. But then she'd met Faruk Aktar, married him, and everything had changed. Her next book, *Screams in the Night*, had been about a serial killer in a small Anatolian village. What so captured the public's imagination about this book was that the killer was a woman who liked to torture her victims. Illiterate and furious, the vengeful widow Handan, the anti-heroine of *Screams*, had been an instant sensation. Feminist groups loved her, ministers of religion and other conservative elements saw the character as a threat, and Lale courted even more controversy when she told the press that some elements in *Screams* were derived directly from her own village background. She'd been raised around illiteracy, forced marriages, honour killings and dangerous folk beliefs that included the likening of strong, independent women to witches.

By the time *Screams* came out, Lale was slim and polished and Faruk had made sure that every liberal media tycoon was right behind her career. Her life was charmed and she knew it. Lale – and Krikor admired her enormously for this – didn't just give money to the charitable causes she supported, she got stuck in. As well as taking time to visit his clinic, she volunteered with a scheme that fed the homeless, visited prisons and hospitals, and continued to write ground-breaking crime novels that challenged the status quo. Occasionally Krikor found himself wondering what, if anything, she did for her family back in her village, or indeed for her father who was serving a sentence for an unspecified crime in a prison somewhere in Anatolia. Krikor never asked her about it and, as far as he knew, neither did her husband.

'Krikor, where's Arto?'

She was back at his side with a champagne flute in her hand.

Krikor looked around and saw his brother leaning up against the bar talking to a small man wearing a red cummerbund.

He pointed. 'Over there.'

'Is that his friend Çetin İkmen with him?' she asked.

Krikor looked back just to check and then said, 'No. I think that gentleman may be something to do with the Chief Rabbi's office. We have several representatives from the rabbinate here tonight. I think that Inspector İkmen is probably outside smoking. Why?'

She smiled. 'I've heard Arto talk about him and I noticed from my list that he's on my investigative team.'

'Is he?' Arto laughed. 'Oh, what a naughty man my Burak is to put Çetin in opposition to his colleague Mehmet Süleyman.' He looked around to try and see where Burak Fisekçi had gone, but he'd sloped off somewhere, probably in an attempt to be alone. Events like this were not easy for him.

'Well, don't change it now, Krikor,' Lale said. 'If I've got a police officer on my team then I'm not complaining.'

* * *

'I want to win for my own self-esteem,' Süleyman said.

It was cold outside the hotel and a light mist was beginning to come up from the Golden Horn. But Süleyman and İkmen, together with other small groups of guests who were also braving the weather, had to smoke somewhere.

Shuffling stiffly from foot to foot in an attempt to keep warm, İkmen said, 'You sure it's not to impress the famous novelist?'

'Well, yes, that too . . .'

'She is married,' İkmen said.

'I know that!'

'Yes, and I know you, my dear friend,' İkmen said. 'Neither time nor misfortune seems to have impinged on the effect you have on women. But I don't have to tell you how bad—'

'Yes, yes, I think I know by now just how tediously disapproving you are of my private life.' He took a drag from his cigarette and then said, 'I'm not going to make a pass at Lale Aktar, Çetin. Apart from anything else, why on earth would someone like her even be aware of a penniless policeman like me?'

'Because you are the opposing team leader.'

He shrugged.

İkmen raised a warning finger. 'Competition can be very erotic,' he said. 'That which we are not can be highly alluring. I shouldn't have to tell you this. Your second wife was a psychiatrist.'

The slightly pained and also chilled look on Çetin İkmen's face made Mehmet Süleyman smile. İkmen really didn't want to be anywhere near this event and so he was complaining about everything and everyone. In an attempt to lighten the mood, Süleyman said, 'What's your room like?'

'I can smoke in *there*,' İkmen said gloomily.

'Yes, but what's it—'

'It has a bed, a bathroom and a cupboard to hang my normal clothes up in,' İkmen said.

There was going to be no lightening his mood, clearly, so Süleyman stopped trying. It was at times like this that the younger man felt the difference in age between them most acutely. İkmen had always been irascible but now that trait was magnified and also he was much more vocal about what he liked and didn't like. Formal occasions were not for him and formal occasions allied to 'fun' were positively poisonous.

And, of course, it was İkmen's birthday. Süleyman knew it, the Sarkissian brothers knew it and everyone, as usual, was tiptoeing around it, and İkmen, as if it was just another day. Mehmet Süleyman put one cigarette out, lit another and then watched what looked like a group of goths get out of a taxi and go into the hotel.

They were, he imagined, the Bowstrings, the murder mystery theatre troupe.

The Grand Pera Ballroom was set up for the banquet which would consist of five courses plus coffee and petits fours. There were a hundred guests who would be seated at round tables set with either six or eight places each. To cater for such numbers was a major, almost military operation, which fortunately boasted an ex-solider as its orchestrator. Ersu Nadir had been a professional soldier for twenty-five years before he became maître d'hôtel at the Pera Palas. Now a handsome and highly organised fifty-year-old, he inspected every place setting on every table while his waiting staff looked on, barely daring to breathe. Ersu Bey was not one to find fault where none existed but if he did find anything wrong he would not hesitate to point out the error to whoever was responsible in front of the whole banqueting team. Finally finding himself satisfied, he called housekeeping to come and brush one of the Murano chandeliers just one more time, then he went into the adjoining Aynalı room where the theatre group had just arrived. To Ersu Bey they looked like a bunch of anarchists.

'Hello, I'm Alp,' a boy who Ersu Bey thought was probably no more than twenty-five said.

'Sir, I am the maître d'hôtel, Ersu Nadir.' He bowed.

'Is it OK if we use this room to get changed in and sort out our stuff?'

'Of course.'

There was one girl and a couple of slightly older women with Alp, plus four other men, and Ersu Bey did wonder whether he should ask if they'd like separate changing facilities but then he noticed that they were already getting undressed. Theatrical people did things like this. On the one hand, he approved – had not Atatürk himself declared that men and women should be equal? – but he was also very embarrassed.

'So what is this, er, this *performance* you are giving tonight?'

'We're doing a piece I wrote myself,' Alp said. 'It's based, loosely, on the novels of Agatha Christie and it's set in the nineteen twenties. We're all playing characters staying here at the hotel. I'm called İzzedin Effendi, I'm a former Ottoman prince, Ceyda there is my wife Nuray Hanımefendi, plus we've İzzedin's younger brother, Yusuf, an Armenian called Avram Bey, a Dr Garibaldi, an Italian, the owner of the hotel, Nicos Bey, an American governess, Sarah, and the housekeeper Sofia Hanım.'

'So one of these characters is killed?'

'Yes.'

'Where is your Hercule Poirot, your Miss Marple or whatever?'

'Ah, it is for the guests to discover who killed whichever one of the company is 'murdered,' Alp said. 'There will be clues both in our performance and scattered throughout the hotel.'

'I see.' Ersu Bey didn't really approve. But then he was hardly on board with either the murder mystery evening or Dr Krikor Sarkissian's drug clinic. In Ersu Bey's opinion, drug addicts belonged not in hospital but in prison.

'We're scheduled to start our performance at ten,' Alp said.

'But you and your company will eat with the guests.'

'Yes. We'll mingle, in character, then when the meal is over, when the coffee is being served, our performance will begin in earnest.'

Ersu Bey didn't even pretend to understand what that meant. No performance area had been set up and so he couldn't really picture what was going to happen. However he smiled and said, 'Well, sir, I will be working until eleven this evening and so if I can assist you in any way at all, please don't hesitate to ask.'

'Thank you. Er, do you know where Dr Sarkissian is?'

'In the Orient Bar, sir. Would you like me to get him for you?'

'Well, actually it's his assistant Burak Bey I really need to speak to,' Alp said. 'Mr Burak Fisekçi.'

Ersu Bey smiled. 'I will have him paged for you, sir.'

'Thanks.'

When Ersu Bey had gone, Alp looked at his colleagues and they all laughed.

'I thought,' one of the women said, 'that men like him were dying out.'

'Oh, no,' Alp said. 'Men like him will always be with us.'

Chapter 4

Ayşe Farsakoğlu looked up at the famous hotel façade and squeezed İzzet Melik's arm a little harder.

'I'm sorry, it was just impossible,' he said. 'But the Emperor Alexis will be nice too. We have the bridal suite, which overlooks the sea, and Fevzi Bey is providing wonderful food.'

'And we've the klezmer band.'

'And we have Sefira, the klezmer band! Everyone will eat, drink, dance and we'll get married and live happily ever after.' He kissed her. 'We will, you know.'

'Yes.' Ayşe looked into his eyes and smiled. 'I love the Emperor Alexis, İzzet, don't think that I don't. It's just Çetin Bey was so grumpy about coming to the Pera Palas tonight it made me angry.'

'He's grumpy because it's his birthday.'

'I know, but he was dismissive about this place too,' she said. 'Going on and on about how he'd rather be at home and couldn't wait for it all to be over. Poor Dr Sarkissian!'

'I think that the doctor and his brother are used to Çetin Bey by now,' İzzet said. 'What worries me is what will happen if Inspector Süleyman doesn't win this detection contest or whatever it's called.'

'Murder mystery evening.'

'If a crime novelist, a woman, beats him, he'll be unbearable.'

'Yes.' But secretly, Ayşe hoped he'd win anyway. She smiled and said to İzzet, 'I love you.'

'I should hope so,' he replied. 'You're marrying me.'

They shared a brief hug and then Ayşe looked at her watch. They were due to meet her brother in nearby Nevizade Alley at sometime between seven thirty and eight. It was nearly seven forty-five now.

'We'd better go,' Ayşe said. 'Çetin Bey and the others will have just sat down for their five-course meal.' She looked through the windows in the art nouveau front doors of the Pera Palas at the smartly dressed security personnel and the arch of the metal detector they operated. 'They're going to have lobster,' she said. 'I like lobster.'

İzzet laughed. 'Well, how will stuffed mussels do as a substitute?' he said. 'Those I can promise you.'

She paused for just a moment then she kissed his cheek and said, 'I love stuffed mussels.'

'Well, that's settled then.'

They began to walk away. But then a taxi pulled up right in front of them, forcing them to stop. İzzet instinctively held Ayşe close. It was dark and there was no need for the taxi driver to pull up so far on to the pavement. As they passed the car Ayşe saw a man get out carrying a very large and, by the light of the hotel entrance, what looked like a gold samovar. It was exactly like the one that had once belonged to Dr Krikor's clinic; she remembered it well because it had such an unfortunate history. He'd sold it to help fund his clinic some years ago. How odd and also blood-chilling that it should turn up outside the hotel where Dr Sarkissian was again raising funds for his clinic. Ayşe frowned. That thing represented nothing but misery.

The entrée, which was a cold meze, had been, to Çetin İkmen's mind, pleasant enough. But he didn't really eat much of it.

'I'm saving myself for later,' he told Arto Sarkissian as he got up from the table.

Arto, looking up at him, said, 'The fish course will be here soon, where are you going?'

İkmen shrugged.

'For a cigarette?' Arto shook his head. 'Are you actually going to eat anything, Çetin?'

'Of course!' But he walked off towards the Kubbeli

Saloon which led to the foyer and from there the great outdoors. Süleyman was sitting at Krikor Sarkissian's table with Krikor's young wife Caroun on one side and Lale Aktar on the other. They were all talking and laughing animatedly and so İkmen banished any thought that Süleyman might want to join him for a smoke.

He walked into the Kubbeli Saloon, the Moorish-style afternoon tea venue where, later on, coffee and petits fours would be served and where the murder mystery thing would start. It was a beautiful room, with a most spectacular multi-domed ceiling. Despite his mood, İkmen took a moment to have a look at it. Above the domes was a vast space and then a glass roof that, in the daytime, allowed the Kubbeli Saloon to be illuminated by natural light. When his daughter Hulya had got married at the Pera Palas, before the refit, it had been a dark and rather dusty place, but then it had also been affordable. İkmen couldn't remember what year Hulya and her husband Berekiah had got married. Their son, Timür, was at school already and so it had to be more than seven years ago. How old was Timür now? He didn't know. He was little and yet he was at school. How old did that make him?

İkmen knew how old *he* was and the knowledge didn't make him happy. His mind was still as sharp as ever but his body was a damn nuisance. When it wasn't aching, it wouldn't always do what he wanted it to and even he had to admit that his lungs were shot to pieces. Stairs, in common with hills and slopes, were now his enemies. But would he stop smoking? İkmen didn't bother to dignify that with an answer even in the privacy of his own mind.

He walked down the stairs into the foyer and made for the metal detector arch and the front doors of the hotel. But then he stopped. There was a man standing in front of the hotel concierge's desk. He was thin, a little shabbily dressed and İkmen didn't recognise him but there was something about him that made him want to stare. The concierge wasn't in evidence and the man was casually looking around the foyer in a non-committal sort of way. Neither ugly nor particularly attractive, he was a middle-aged man just like thousands of others.

Except that he wasn't because he was giving Çetin İkmen one of those feelings that he had from time to time that always reminded him of his late mother. Ayşe İkmen had been a witch who read coffee grounds, tarot cards and effected cures and curses for her many devotees. İkmen's father Timür, an academic, had never understood or even really approved, but he'd loved her and her early death had brought a sadness into his life from which he had never really recovered. It was acknowledged both within the family and beyond that Çetin had inherited Ayşe's powers of observation and insight, what some called her 'second sight'. Now this unknown man was making something inside İkmen twitch – and not in a good way.

He was on the point of going up to him and opening a conversation when the concierge returned to his desk and handed the man a piece of paper.

'Here's your receipt,' he said. The man took the document. The concierge smiled. 'I put it safely into his hands,' he said. 'You need have no worry.'

'Thank you.' The man's voice was slightly mucoid, as if he had the tail end of a cold.

For just a moment, İkmen wondered whether he ought to approach the man but then thought better of it. What was he going to say to him, *my insides are twitching, can you tell me why you might be having that effect on me?*

The man left and İkmen followed him out of the front door only because he wanted to go and have a smoke. But once outside, he watched him. The man hailed a taxi and when he got in he asked the driver to take him to the smart Bosphorus village of Yeniköy. What had he just delivered and why?

* * *

The pretty young woman in the 1920s flapper dress pointed towards a handsome man at the next table and said, 'My husband is a prince. Aren't I lucky?'

She'd come to sit beside Krikor Sarkissian and opposite Mehmet Süleyman, who was charmed. Had the country not become a republic back in 1923 he would have been a minor prince of the Ottoman Empire himself. The handsome man at the next table wore a long frock coat, known as a Stambouline, and a red fez.

'I am actually a distant relative of the Imperial Family myself,' the pretty young woman, Nuray Hanımefendi, said, 'but I'm from Antep and so all of this big city sophistication is still new to me.'

Entering into the spirit of the murder mystery event, which was set in 1925, Krikor asked her, 'So, Hanımefendi, you and your husband remain in İstanbul even though the Sultan has fled?'

She smiled. 'Ah, yes, but sir, my husband, although related, was never a member of the royal household.'

Very much like the Süleyman family, Mehmet thought. Atatürk and his government had allowed his great-grandparents and their children to remain in the country for just that reason. And because they had rescinded all and any claims to titles, money and property beyond a couple of very shabby wooden palaces, they had been left alone, overlooked and forgotten.

'So you're staying in the Pera Palas . . .'

'Tomorrow we will take the train to Paris,' she said.

'The Orient Express?' Lale Aktar's eyes shone with the romance of it.

'Yes. Have you been on it, madam?'

'No, I'm afraid I haven't,' Lale said. 'But I've heard it's very luxurious.'

'Oh, it is indeed – or so I am told. We are going to Paris to deliver my husband's young brother to his studies at the Sorbonne,' Nuray said.

'Will you also go shopping?' Caroun Sarkissian asked.

She giggled. 'Oh, I do hope so!'

'I hope so too,' Caroun said. 'Paris has some of the best shops, especially for clothes and accessories, in the world.'

'I know. I am so excited!' Then she put her head to one side, looking a little sad now, and she said, 'I just hope that my husband will be able to accompany me if I do go shopping. He is always so busy.'

'He is in business?' Süleyman asked.

Nuray Hanımefendi pursed her lips slightly. Ottoman gentlemen, even in the mid-1920s and down on their luck, would not generally have been 'in business'. 'There are cotton fields, in Anatolia,' she said. 'But that is not his concern. No, my husband has literary interests, sir.

He attends a great many literary salons in İstanbul. Now he intends to investigate Paris.'

'He's published?'

'Oh, no!' She looked at Lale as if she'd just asked whether her husband was some sort of pervert. 'No, it is just a fascination, madam.'

'But it's one that takes up a lot of his time?'

She lowered her head. This girl was, Süleyman felt, a very good little actress. 'It does, yes,' she said. 'I am quite frequently left to my own devices and it is . . .' She leaned forward across the table and whispered, 'Sometimes I entertain fears that maybe İzzedin has a mistress or perhaps he visits loose women of the streets! Men do such things. I know that this is probably madness on my part, but I cannot get it out of my head! I must always please my husband and be everything that he wants me to be. If I lost İzzedin I would have nothing to live for. Nothing!' She put a small handkerchief up to her face and then stood up. 'I'm so sorry!' she said. 'I have said too much!' And then she ran from the table back to her previous place at another table at the rear of the room.

Süleyman smiled. 'So İzzedin Effendi may have interests that go beyond the mere literary,' he said.

Krikor and the two women laughed.

During the meal, which was currently between the

fish and the meat courses, the characters moved around the tables, making themselves known to the guests. So far Krikor and his party had spoken to Nuray Hanımefendi and a character called Nicos Bey who 'owned' the hotel. He was an anxious and somewhat volatile Greek whose mind was almost entirely taken up with planning what was going to be Turkey's first ever fashion show.

'It actually took place in nineteen twenty-six,' Krikor said after Nicos had gone. He and Arto had always been passionate local historians. 'Apparently every guest was given his or her own nargile pipe and the only drink served was champagne.'

Süleyman was rather more interested in what clues Nicos might be planting in their minds. Nicos had revealed that he was worried that İzzedin Effendi might not be able to pay his bill. Apparently it was well known in the city that although he sent his brother to the Sorbonne and employed servants and governesses, he was bankrupt.

A strong smell of tobacco accompanied by a cough heralded the arrival of İkmen. He stopped at Süleyman's table on his way back to his own and sat down next to Krikor. 'A woman in a severe black gown is sitting in my chair,' he said.

'Oh, that's one of the actors,' Krikor said. 'You should go back to your table, Çetin. This is when we get some clues about the personalities and problems or issues that surround our characters. You should go back and listen.'

'She's in my chair.'

'Well, there's another, empty chair at the table,' Süleyman said.

'And it's not as if you're actually eating, are you, Çetin?' Krikor added. 'I don't think I've actually seen you put food in your mouth since we were children.'

But then İkmen got to the real point of his visit to their table. 'Krikor,' he said, 'did you order anything to be delivered here tonight?'

'No,' Krikor said. 'Why?'

İkmen told him about the man at the concierge's desk and Krikor said, 'Oh, I expect it was something for the hotel. Unless a guest has had something delivered . . .' He shrugged.

But İkmen still wasn't easy about it.

The far end of the Kubbeli Saloon was just far enough away from the dining area for Alp to be able to talk in private. Söner Erkan, who was playing his brother Yusuf Effendi, was hassling about money. This wasn't unusual.

'Söner, we'll get paid tomorrow when the performance is over,' Alp said.

'Bowstrings, the company account, will be paid, not

me! How am I supposed to get home tomorrow with no money?' the boy asked. He was an eighteen-year-old student who lived in a shared flat in Ortaköy and, in spite of having rich parents, he was always hard up for cash.

'You use your Akbil to get on a tram,' Alp said. 'Then get a bus.'

'I've got no money on my Akbil,' he said.

Alp sighed. To let his Akbil, İstanbul transport pass, run down to nothing was typical of Söner. He never had any money because he spent it all on clothes and entertainment. Alp, at twenty-three, was a little older and wiser and he really wanted the Bowstrings to be successful. But Söner, in spite of his avowed love of acting, his obvious talent and the funding he'd brought to the project via his rich parents and their friends, was a liability.

'I'll pay you as soon as the money has gone into the account,' Alp said. 'And in the meantime I'll lend you some money to put on your Akbil.'

'I need cigarettes and some food too.'

'All right, I'll lend you enough for a pack of cigarettes and something to eat. But you must get back to the guests. We have a job to do, Söner. We need to be professional.'

'Don't speak to me like that,' Söner said. 'Bowstrings wouldn't even exist without me. You only run things because I let you, Alp. I've people in my life beside you, you know. People who like me.'

Alp bit his tongue both because he was angry and because what Söner said was true. He put a hand on the younger man's shoulder and said, 'Come on, let's get back in there.'

Chapter 5

The woman in the severe black gown was the young Yusuf Effendi's governess. She was American, from Chicago, and she'd been with the boy ever since he was a small child. But to Çetin İkmen that didn't make any sense.

'If Yusuf Effendi is going to the Sorbonne then he must have had tuition other than from you,' he said.

'Oh, Yusuf Effendi attends the Galata Lycée,' Sarah said.

'And so what is your purpose? Your role?'

She smiled. She wasn't American in reality of course, but she was blonde and quite tall. 'When one has been with a family for a long time, one becomes part of that family,' Sarah said. 'I have continued to tutor Yusuf Effendi, while also helping Nuray Hanımefendi around the house in these difficult times. Since the . . . since the end of the Great War, we have lost many servants. Hanımefendi cannot run the house alone.'

This was a good point. After the First World War a lot of aristocratic families had lost many members of their domestic staff but İkmen wondered whether there was more to it than that. Sarah was an attractive woman and, according to Süleyman, who had graciously filled him in on conversations with other characters he'd missed while he was smoking, İzzedin Effendi was a man who spent very little time with his wife. Süleyman had also pointed out that, in spite of having been married for four years, İzzedin and Nuray still didn't have any children. Was he spending some time, maybe, with American Sarah? In spite of himself, İkmen was actually beginning to show an interest in this murder mystery thing.

Sarah moved on and, whilst waiting for the meat course plates to be cleared away, İkmen found himself alone at his table with Hovsep Pars. He hadn't seen the elderly Armenian for more years than he cared to remember. But then the last time he'd seen him it had been at Hovsep's sister's funeral. The poor woman had killed herself a couple of years after her son had been murdered and her death had been closely followed by that of her husband, also a suicide. This family tragedy had led to Hovsep having a breakdown and had subsequently turned him into a virtual recluse. Those had been dark days for a lot of people, including Çetin İkmen.

They looked at each other in silence for a moment and then the old Armenian said, 'Do you keep well these days, Inspector?'

İkmen smiled. 'I'm fine thank you, Mr Pars.' He'd always liked Hovsep Pars even if he'd had issues with his brother-in-law Sevan Avedykian. But then he'd been a lawyer and İkmen didn't generally like those much – especially if they were stiff-necked and arrogant.

'You must think it odd that I should come to a murder evening,' the old man said.

'I think it's even odder that I'm here,' İkmen said.

'I came for Krikor,' Hovsep said.

'Yes.'

All around them people were leaving to go out for cigarettes, women were disappearing to repair their make-up and, under the watchful eye of the maître d'hôtel, the staff were clearing the plates and setting up for dessert as quickly as they could.

'When I die, Krikor, or rather his clinic, will inherit my estate,' Hovsep said.

İkmen was taken aback. Apart from the fact that his own death was a strange thing for the old man to bring up at this time, he was astonished that he'd decided to leave his property to Krikor.

'He's been very kind to me over the years,' Hovsep, a lifelong bachelor, continued. 'And who else do I have to leave it all to?'

In the normal course of events, Hovsep's property would have passed to his only nephew. But he was dead and with no nieces to pass it on to, that left only his sister's husband's family, and he'd never liked them.

'That's very generous of you, sir.'

He smiled. 'Not really. My parents' poor old house is . . . well, it's not what it was. I fear poor Krikor will have to spend a considerable amount of money on it in order to be able to sell it.'

'I'm sure that's a long way off yet, Mr Pars,' İkmen said, not really believing what he was saying but saying it anyway. The old man looked pale and sick.

'Then you're wrong, Inspector. I'm dying,' the old man said.

Shocked at his frankness, İkmen was left temporarily speechless.

'I have cancer,' he said. Then he looked about to see if anyone else was listening and he said, 'Tell me, Inspector, does that monster still live?'

İkmen thought for a moment, wondering whether he could get away with a lie of kindness. But he knew that he couldn't. The death of the man who murdered Hovsep's nephew would be reported in the media.

'Yes, Mr Pars, he does,' İkmen said. 'I hear he is a reformed character now. A good Muslim, I understand.'

'Is he?'

'He is also in prison for life, Hovsep Bey. That does mean until he dies. He's never getting out.'

'Is that supposed to make me feel better, Çetin Bey?' the old man said.

And then Hovsep Pars gave İkmen such an accusing look that İkmen was forced to turn away. He should never have engaged in conversation with the old man and so he moved across the room so that he could hear what the fictional prince's brother was saying. Not that he could concentrate on it. As if being at another of Krikor's benefit events was not enough, now he had Hovsep Pars reminding him of that terrible murder he'd investigated all those years ago. Pars's nephew had been murdered by his lover, a psychopath whom İkmen could have killed – but he hadn't.

'I am Venetian.'

Via İzmir, Mehmet Süleyman thought uncharitably.

'My name is Dr Enzo Garibaldi,' the actor said, 'and I will be travelling on the Orient Express tomorrow to go back to my home in La Serenissima.'

'Have you been working in İstanbul, Dr Garibaldi?' Lale Aktar asked.

'Yes, I have.'

'For the family of İzzedin Effendi?'

He frowned. 'I do not know such a person, madam,' he said.

'Oh, he's over there,' Lale said, pointing to the 'prince'.

The fake Italian looked to where she was pointing and said, 'No, he isn't known to me. I haven't been working in the city for long and so I know few people.'

'Where were you working before?' Süleyman asked.

'Various cities.'

'Where?'

'Oh, Urfa, Antep, İskender.'

'Rather dangerous places in what has been a theatre of war,' Süleyman said. The Italians, along with the British, the French and the Greeks, had attempted to partition what was now Turkey after the First World War. The Turks had only finally tasted complete victory in 1923 when Atatürk founded the republic. One would have thought that someone like Dr Garibaldi would have either been killed in the conflict or gone home a lot sooner than he clearly had. So there had to be a reason why he had stayed.

'Prince İzzedin's wife, Nuray Hanımefendi, comes from Antep,' Süleyman said. He pointed her out. 'That lady, there.'

The Italian barely glanced in her direction. 'No,' he said. 'I don't know her.'

'Are you sure? Look again.'

He did, shrugged, and then repeated, 'I don't know her.' Then he walked away.

'Mmm.' Lale Aktar gave Süleyman a meaningful look.

'We are on opposite teams,' he said to her. 'You should not be so much as looking at me in case I can read your thoughts.'

She laughed. He noticed how beautiful, and perfect, her teeth were.

'So policemen can mind-read now, can they?' she said.

'Not exactly.'

'I may be giving you false signals,' she said as she moved closer to him and smiled. She took a sip from her champagne flute. 'Maybe I want to confound your investigation.'

'Mmm. Maybe you do.'

'Or perhaps I just like looking at you,' she whispered.

He felt himself go cold. Women flirted with him all the time and he found Lale Aktar extremely attractive in her shimmering gold sheath dress with her lovely face and her tiny, perfect teeth. But in this context, it wasn't right. She was in Krikor Sarkissian's circle, she was married to one of his friends. Maybe she was merely trying to cloud his mind so that she could win.

'I am afraid,' he said, slowly, 'that I can see right through your flattery, to a woman who is determined to beat me.'

She laughed and held her hands up. 'Ah, you have the better of me, Inspector.'

'I thought so.' He hid his disappointment carefully although maybe not quite carefully enough.

Either she sensed what he felt or she was just continuing to tease him when she said, 'But I do like looking at you. And that is not me trying to mess with your mind.'

The meal finished with fruit and a massive cheeseboard which included the famous (according to Ayşe Farsakoğlu) Circassian smoked cheese. Because his sergeant had mentioned it, Çetin İkmen did try a piece but he wasn't that impressed. It was, to his way of thinking, rather dry. Still a little shaken by his conversation with Hovsep Pars, he looked around the ballroom to take his eyes away from the old man. Soon they'd all go into the Kubbeli Saloon for coffee and liqueurs and he'd be able to get away. But for now he just had to distract himself.

To his chagrin he noticed that Süleyman and Lale Aktar were enjoying each other's company rather more than was good for either of them. But then years ago he'd decided that his friend had to have some sort of unique pheromone that made him irresistible to all women, except lesbians. In fact, watching women with

Mehmet Süleyman was a good way of finding out who was and was not a lesbian – not that that was germane to anything. He looked at them again and saw the familiar stars in Lale Aktar's eyes. He'd have to have words. If Süleyman and Mrs Aktar ended up falling into bed together and Krikor Sarkissian found out, he'd be both hurt and disgusted. Faruk Aktar was his friend and he'd never be able to look him in the face again if Süleyman had an affair with his wife.

Over the other side of the room, both Sarkissian brothers had joined forces to talk to a man İkmen knew to be a very wealthy landlord. He was a Kurd – İkmen couldn't recall his name – from somewhere in the east, the coastal city of Adana sprang to mind, but İkmen couldn't be sure that was right. What he did know was that the man's son had been shot by police in a drugs bust in Edirnekapı over ten years ago. It had been some sort of inter-gang incident and the boy, a small-time dealer, had been collateral damage en route to the big-time players who had also been taken down that day. İkmen had not been involved, but he felt for this man whose son had died. There was a sad connection between people who had lost children and İkmen had to be hard on himself not to think about his own dead son, Bekir. He too had been killed by police in the distant far eastern Turkish town of Birecik. And also in common with the Kurd's son, he had been a drug dealer.

As far as he could tell, all of the guests were wealthy, with the exception of himself, Süleyman and several groups of divines – Armenian priests, Greeks, representatives from the Chief Rabbi's office. There were nightclub owners, landlords, fashion designers, film stars, plastic surgeons, publishers and industrialists. Some he knew, some he knew of; all of them were smiling or laughing and having a good time, which was nice. Not for the first time, Çetin İkmen wondered why he couldn't do likewise at events like this. There was that twitch he was feeling inside brought on by the man he'd seen at the concierge's desk. But was that just his mind wanting to make a mystery out of this innocent evening to somehow justify his presence at it?

İkmen didn't do relaxation, he never had. In a sense that was the way he liked it but, as he got older, it was annoying too. Not being able to sit still at nearly sixty was tiring, for him and for those around him. But there was little point in trying to force himself into it.

His restless eyes and ears found the younger brother of İzzedin Effendi, Yusuf Effendi, and he listened in as the boy spoke to a woman who played a bit of a flighty piece in a popular evening soap opera.

'Our parents died when I was just a child,' he said. Then he lowered his voice to almost a whisper. 'My mother, thinking that my father had died fighting in Arabia, took her own life.'

'Oh, how sad!' The woman had that excessive emotional edge to her voice that so many theatricals seemed to have.

'Then my father returned.'

'Allah!'

'Not knowing that my mother was dead, he came back expecting to see her.' He shrugged. 'He was weak from fighting the Arabs in the desert and he had an accident. He hit his head and he died.'

'Oh, so you were brought up by . . .'

'My dear brother, yes,' he said. 'He has always taken care of me. Not a single kuruş has been spared on either my comfort or my education. And tomorrow I will go to the Sorbonne in Paris. It is my sincerest hope to train as a linguist and so help our new nation to reach out into the world anew.'

'That's a wonderful ambition!' the actress gushed.

But İkmen found himself a little confused. İzzedin Effendi, so he'd heard, was supposed to be bankrupt. How was he going to afford tuition fees at France's top academy? And wasn't this story rather too similar to one he'd heard before, one that hadn't been fiction?

* * *

Ayşe couldn't believe that it was the stuffed mussels that were making her feel bad. She had the constitution of an ox. That said, her stomach felt curdled and uncomfortable and she'd had to use the lavatory at the restaurant rather more than she'd wanted to. Both İzzet and her brother, Ali, were concerned.

'Are you all right?' Ali asked the third time she returned from the tiny restaurant lavatory.

'Yes.' She sat down next to İzzet who frowned when he looked at her.

'You're pale.'

'Wedding nerves,' her brother said with a misplaced tone of authority in his voice.

Ayşe rolled her eyes but said nothing. On occasion, Ali liked to pretend his younger sister was some sort of blushing virgin bride, which everyone – including him – knew she was not.

İzzet poured her some water and encouraged her to drink it. She'd only had one glass of beer with her meal and so she was by no means drunk but it still wasn't a bad idea to drink water. The two men, like most of the revellers at the tables outside the small restaurants on Nevizade Alley, were getting stuck in to a bottle of rakı. As the night had progressed, the noise level had risen considerably as people began to indulge in long, rambling story-telling sessions punctuated by bouts of happy singing. Some character down at the end of the alley periodically sang 'Jingle Bells' in Turkish, to the obvious delight of everyone at his table. But Ayşe was not amused, either by the 'Jingle Bells' man or by her patronising brother. Her mind was elsewhere.

The gold samovar she'd seen that man take into the Pera Palas bothered her. It had looked so like the one that had once belonged to Dr Krikor Sarkissian, the one he'd been given by a murderer. His name had been Muhammed Ersoy and he'd killed several members of his own family as well as his lover. He would have killed Inspector İkmen, Dr Sarkissian and Mehmet Süleyman if they hadn't captured him and put him in a psychiatric unit and then prison. She'd been sleeping with Süleyman at that time and when she'd heard that Ersoy had been holding him hostage she'd almost collapsed. Even though Süleyman was married then and so he wasn't hers in any sense, she'd been terrified that something bad might happen to him.

Seeing the samovar had brought it all back. Not that 'it' had ever actually gone very far away. In one sense that period had been both the best and the worst time in her life. Certainly no one since excited her as much as Süleyman had, and that included İzzet Melik, the man who was going to be her husband. She began to wonder whether she should call İkmen and tell him about the samovar. If one of the hotel guests was going to display it in the hotel for some reason, it might come as a rather unpleasant surprise for her boss. But then she decided against doing that. Inspector İkmen was a grown man, he could take care of himself.

Chapter 6

'Now that Mustafa Kemal Paşa has created this new homeland for the Turks, we get few guests who are not of their kind in this hotel,' Sofia, the 'Greek' housekeeper, said.

The guests were now all seated drinking coffee and liqueurs in the Kubbeli Saloon, watching the actors perform soliloquies and play out scenes in character.

'An Armenian man is in room four thirteen. Şeymus, one of the drivers here, says he was an arms dealer to the Russians during the war.' Looking over her shoulders to make sure that she wasn't being overheard, Sofia went on, 'Ourselves and the Armenians had hopes that the Russians would save us back then. But they didn't. The Turkish princess who is staying here tonight, her father and brothers fought the Russians in the east. The governess, the American, she told me that all the men in the princess's family were killed in battle with the Russians. I don't know how a person gets over such a thing – if they ever do.'

Çetin İkmen looked at his watch. The meal had overrun and it was now ten fifteen. He was actually ready for his bed and would have just sneaked off to his room had Krikor not put him on Lale Aktar's investigative team. She was, so she had told him, relying on his investigative skills to help her win.

'The young prince, the one the older prince and his wife are taking to Paris tomorrow, is, so the Armenian, Avram Bey, told the concierge, Monsieur Maurice, very wealthy. When his father died he left separate sums of money to each of the sons and the boy apparently has a lot,' Sofia continued. Then her face dropped into a frown. 'How I resent that! The Turks lose the Great War, they take my home in Fener away from me and make me work like a common servant! I am not just some Greek woman from the country! I am a Fenariote, a Greek of old Byzantium! We were here a thousand years before these Turks and now they want us out. I hate them! But I especially hate the old Ottomans who ruined this country and made way for people like this new government in Ankara. Princes like these young men who are staying here tonight deserve to die for what they did to this country!'

Albeit in a fictional form, these old enmities that Sofia and others were displaying were still, İkmen knew, very alive in the present day. It was sad to think that Turkey still had issues with Greece and Armenia but it was a fact, and it was one that not all of the audience appeared to be comfortable with. But then Sofia left the Kubbeli Saloon and, from different ends of the chamber, İzzedin Effendi and Avram Bey the Armenian approached one another. When they got close, the prince put an arm out as if to ward off the Armenian.

'I have nothing to say to you, sir!' he said as the other man eyed him narrowly. 'Tomorrow I will be on my way to Paris and there will be an end of it.'

'I do not think that is so, effendi,' the Armenian said.

The prince put his nose in the air. 'Oh? And why is that, Avram Bey?'

He smiled. 'Because you need me, effendi,' he said.

'I do not!'

The Armenian moved closer to the prince. 'I think you will find that you do,' he said. 'I think you will find that if you try to continue without me, that will not be possible.'

The prince scowled. 'What do you mean?' he said. 'Are you threatening me?'

Avram Bey shrugged. 'I would not use such a word myself, effendi,' he said. 'But without me it is possible that bad things may happen. I would not like it to be so but . . .'

'I will not listen to any more of this!' the prince said as he stormed past the Armenian and out of the room.

İkmen noticed as he passed that he had tears in his eyes.

Beyond the fact that the racial types on show were stereotypical (the slimy Armenian, the hate-filled Greek), the performances were good and İkmen, at least, could deduce some subtlety and layering in their acting. On the face of it the exchange they had just witnessed seemed to have been about money. The prince was bankrupt and had, possibly, borrowed money from the Armenian. But there had also been a fairly heavy dose of sexual tension between the two characters as well and İkmen wondered if the prince and the Armenian were lovers. But then he found that he wasn't comfortable with that notion and he decided that it couldn't possibly be so.

Now that the kitchens were clean and tidy and the head chef had gone home for the night, Ersu Bey decided to let all but two of his staff members leave early, just over half an hour before the night shift came on. He himself would stay until every cup and liqueur glass was safely back in the kitchens but most of the guests had finished their drinks now and so there was very little left to do except pick up the odd cup and saucer.

He didn't trust the night shift, which was even smaller than usual for this one exclusive party, to do a proper job, not really. They were only casual staff anyway and he lived in fear of coming into the kitchens the following morning and finding dirty cups and glasses all over the work surfaces. Apart from anything else, Chef Roberto would go insane with fury.

Ersu cleared away a few more cups and then he told his remaining two waitresses to go. With no wife or family waiting for him at home, Ersu Bey wasn't in any great hurry to leave and so if he did stay on after 11 p.m. to wash up the remaining cups and glasses, that was up to him.

He managed to gather up ten small liqueur glasses and four coffee cups and made his way down to the kitchens. Büket, the last of his waitresses, was just slinging her bag over her shoulder and going out of the back door when he got there.

'Goodnight, Ersu Bey,' she said as she passed a couple of young men, night staff, walking in the opposite direction.

'Goodnight, Büket,' Ersu Bey said. 'See you tomorrow.' Then he pushed his tray of dirty glasses and cups at one of the young men and said, 'Wash these up.'

'OK.'

Ersu Bey went back up to the Kubbeli Saloon smarting a little at the casual language that the boy had used with him. It was OK, *Ersu Bey* to people like him! He shook his head with irritation and had to take a moment to compose his features before he faced his guests once again.

* * *

'Burak!' İkmen beckoned Krikor Sarkissian's assistant over and Burak Fisekçi duly lumbered across the Kubbeli Saloon towards him.

'Çetin Bey?'

'Now that all of our fictional villiains and innocents have apparently gone to their beds, do I have time to slip out to have a cigarette?' he asked. Soon, or so he imagined, something grisly would happen.

Burak looked at his watch. As principal organiser of the event he of course knew how the evening was going to proceed. 'Yes,' he said. 'You have time.' Then he smiled. 'But don't walk all the way out to the front entrance, go out the back door, through the ballroom, it's closer.'

'I will.'

When İkmen got outside, he found that he wasn't alone. An elderly rabbi he knew by sight, plus a lot of rather elegant-looking men that he didn't know at all were also availing themselves of the ashtrays outside the ballroom. And then there was Süleyman.

'Saw you deep in eye-to-eye contact with Lale Aktar,' İkmen said as his friend came and joined him.

Jumping up and down on the spot in order to keep warm, Süleyman said, 'Just chit-chat.'

'Yes, and I am the Shah of Iran,' İkmen replied acidly. 'I know you, Mehmet, don't even try to fool me.'

Süleyman lit a cigarette and then smiled.

'Even if she offers herself to you on a plate, you mustn't do anything,' İkmen continued. 'Krikor is very good friends with her husband, he'd take it as a betrayal. I'd take it as a betrayal.'

Süleyman didn't answer. He looked up at the elderly buildings that remained on Meşrutiyet Street and wondered whether the old Londra Hotel, diagonally opposite the Pera Palas, was still like some sort of dusty belle époque museum. He didn't want to think about what İkmen had just said to him and he certainly didn't want to make him any sort of promise. Lale Aktar was a very attractive woman who had run one of her smooth, slim legs up against his thigh several times during the course of the dinner. But luckily for him, İkmen changed the subject.

'So who do you think is going to get killed?' he asked. 'Will it be the prince? The princess? The young brother? The Armenian? The governess? The Greek woman?'

Süleyman, glad to be far away from the subject of Lale Aktar, said, 'Mmm. I've a feeling there is some serious business between the prince and the Armenian.'

'The prince is bankrupt and it may well be that he is indebted to the Armenian.'

'Stereotypical, but it may be true,' Süleyman said. 'But, you know, I wondered whether they were lovers.'

'So did I.'

'Not something that many of the clerics in our party would approve of, but the actors are young and maybe they're keen to push the boundaries and sensibilities of their audiences. I can't see Dr Krikor having a problem with that either.'

'So the Armenian may kill the prince because he has defaulted on a loan?'

Süleyman shrugged. 'A bit obvious. Maybe he'll kill the princess . . .'

'I think she might have had some sort of liaison with the Italian tutor,' İkmen said. 'He worked in Antep in the past, which is where she comes from, and yet he protested, I felt, rather too vehemently about not knowing her or her family. People like the princess and her family are, or were, just the type who would have had an Italian tutor on their staff.'

'And Italians are very attractive to woman.'

İkmen smiled. 'Something of a generalisation, but I know what you mean.'

'It's partly the language, of course,' Süleyman continued. 'It sounds so beautiful.'

'Makes you wonder whether your Sergeant Melik wooed my Sergeant Farsakoğlu in Italian,' İkmen said and then instantly regretted it. İzzet Melik did indeed speak perfect Italian but İkmen was sure Süleyman didn't want to be reminded of that. He was not, so İkmen had heard on the grapevine, going to attend his ex-lover's wedding to the sergeant. He'd made some sort of excuse about having to go and visit relatives out on the Princes' Islands.

Süleyman didn't want to talk about İzzet Melik. 'The princess could kill the Italian in an effort to silence him if she did have an affair with him in the past.'

'So that the prince didn't find out?'

'She clearly loves her husband. Yes.'

Mehmet Süleyman didn't love Ayşe Farsakoğlu any more but İkmen knew that he was still not happy about her marriage. He was possessive rather than actually attached to women he had once either dated or been married to. It wasn't a trait that İkmen felt was in any way attractive, shedding as it did a rather selfish and arrogant light on his friend whom he nevertheless, and for all his faults, loved.

'But is she capable of murder?' İkmen asked.

'What, you mean because she's so pretty?'

İkmen laughed. 'No, you know me better than that!' he said. 'Since when was I ever taken in by a pretty face?' He wanted to add, *that's your weakness, not mine*, but he stopped himself. 'And what do you think of the notion of İzzedin Effendi killing his younger brother for his money? You know that Yusuf Effendi has a lot of money, don't you?'

Süleyman didn't reply but he did frown.

* * *

Some of the casual members of staff drove him crazy. There were two lads who were supposed to be stacking the dishwashers, but neither of them seemed to know how to stack properly. Plates, cups and glasses were just chucked in randomly. Left in that sort of state, they'd break! Ersu Bey saw no other option but to do it himself. The night staff were not generally his concern and he didn't want to get involved with them, but he'd tell management about them at the earliest opportunity. Sitting about on work benches were about eight of them in total and they looked like a bunch of lazy articles to Ersu. If any of the guests wanted room service in the middle of the night they'd have quite a wait with people like these at the helm.

And then there was the butter! A boy, a dark, Kurdish-looking character, had come straight in and made himself a sandwich using smoked salmon leftovers. Fair enough, but he'd taken butter out of one of the fridges to make the sandwich and had then failed to put it back. Although no actual cooking was taking place, the kitchen was still warm and, if left out on a bench, the butter would melt.

Shaking his head in silent frustration, Ersu Bey picked the butter up and took it through the kitchen to the fridges and freezers at the back. Butter was kept with all the other dairy products in a walk-in fridge. Ersu opened the door and went inside.

Because the fridge was dedicated to milk and its

various derivatives, it was a somewhat colourless environment. Cream, butter in white cartons and cheese made the place look like a cross between an industrial unit of some sort and a version of CS Lewis's fictional frozen land of Narnia. Ersu put the butter back on the correct shelf and was just about to leave when he heard the door into the fridge close. He knew from long experience of working in hotels that fridge doors like this could only be opened from the outside. He also knew that such devices were virtually soundproof. Ersu Bey, old soldier and consummate professional, told himself that he would have to keep his wits about him. In all probability the stupid kids who were on duty had either carelessly knocked the door or were just having a laugh at his expense. But there was something at the back of his mind that didn't quite believe that.

There was an air of anticipation in the Kubbeli Saloon that İkmen found both completely understandable and also very odd. Everyone was waiting for some entirely fictitious murder to occur and yet there was a tension in the room that was almost ominous. It bore some relation to the anxiety he'd felt when he'd first gone to see the film *The Exorcist*. There had been so many accounts in the press about revolving heads and projectile vomiting that İkmen had both wanted and not wanted to see it. He'd gone with Arto Sarkissian and, although he'd been a married man with children at the time, he'd watched most of *The Exorcist* through his fingers. Now again he found he had an unreasonable urge to lie low and shield himself from what was about to happen.

'Do you think it will all start off with a scream?' Arto Sarkissian eased himself down into the chair next to İkmen's and smiled. 'Krikor has told me nothing about any of this, you know,' he said. 'I've no idea what to expect.'

'Nor I,' İkmen said. 'But then thankfully we don't have to worry too much about it, do we? It's for Süleyman and the novelist to work it out.'

'I think we have to help,' Arto said. 'And anyway, it's supposed to be fun.'

'I've told you, I don't like fun.'

'But my brother's guests do and so if you can be a little bit convivial . . .'

'Arto, my dear friend, I will strain every nerve to make sure that everyone except me has a wonderful time,' İkmen said. Then recalling his recent conversation with Mehmet Süleyman, he added, 'I've already done my bit in terms of my colleague and his apparent fascination with Mrs Aktar.'

'Süleyman and Lale Aktar?'

'Don't look so shocked, you know what he's like,' İkmen said. 'You also know how most women can be around him too.'

'But Lale loves her husband, he—'

'I put him straight,' İkmen said. A long discussion about Lale Aktar and her husband was not something he wanted to have. 'It's OK – now.'

The Armenian sighed. He'd drunk far too much whisky and eaten much more than was good for him and he felt really rather uncomfortable. İkmen knew the signs, Arto wanted to go to bed and sleep it all off. But he wasn't going to be able to do that. İkmen looked across the room for Krikor Sarkissian's assistant, Burak Fisekçi, but he wasn't about. The whole event had largely been his work. Burak, the son of Armenian parents, was single. Dedicated to Krikor and his clinic, he seemed to have very little life outside of his work. In that respect, İkmen could relate to him, but İkmen had a family. Voices could be heard in his apartment twenty-four hours a day. What, he wondered, could Burak, who lived alone now that his mother was dead, be feeling in this place so full of people and their noise?

'Oh, I do wish they'd get on with it!' İkmen said. 'Having to keep getting up to go outside for a cigarette is making me tired.'

'Then stop smoking,' Arto said. 'I've been telling you to stop for over forty years, indulge me for once.'

'And lose my reputation as the man who chooses not to listen to his doctor?' İkmen stood up.

'If I were your lungs, I'd leave home,' Arto said.

'Ah, but you're not, are you, you're . . .' And then he stopped talking, as did everyone else in the Kubbeli Saloon. He looked where they were looking and he had to admit that he was impressed.

Like some of the other guests, İkmen had expected the murder to be a bit farcical – a bloodless, almost comic affair, complete with unconvincingly fainting ladies. But this was in a whole other league. It was also, in terms of suspects and players, entirely unexpected.

Lale Aktar, her face trembling with an emotion she could barely hold in check, stumbled into the Kubbeli Saloon with both her bloodstained hands held out in front of her. Her gold sheath dress, her hair and even her face were also spattered with blood. İkmen was just thinking what excellent make-up had been used on her when he smelt something that was most definitely not make-up.

Chapter 7

Someone gave her water, probably because they thought that's what you should do. İkmen wiped one of her bloody hands on a tissue which he then turned away to examine and to taste. His suspicions confirmed, he pushed aside all the other men who were coming to Lale's aid and asked her, 'Where did this happen?'

'Happen?' She looked at him as if he were speaking a foreign language. İkmen led her to a chair.

'Come on, Lale, tell us what you found and where?' one man asked jovially.

People were laughing, but then why shouldn't they? It was an entertainment, a performance. Wasn't it?

'My room . . . four hundred and eleven. The young prince!' the novelist said.

Süleyman, who was now at İkmen's side, said, 'This is odd.'

İkmen looked at him.

'Odd that Lale should find the body,' Süleyman

continued. 'I thought she was supposed to be leading the other team.'

İkmen took his arm and led him to one side. 'I want you to keep everyone away from her,' he whispered.

'Why?'

'Because the blood on her hands is real,' İkmen said.

For a moment Süleyman seemed to wonder whether he'd heard İkmen correctly, but when he realised that he had, he got to work rounding up members of his team who were nearby and assembling them next to a group of tables in a corner. And although other people did come up and attempt to speak to the novelist, İkmen managed to get them to move away so that he could speak to her.

'The young prince is just a fiction, Mrs Aktar,' he said. 'Do you mean the boy who's playing that part? Is he dead in your room?'

Lale Aktar moved her head slowly up and down once and then she whispered, 'On my bed.'

Later, Çetin İkmen would bitterly regret the fact that he didn't call for back-up there and then, but like everyone in that place, he was still half in a fantasy. He'd have to at least check room 411. Süleyman saw him leave the Kubbeli Saloon and followed him.

* * *

Years before, when he'd been a young private, Ersu Bey had had an accident. His company had been on patrol just outside the eastern city of Mardin in an area known to be rich in archaeological sites. Over the centuries Mardin and its environs had been conquered by the Byzantines, the Persians, the Arabs and the Turks, and all of them had left evidence of their civilisations behind them. His commander had told them to be careful where they trod, but Ersu had taken his eyes away from where he was walking just for a second, to look back at the fortress city of Mardin, and had fallen through the earth into what had turned out to be a Persian cistern. Then, as now, he had been entombed, alone. Then he'd broken his leg and now, as he recalled those old events of the late seventies, his right calf duly began to ache.

It had taken his brothers in arms the best part of a day to get him out. The roof of the cistern had been unstable, hence his fall, and they'd had to first locate where the firm ground was and then send men down to get him. Because he'd broken his leg, lifting him out had not been easy. He still remembered how claustrophobic he had felt in the cistern, how scared he'd been and the pain he'd suffered. His broken leg had been fixed and he had made a rapid recovery, but it had always been a struggle not to limp ever since. Now he was trapped again and this time it was not in a damp cistern but in a cold fridge.

Ersu knew that if he cried out no one would be able to hear him. The vindictive or careless night staff (he couldn't decide which they were) wouldn't let him out until either they'd had their fun or one of them needed milk, butter, cream or cheese for some reason. Intellectually Ersu knew that he wasn't in mortal danger. Had he been trapped in one of the freezers, that would have been another matter. But he was cold and uncomfortable and in spite of the fact that someone had to let him out in the end, he felt scared. Alone with his own thoughts was not a place that Ersu Bey liked to be and there was a limit to the number of times one could distract oneself by reading butter wrappers and cream cartons. After a while he began to sing. Strangely, the songs that came to mind most readily were some of Stevie Wonder's greatest hits from the seventies.

The room that had once been Agatha Christie's favourite was larger than the one the Pera Palas had allocated to Çetin İkmen. Decorated in modern pale tones of white, pale grey and warm gold, the room was nevertheless furnished in dark wood and decorated with pictures and articles about the famous author, as well as a desk supporting her typewriter. The bed, which was new, like all the beds in the refurbished hotel, had the body of the young boy who had played the prince's younger brother sprawled across it, face up. By the look of him, he had been stabbed at least five times, once in the throat.

İkmen, bending as low as he could over the body without touching it, said, 'So fiction becomes reality.'

'Makes you wonder if this character was the one that was supposed to die in the land of fictional crime and mystery,' Süleyman replied. Then he said, 'I suppose he really is dead . . .'

'Oh, he's dead all right,' İkmen said. He checked his watch, it was ten past eleven. 'Although we will have to get Dr Sarkissian up here in order to confirm that.' He moved his head the better to see the deep wound in the neck and then looked at the bed and the headboard. 'Must've still been alive when he was stabbed in the carotid or whatever artery that is in the neck. Blood spatter.'

'I wonder how Mrs Aktar is managing downstairs,' Süleyman said. 'I left Dr Sarkissian in charge of her but if she starts telling everyone about this . . .'

'You go down and send Dr Sarkissian up here,' İkmen said. 'We'll have to secure the building until we can get a team in here.'

Süleyman left and İkmen began looking around the room, moving as little as possible. The prints from Lale Aktar's stiletto-heeled shoes were easy to see retreating across the floor from the bed to the door of the room. There were splashes of blood on the walls and even a few handprints where the novelist had probably tried to steady herself against the wall.

What, İkmen wondered, had the boy been doing in Lale Aktar's room? Unless she had invited him in, how had he got into room 411 and why? Had he perhaps tried to rob her and then been killed by her when she tried to stop him? Given the ferocity of the wounds he had sustained, this seemed to be unlikely. But if Lale Aktar hadn't killed the boy, and turning up with his blood all over her did seem to be a bit of a giveaway for a cold-blooded killer, then who had?

Whether it was the sound of a woman's screams or the gunshots he heard coming from somewhere down on a lower floor of the hotel that made İkmen sprint for the door, he didn't know. But he was out of room 411 and on to the landing before he could really think about what came first. He got there just in time to see a tall man dressed in black, his face covered by a balaclava helmet, coming towards him. İkmen reached inside his jacket pocket for his phone. But then the man in black pointed a gun at him and said, 'Take your phone out and throw it on the floor or I'll kill you.'

İkmen did as he was told. The phone, when it hit the floor, skittered along the surface until it hit the man's boot. He crunched his heel down on it and said, 'Now you come with me.'

* * *

It was an absolutely textbook psychological technique. They shot four people, three men and a woman, straight away, dragged their bodies into the bar and then stood in the middle of the saloon panning their guns around the survivors, asserting their dominance. People screamed in terror, some even tried to hide underneath furniture, which was exactly the effect these people had wanted. There were ten of them, that Süleyman could see, and they all wore black, anonymous jump-suits or shirts and trousers and balaclava helmets. One of them wore a headset which Süleyman recognised as the type that included a camera, and they all wore microphones. Through his fear, Süleyman wondered what terrorist organisation the nine men and possibly one woman represented. Was it a knee-jerk assumption to brand them as terrorists? Süleyman thought not but then he remembered a recent report he'd read on the finances of one of the city's most powerful criminal gangs and realised that perhaps his first thought had been a rash generalisation. These people could be anyone.

Everyone, including Süleyman, was down on the floor. The only exceptions were Lale Aktar who was still sitting, covered in blood, in the chair İkmen had guided her to, and Dr Arto Sarkissian who was standing next to her. Süleyman could just see the four bodies of the dead through the doorway into the bar. Laid down or slumped, they had the look of drunken sleepers – or they would have done if they hadn't been covered in blood. One of them Süleyman thought he recognised as the owner of some sort of health club. Why him? But then why not him? When one asserted dominance through terror, it didn't matter who got killed.

'I want all your phones, cameras and any other mobile devices in the middle of the room now.'

The one who spoke was shorter than the others. The timbre of his voice was of a man in his middle years and when Süleyman raised his head to look at him, he saw that he was also more thickly set than his colleagues. Was he the oldest? Was he also, therefore, the slowest and least agile as well?

With shaking hands people began to throw their phones and cameras into the middle of the floor.

'Don't try to conceal anything from us,' the man said as he watched the people empty their pockets. 'We'll be searching every one of you. Hold anything back and you'll end up like them.' He pointed at the dead bodies.

Süleyman threw his phone into the middle of the room but not before he'd put the device on and pressed 155. Hopefully the operators at the police emergency control room would hear what he was hearing, at least for a short while. But as the phone flew through the air one of the masked men shot it and his colleagues all laughed.

Then their leader walked over to Süleyman, and said, 'Nice try, Inspector Süleyman.'

Every cell of Süleyman's body turned cold. 'How do you know who I am?' he said.

The man poked the side of his head with the muzzle of his submachine gun. 'Everything will become clear soon enough,' he said. Then he beckoned one of his subordinates over and told him to search the policeman. He pulled what had been an expensive jacket so hard that one of the arms ripped at the shoulder.

'Even when my daughter got married here I never actually used this beautiful lift,' Çetin İkmen said as he climbed into the Pera Palas's glamorous wooden elevator. He realised that he was babbling but then what else could he do under the circumstances? A faceless man was pointing a gun at his head for no reason that he could as yet understand.

'Sit.' The man pointed to the velvet-covered seat at the back of the lift and then shut the doors and started the mechanism.

İkmen sat. Under normal circumstances this short journey to the ground floor in the historic Pera Palas lift would have been a joy and a delight. But with guns and screams and at least one murder already committed, there was very little levity to be found in the situation. Just before he'd been pushed into the lift, İkmen had seen two of the actors, the ones playing the older prince and the Armenian gentleman, being hauled out of a room on to the landing and pushed to the floor by two other anonymous creatures in black. He'd heard at least one of them grunt with pain but what had happened after that he didn't know.

The lift creaked. 'Amazing how this thing has kept going all these years,' İkmen babbled. The eyes above the balaclava face mask looked at him with what the policeman interpreted as pity. He probably thought he was a stupid old bastard, way past his prime. He was wrong – probably – but İkmen was quite happy for that to be the impression he gave.

'Of course we could observe the normal pleasantries and I could ask you your name, but I don't suppose you'd tell me,' İkmen continued. 'I could just call you "faceless, frightening person who wants to kill me" but that is somewhat long-winded and also I don't actually know that you actually want to kill me per se—'

'Shut up.'

'In reality I have absolutely no idea about your motives at all. To me this all looks a bit like that film. The one with Bruce Willis. What was its name?'

The masked man didn't respond.

'I can't remember,' İkmen said. 'But he was in some office building when a group of people who at first seemed like terrorists attacked and Bruce got into all sorts of terrible situations as he tried to stop them. Then it turned out that the villains weren't terrorists at all—'

'Shut up!' This time he shoved the muzzle of his gun up against the side of İkmen's head. Then he leaned down and whispered in his ear. 'Don't try the silly old man act with us, Inspector. We know you.'

İkmen said nothing. The lift creaked to a halt on the ground floor and he got out without another word. So whoever these people were, they knew him. Whether that was a good or a bad thing, İkmen didn't know. But what he had deduced was that the man in the lift was on a hair trigger, which could or could not work to his advantage.

Chapter 8

Ayşe Farsakoğlu got all the way home and had even put the television on before she decided that she didn't want to be in her apartment. Her brother hadn't returned with her but had gone out to a nightclub with a group of his friends from work and probably wouldn't be home until the morning. İzzet had headed back to his own place in Zeyrek.

The stomach upset she'd apparently developed during the course of the evening wouldn't go away. Uncomfortable rather than painful, she knew it wouldn't let her rest easily and so Ayşe decided to go back up to İstiklal Street again and see whether she could walk whatever it was off. She put her coat on and just took her keys and cigarettes out of her handbag. Her mother, had she still been alive, would have prescribed yoghurt for a stomach upset, but then her mother had recommended yoghurt for everything from colic to cancer. Inspector İkmen called yoghurt 'Turkish antibiotics', which always made her smile.

Ayşe walked up İnönü Street and into Taksim Square. It was just after eleven thirty and so the town was still heaving with revellers making for home, as well as more robust souls heading into clubs and late-night bars. As she skirted around the edge of the square, Ayşe saw a couple of transsexuals she knew by sight melt into doorways as she approached, their eyes expressing both fear and resentment. They had to know by this time that she, of all people, wouldn't bother them unless she had to. She actually liked most of them. But she was still 'the police' and so of course they'd feel at the very least ambivalent towards her. Most of them, after all, were street prostitutes. With the exception of a few high-profile entertainers, it was almost the only profession that was open to them. Even Inspector İkmen's cousin, Samsun, had worked the streets when she was young.

Ayşe turned on to İstiklal Street and found herself almost immediately surrounded by a group of young tattooed and pierced students. They hardly noticed her but she was impressed by their energy and their joy as they cavorted underneath the festive lights that were strung across the famous thoroughfare. Some people called them 'Christmas' lights, others 'New Year' decorations. But it didn't really matter. They cheered up the dark winter nights and were appreciated by all but the most austere Muslims and there weren't many of those wandering about on İstiklal in the middle of the night.

Walking at a steady pace, Ayşe found that as she drew level with the Catholic Church of St Antoine, she was beginning to feel a little better. Sometimes being with her brother *and* with İzzet at the same time could be a strain. They both so wanted to look after her and, if she was honest, she didn't really appreciate it. Maybe she'd been single for too long.

She turned off on to Kallavı Alley. It wasn't until she was over halfway down that she realised where she was going. Kallavı joined directly on to the end of Meşrutiyet Street, which was where she'd walked arm in arm with İzzet some hours before and where the Pera Palas Hotel was. As soon as she'd acknowledged it, she felt the pull of the grand old hotel, or rather the lure of who was inside. İkmen and Süleyman, especially the latter.

When she reached Meşrutiyet, Ayşe stood and stared down the street at the hotel and wondered what she thought she was doing. Süleyman was at a private party that was probably in full swing and to which she had not been invited. The hotel security staff weren't going to let her in and even if she did get in, what was she going to say?

The truth was that beyond some vague notion about wanting to tell İkmen and Mehmet Süleyman about the gold samovar she'd seen going into the hotel, she didn't know. Was it even the same gold samovar that had once belonged to Dr Sarkissian? She was about to be married and yet here she was wanting to talk about a piece of ornate kitchen equipment to a man who had once been her lover.

She loved İzzet, she felt safe with him, he was kind and generous and he loved her with all his heart. But she didn't *want* him. There had only ever been one man she had wanted so much she would have crawled over open cans to get to him and he was in the Pera Palas Hotel no doubt making big brown eyes at some other woman. Ayşe had to put a hand up to her mouth to stop herself from screaming.

Putting aside the great pile of broken mobile phones and cameras in the middle of the room, İkmen could have imagined himself inside some sort of Agatha Christie novel. A lot of very elegantly dressed people – as well as some Pera Palas staff – were sitting and standing around, looking anxious, in a most impressive orientalist saloon. Some of them, the actors, even wore clothes from the 1920s. It was all very . . . theatrical. İkmen, now mercifully free of his personal captor, sidled up to Süleyman.

'Ideas?' he whispered.

'They know my name,' Süleyman replied.

İkmen had a feeling they knew his too, although none of them, as yet, had actually used it. But now the one figure who could have been female was looking straight at them and so they both became silent.

There was a moment of absolute stillness, punctuated only by some muffled weeping. It was ultimately broken by the leader of the terrorists or whoever they were who said, 'Your game just finished. Well, it did for most of you.' Then he put his hand in his pocket and withdrew a piece of paper. 'In a minute my associates here will take most of you back through to the ballroom. But these people are to stay in here.' He looked down at the paper and read, 'Dr Arto Sarkissian, Dr Krikor Sarkissian, Inspector Çetin İkmen, Inspector Mehmet Süleyman, Mrs Lale Aktar and Mr Hovsep Pars.'

İkmen, instantly alarmed for the elderly and terminally ill Armenian, couldn't stop himself from saying, 'Mr Pars is—'

'Mr Pars is going to play the same game as you,' the leader cut in. 'Or rather, he'll watch you do it.'

'Game?' İkmen looked across the saloon at the small, ailing man and felt his heartbeat rise.

'You six, although more accurately and realistically İkmen and Süleyman, are going to solve a mystery for us,' the leader said. 'Unless of course one of you six perpetrated the crime yourselves.' Whether or not he was smiling underneath that balaclava helmet, İkmen couldn't see, but he could tell that he was gleeful by the tone of his voice.

'What mystery?'

'The mystery of who killed the young prince,' the man said. 'Get it right and you all get out of here alive. Get it wrong and everybody dies. The game for you is far from over.'

Çetin İkmen suddenly felt cold and his body started to shake. He looked at Süleyman whose face was so white it was almost blue. From the other guests came muted crying, little whimpers of fear and soft appeals to Allah to help them.

'Take them through.' The leader directed his team to get all but the policemen, the novelist, the doctors and Hovsep Pars back into the ballroom. As he left, one man said to İkmen, 'You'd better get this right!'

Only when they'd all gone did Çetin İkmen feel able to speak again. He said, 'But there is no young prince, is there? There's a dead boy, an actor. I don't know who he really is.'

'Well, you'd better find out, hadn't you?' the leader said. Then he told his men to clear up the mobile telephones and cameras.

* * *

Nar Sözen had tried her best to keep up with that bloody policewoman but her fucking shoes just hadn't let her. Ayşe Farsakoğlu had always been one of those cops who was generally sympathetic to people like Nar and so she, as well as all the other girls, had wanted to know what she'd been doing sniffing around doorways in Taksim. If Nar and her sisters were going to be subjected to some sort of police crackdown or if the law was looking for someone in particular then Nar wanted to know about it. And Sergeant Farsakoğlu was generally a safe bet when it came to dropping hints.

The 'fucking shoes' put Nar at well over two metres tall and so she stuck out like a beach ball in a snowdrift. Not that it mattered on İstiklal Street. Where İstanbul's alternative society met was not a place that Nar or any transgendered person had to be too worried about. Most of the late-night revellers on the street were either students who didn't give a damn who anyone was provided they could do their thing, liberal Turks and tourists. Only when Ayşe Farsakoğlu peeled off the main road did Nar feel a twinge of fear. But she followed her anyway.

When she got on to Meşrutiyet Street, Nar spotted Ayşe Farsakoğlu making for one of the flanks of the old Pera Palas Hotel. People had to smoke outside these days and so Nar had seen people lurking down the side of the hotel bar on several occasions. She wondered if Ayşe was meeting someone there or whether she was going to enter the hotel via the bar for some reason. As Nar got closer she waved an arm and shouted, 'Hey!' But Ayşe Farsakoğlu didn't respond. She seemed to be fixated on one window. Breathlessly Nar jogged towards her and said, 'Sergeant, what do you want with the girls?'

Ayşe Farsakoğlu turned and, even by the dim light from a street lamp, Nar could see that her face was unusually pale.

'What—'

The policewoman clamped a hand over Nar's mouth and said, 'Sssh!'

Nar tried to talk but Farsakoğlu just pushed her hand still harder against her mouth. 'I think there may be something wrong,' the policewoman whispered. Nar's eyes widened and she mumbled against Farsakoğlu's hand. 'Not with you, Nar!' she continued. 'No, in the hotel. Look.'

She pulled Nar closer to the window she had just been looking through. Nar saw the ornate and comfortable bar of the Pera Palas Hotel and at first she could see nothing wrong with it – apart from the fact that it appeared to be empty. Aware that Nar was not seeing what she had seen, Farsakoğlu said to her, 'Over on the left, in front of the pillar.'

And then Nar saw the figure of a person, possibly a man – she wasn't sure because she never wore the glasses that she needed – on the floor, covered in what could be blood. Slowly Ayşe Farsakoğlu let go of her mouth and then she said, 'Did you see?'

'Was it a dead . . .'

'It could be,' Ayşe said. 'Then again, there is a murder mystery evening taking place in the hotel tonight.' She looked back through the window once more then and added, 'But it looks so real to me. He, the dead man, looks really dead.'

Nar said nothing. She'd seen a few dead bodies in her time and she'd seen even more people who were dead drunk or dead drugged.

'I think I'll go in,' Ayşe said.

'Alone? Aren't you going to call for support or whatever it is the police do?'

Ayşe knew that strictly that was exactly what she should do. *Strictly* she could just march up to the front door of the hotel, present her ID and demand entrance. But if the 'body' was just part of the murder mystery evening, doing that or, worse, stomping in with a load of lairy constables was not a prospect that she relished. The humiliation just didn't bear thinking about. And Mehmet Süleyman was in there. But then that cut both ways. If he was in the hotel and a murder or murders had been committed then he could be in danger at this very moment.

'Inspector İkmen and Inspector Süleyman are in there,' Ayşe said, 'at a party. I've tried to call both of them, but their phones just go to voicemail.'

Nar knew them both. Süleyman had arrested her once for soliciting and İkmen was the cousin of that weird old girl called Samsun who lived over in Beyazıt. 'Do you want me to come with you, Sergeant?' she asked.

Ayşe looked up at her. Nar was a great deal bigger than she was and was also well known for being very handy in a fist fight. She had one conviction for assault to prove it. Officially she was a criminal but having Nar along wasn't a bad idea. 'OK,' Ayşe said. 'But we will have to go in through the back of the building, if we can, because if something dangerous is going on we can't take the risk of going through the front door.' She began to move to where she knew the entrance to the kitchen was, Nar's skyscraper stilettos clacking on the paving stones behind her. The sound of them made Ayşe stop and then turn round. 'You'll have to take those off, Nar,' she said. 'Sorry. But if we have to move quickly for any reason . . .'

Nar gave her a very unamused look but she did take the shoes off. Her feet, Ayşe noticed, were enormous. Nar herself, on the other hand, was now a lot less intimidating than she had been. 'Happy now?' she said as she stood in her stockings, her fingers wrapped around her stilettos.

'So this is how it's going to go—'

'Excuse me,' İkmen raised a hand in the air and then smiled. 'We don't know what your name is. If we don't know how to address you, how can we attract your attention if we have any questions?'

The man behind the balaclava helmet knew that he was being played with and he didn't like it. İkmen could see the anger in his eyes.

'There won't be any questions,' he said. 'You'll do as you're told or we'll kill you.'

'Oh, well, that's all nice and clear then. Thank you.' İkmen subsided into what to the outside world looked like a satisfied silence. Inside he was quite another creature. Inside, his mind was screaming to know what exactly was happening and why. But now he'd managed to regain his outward composure he had to hang on to it. Whatever they were facing, at least one cool head would be needed and so it might as well be his.

'You can interview any of the guests or the actors or the hotel staff who are in that ballroom now,' the masked leader said. 'And you, Inspectors İkmen and Süleyman, may also interview the doctors Sarkissian, Mrs Aktar and Mr Pars. Someone in this hotel killed that boy and whoever did it didn't just do it for a laugh or for effect. You have to uncover the motive behind the killing as well as the culprit. Then, and only then, will we let you go.'

'By *you*, you mean . . .'

'All of you. Decide who you want to interview and we will bring that person to you. This isn't just your show, Çetin Bey. You have a team with Inspector Süleyman, Mrs Aktar, Mr Pars and the two doctors. You must whip your team into shape. Or not.' A muffled laugh came from the mask. 'Because you know what? You have a time limit.'

'A time limit?'

'You must solve the case before the sun comes up, which tomorrow will be at seven twenty a.m.'

'And if we haven't done it by that time, you'll kill us and everyone else?'

'We will.'

'Why?' Even İkmen himself didn't know where that had come from. It was a fair question but they were all in mortal danger from what seemed to be a bunch of terrorists. Not exactly people one questioned closely.

Those eyes looked angry again. 'Why?'

'Yes,' İkmen said. 'Why are you making us do this? Why has he,' he pointed to the man standing behind the leader of the group, 'got a camera on his helmet? And also, how did you know that a real murder was going to happen here tonight?'

The man said nothing and so İkmen, emboldened, continued. 'You could have killed the young prince yourselves. In fact, at the moment, I can't think of anyone more likely to have done that.' He saw Süleyman looking across at him with fear on his face, but he went on anyway. 'And besides, if we do solve this crime or whatever you care to call it, what are you going to do with the perpetrator? Are you going to hand him over to the police? Kill him, or her, yourselves? Just walk out of here as if nothing had happened?'

İkmen was angry. People had been killed for reasons he couldn't even begin to understand, Krikor's event had been ruined and now they were all on some sort of insane time limit. He wanted to say, *Solve the damn case yourselves*, but he didn't, even though he surmised that these people had to know who the murderer was. Because if they didn't know, how could they assess whether or not İkmen and his fellows were right or wrong? They couldn't.

'Well?' he asked. 'Are you going to answer my questions or not?'

The leader stood up. As he walked across the Kubbeli Saloon towards İkmen, Süleyman put a protective arm across his colleague. But contrary to expectation the man didn't hit or even touch Çetin İkmen, he just leaned across his submachine gun at him and said, 'You do your job, I'll do mine and we'll all get along well. Now tell me, Çetin Bey, have you ever read any novels by the late great British author, Agatha Christie?'

Chapter 9

Ersu Bey just couldn't get Stevie Wonder tunes out of his head. Over and over and over again – an endless Stevie Wonder loop that he had even, he was ashamed to admit to himself, started to dance to, albeit rather painfully. But then that had been purely practical. Locked in the fridge he had to keep warm somehow.

The night shift had looked like a bunch of reprobates. But then a lot of young people did look a bit thuggish, especially if they had piercings and tattoos, or so Ersu Bey thought. Not that all of the night staff had been young or unfamiliar to him. He'd seen some of them before even though he didn't know who they were. A very attractive woman probably in her late thirties was the standout person for him. She had a rather boyish figure which he found particularly appealing. He wondered whether she was married.

Ersu Bey had been divorced seven years ago. He and his wife had never had any children and so it had been a relatively straightforward affair. She'd tired of what she always called his 'fussy ways'. But folding napkins so that they made perfect triangles or organising the washing machine in proper sensibly stacked loads were important functions. His wife's divorce papers had described him as 'obsessive compulsive', which had made him sound like some sort of lunatic. But that hadn't been him, that had been her. How he'd managed to live with a woman who thought it was OK to do no housework and spend all her time when she wasn't at work drinking alcohol with her friends he didn't know. Not now. His ex-wife, Tania, had been Russian and because she was Russian not even his lawyer had bothered to question her drinking and carousing. They weren't Muslims, they could do that and, besides, everyone knew that Russians liked a drink. Ersu Bey had known that well before he'd married her. But Tania, like the unknown woman who had come in with the night shift, had possessed the type of tight, boyish figure that he'd always liked. He'd married her before she'd been able to speak more than two words of Turkish, just because he'd found her so alluring. After she left him she'd taken up with some gangster who worked out of a down-at-heel nargile salon in Tophane.

Ersu Bey looked at the sell-by dates on the packets of butter on the shelves and put them in strict order of use. So many people were slack about such things and they mattered. Using older butter before new stock just made sense. He began humming.

Tania had called him superstitious too. She'd said that his habit of always making up their bed in exactly the same way every morning was the same thing as people wearing boncuks and Maşallahs to ward off the Evil Eye. She'd been brought up under the Soviet system and so anything that smacked of superstition or religion was anathema to her. Not that she'd really believed that Ersu had been doing anything occult. She'd just used his very particular nature against him when someone with more money came along.

Ersu Bey began sorting the cheese. He didn't miss his wife, except for the sex, very much at all, if he was honest. The only thing that gave him any real pause for thought about his current state of mind was the fact that, given the choice between life and death, he would occasionally select the latter. A lot of people wanted to die but that didn't mean they actually planned to do anything about it. Currently he was locked in a fridge which probably wouldn't kill him, but he was, deep down, quite indifferent as to whether or not that would really happen, even if he was a little scared. He cared about his guests up in the hotel and hoped that they were being properly looked after by the night staff. That did bother him, he had an anxiety about that. Allied to the deep sense of pride he felt at being employed by the Pera Palas, this did not make for a settled state of mind. So when the door of the fridge did eventually open, Ersu Bey was in fact quite relieved. He would just have liked a little more time to sort out the cream.

'Do you know what he was doing in your room, Lale Hanım?'

Their captors hadn't allowed Lale Aktar to clean herself up after she'd found the boy's body in her hotel room, which meant that when she looked up at İkmen he could see a long smear of blood along her jaw and down her neck. It made her look as if she'd been savaged by a vampire.

'I've no idea.'

İkmen, who had just lit up a cigarette in the no-smoking Kubbeli Saloon, flicked his ash into a dirty coffee cup. None of the masked creatures around them made any comment. 'As far as you know, he hadn't obtained a key to your room?' İkmen asked.

'No.'

He wrote on a notepad their captors had given him. 'And you didn't give him a key?'

'No. Why would I?'

The boy, whose name, Söner Erkan, he had discovered from one of the other actors, had been sweetly attractive. With his trim figure, his razor-sharp cheekbones and

113

full if slightly sulky mouth, he had been the sort of male who could very easily turn a woman's head. In the normal course of events, İkmen wouldn't have pursued this line of inquiry until later on in the investigation. But in this instance there was no time for niceties.

'You might give him a key if you wanted to talk to him for some reason,' İkmen said. And then he looked her straight in the eyes. 'Or if you intended to have sex with him.'

She returned his gaze with rock-solid steadiness. 'No, on both counts,' she said.

'You didn't find Mr Erkan attractive?'

'I didn't know him,' Lale Aktar said. 'My understanding is that he was an actor in what was going to be a murder mystery evening. What he was doing in my room, I can't imagine. Their performance, or whatever you call it, was just about to get going, wasn't it?'

İkmen didn't answer. The performance had actually started during dinner, as Mrs Aktar well knew. What they had all been waiting for in the Kubbeli Saloon had been for the 'murder' itself to actually happen. 'So why were you in your room when the event was just about to get into its stride? You were a team leader, weren't you?'

'Yes. But I had to . . .' Lale Aktar put her head down, then raised it but this time looked away from İkmen. 'I had to . . . get something . . .'

'What?'

'Well, something, er, personal.'

'Something personal? What?'

She didn't answer.

'What, Mrs Aktar?' İkmen asked again. 'Tell me. Whatever it is, I can assure you I will not be shocked, embarrassed or disturbed in any way.'

Lale Aktar looked as if she might be about to cry. But İkmen ignored this and said, 'Mrs Aktar? Please.'

Only Arto Sarkissian and Mehmet Süleyman had ever seen İkmen interview a suspect before and both Krikor Sarkissian and Hovsep Pars now looked visibly uncomfortable. Neither of them realised that this was very gentle probing. Krikor Sarkissian walked away.

Lale Aktar turned to face İkmen and whispered. 'A sanitary towel.'

İkmen didn't miss a beat. 'For menstrual blood?'

Old Hovsep Pars turned away. No one, in his world, ever spoke of such things.

'Yes,' Lale replied.

İkmen smiled. 'Thank you.' He drew on his cigarette and then looked at the notes he'd already taken. 'So please describe to me, Mrs Aktar, what happened when you went back to your room in order to get what you needed. What happened when you first entered room four eleven?'

Lale Aktar swallowed. 'You have to use a swipe card to get into rooms in this hotel, so I swiped my card and let myself in. I flicked the light switch that puts on the light in the little entrance vestibule and made my way through the bedroom and into the bathroom.'

'Did you put the light on in the bedroom?'

She frowned. 'I don't think so. The bathroom is behind the vestibule and so to get to it you just sort of skirt around the edge of the bedroom. And there's a short corridor between the bedroom and the bathroom which is where the wardrobes are. There's a light for that somewhere too, maybe outside the bathroom, but I can't really remember.'

'So the corridor is what is actually behind the vestibule,' İkmen said.

She shrugged. 'I guess so. But the bathroom is behind that – if you see what I mean.'

'But it would have been dark in the room,' Süleyman put in. 'Which means that light from a vestibule that is separated from both the corridor and the bathroom by a wall wouldn't penetrate. Another light source would have been needed, wouldn't it? Unless you just stumbled around in the dark.'

This time she smiled. 'Oh, no.' Then she shrugged again. 'I don't know. I was in a hurry. I may have put the bedroom light on or I may have just put the light on in the corridor . . .'

'But you don't remember seeing the body of Söner Erkan on your bed until you came out of the bathroom?' İkmen said.

'No.' She swallowed. 'No. I came out of the bathroom and walked into the bedroom . . .'

'Did you put the bedroom light on?'

'I don't know. I can't be sure.'

'But the room was illuminated?'

'At some point – before I found, er, the . . . yes.'

'So you came out of the bathroom, down the corridor outside the bathroom, into the bedroom . . .'

'And he was lying on the bed, right in front of me.' Again she turned away.

İkmen looked at Süleyman. The famous novelist clearly needed a moment to herself as she relived her one and only encounter with real, non-fictional death. After about a minute, İkmen cleared his throat. 'So what happened next?'

Her head still turned away from him, Lale Aktar said, 'I was shocked.'

'Obviously.'

She turned and looked at him and her eyes began to visibly fill with tears.

'What did you do first, Mrs Aktar?'

'First?'

'Take it step by step,' Süleyman said. 'What was your first impression of the body on the bed? Were you frightened? Did you think that Söner Erkan was alive or could you see that he was dead?'

For a moment she just sat with her mouth open, as if she were in some way trying to catch the right words. Then she said, 'There was so much blood!' She looked directly at Süleyman. 'I'd never seen blood like it!'

'So you knew that Mr Erkan was dead?'

'I must have done, I suppose.'

'So the light must have been on for you to see the blood.'

'I don't know, I . . . Yes, I imagine so . . .' She began to cry.

Krikor Sarkissian, returned now from his short walk, addressed their captors. 'I want to comfort her, she's a friend,' he said.

The leader of the gang nodded his assent and Krikor went over to sit beside his friend and took one of her hands in his. 'It's OK,' he said as he squeezed her fingers. 'They have to do this.'

'I know.' She smiled though her tears at him and then she looked at İkmen again.

'Could anyone have left your room while you were in the bathroom?' İkmen asked. 'Was there time for a person to do that? Did you hear any sort of noise from the bedroom or beyond when you were in the bathroom?'

'No,' she said. 'I didn't hear anything. As for someone leaving the room . . . I was in the bathroom for a minute, maybe a bit more. I suppose it's possible . . .'

'When you came back down to the Kubbeli Saloon,' İkmen continued, 'your dress and your hands and arms were covered in blood. Can you confirm to me that it was blood from Mr Erkan?'

'Yes.'

'And how did it get on to your body and your clothes, Mrs Aktar?'

She looked at Krikor Sarkissian and for a moment it seemed as if she might be about to cry again. Krikor said, 'Go on, my dear.'

She shook her head. 'You are going to think I'm so stupid!'

'No . . .'

'You will.' She took a deep breath and then she said, 'Because I moved him.'

'You moved him.'

'When I found him, he was face down on the bed. I wanted to see who he was and so I rolled him over,' she said. 'I pulled his shoulders and as he flopped over I got covered in his blood.'

* * *

Piles of cigarette butts outside doorways were a common sight in post-smoking ban İstanbul and so Ayşe Farsakoğlu was not surprised to see them even outside the Pera Palas kitchen door. What did come as a shock, however, was the sight of a man with his back to her, standing in the inner doorway that led from the corridor she was now in to the kitchens. And he was armed. Ayşe Farsakoğlu knew a Kalashnikov rifle when she saw one.

'What is it?' Nar, who couldn't see around Ayşe's body, hissed at her.

Ayşe began riffling though her coat pockets to try and locate her phone. 'Sssh!'

Nar attempted to move past Ayşe to get a look at the inner kitchen door.

But the policewoman held her back. 'Do you have a phone with you?' she whispered.

'A phone? Yes. Don't you?'

'I left it at home,' Ayşe said.

'Well, that was a bit—'

'Just give me your phone!' Her frustration, mainly at herself, was causing her voice to rise. She looked towards the kitchens to make sure that the gunman wasn't coming towards them.

Following an instinct that was more to do with wanting to protect her one-time lover from whatever danger lurked inside the hotel, Ayşe moved forward, pulling

Nar – who had put her precious shoes down and was desperately trying to extricate her phone from the top of one of her stockings – behind her. To both sides of her were doors, possibly to store cupboards or fridges. She heard men's voices from the kitchen.

'What are you going to do?' a young voice said.

There was a laugh, then an older more smoke-dried voice said, 'Bodrum for me. A boat, a bottle of rakı, maybe a girl . . .'

'In your dreams,' a third voice said.

'What? The boat, the rakı or the girl?'

'What do you think!'

They all laughed. Frozen, Ayşe wondered what to do next. She could hear Nar behind her, breathing heavily. She hoped she'd found her phone. But then she heard the young man say, 'It's quiet outside, I'm going out for that cigarette now.'

'Oh, have one in here!' the older man said.

'No,' the young man said, 'I can't smoke in a kitchen, it just isn't nice.'

'OK.'

Ayşe grabbed the handle of the door nearest to her and opened it. She pulled Nar after her. The blinding whiteness of the room was the first thing that hit her. It was some kind of fridge or freezer. Once Nar was in, Ayşe pushed the door to, but not shut. She made Nar keep it open with just one finger.

Hiding in a fridge was certainly a novel experience but the real surprise for Ayşe and Nar came in the shape of a rather urbane-looking man who appeared to be moving blocks of cheese around.

Chapter 10

The boy, Alp İlhan, was clearly frightened but in spite of his fear, his love for what he did shone through.

'Murder mystery events are only part of what we do,' he told İkmen, Süleyman and the others. 'We put on plays, our own work and others, anywhere that will take us.'

'You all go to Boğaziçi University?' İkmen asked.

'Yes.'

İkmen looked down at his notebook. 'And you started Bowstrings the summer before last?'

'Yes. With Ceyda Ümit and Söner Erkan. It was my idea.'

He was a pleasant enough young man but there was a streak of what might be quite ruthless ambition there too. His fictional guise as an Ottoman prince rather suited him.

'I assume that, being students, you needed to raise some capital to start Bowstrings,' İkmen said. 'You must need to pay for costume hire, publicity, for rehearsal time for your plays. Is that right?'

'Yes.'

'So how did you do that?'

He sighed. 'I work as a tour guide in the summer,' he said. 'I can speak English and so I get some work through a travel agency in Sultanahmet. But that's not much. Most of the money that Bowstrings have had so far has come from Söner's parents. They're rich.'

'Would you say that Söner's parents basically own Bowstrings?' İkmen said. Alp was a good-looking boy but now that İkmen regarded him closely he could see that for all his beauty he was just a rather ordinary lower-middle-class İstanbul lad. He was the type of kid whose dad probably had a middle management job in a bank and whose mum stayed at home and wore a headscarf. Not unlike İkmen's own children.

Alp looked down at the floor. 'Yeah.'

'And is that a happy arrangement?' İkmen asked.

'Yeah. Sort of.'

'Sort of?'

'They pay all our bills but . . .' After casting a glance at their captors over one shoulder, he leaned forward in his chair and said, 'Söner could kind of hold that over everyone's head from time to time. Like, if we didn't want to do what he wanted to do he could say he was going to tell his dad . . .'

'Who would cut off your money?'

'Maybe.'

İkmen looked at the boy, who was obviously frightened for all sorts of reasons, and then he said, 'Did you like Söner, Alp?'

He had to think about it for a moment but then he said, 'Yes.'

'Are you sure about that?'

The black-clad ghoul with the camera on his helmet moved in closer and İkmen lost his temper. He glared into the man's eyes and said, 'What are you filming for? Posterity? Your own amusement?'

The man moved in even closer and Hovsep Pars put a hand up to his chest in a vain attempt to still his wildly beating heart.

'What kind of sick—'

'Your job, Inspector İkmen, is to question suspects and then make a judgement,' the leader of the masked gunmen interjected. 'Don't speculate about me or my team. Get it right and you'll never hear from us again.'

'Yes, but what do you want?' Krikor Sarkissian burst out. His face was red with tension and even İkmen, across the other side of the room, could see the veins in his neck pulsating. 'You come here—'

'Shut up.' The leader said it quietly but with an insistence that carried with it a definite layer of menace.

'Your job is not to ask questions. Your job is to watch Inspectors İkmen and Süleyman go about their work and then help them with their judgement at the end.' Then he turned to look at İkmen. 'Time is ticking, Inspector. Do you have many more questions for this witness?'

'A few.' İkmen returned his gaze to Alp's face. 'I get the impression that your liking for Söner was not exactly wholehearted.'

'I didn't kill him, Inspector. You have to believe me.'

Carefully sidestepping the issue, İkmen said, 'What didn't you like about him?'

'Oh.' Alp flung his arms in the air in a gesture of exasperation. 'He was bossy, lazy and he was terrible with money. Always borrowing cash or Akbils or cigarettes from everyone else. Kenan, he plays the Armenian Avram Bey, he's even paid Söner's rent in the past.'

'And yet Söner has rich parents?'

'Yes, but he has – had – rich tastes too,' Alp said. Then his features grimaced and he began to cry. Arto Sarkissian, who was sitting next to the boy, put a fatherly arm around his shoulders.

Under cover of the sound of Alp's crying, Süleyman whispered to İkmen, 'There's an old telephone over by the Christmas tree. I don't know if it works. But if I can get close enough maybe I can find out.'

'What are you talking about?'

They both looked up just in time to see the leader walking towards them.

'Oh, just the case . . .'

He struck İkmen on the cheek with one hard, open hand. It hurt. 'Discussion will come after you've finished all your interviews,' the leader said quietly. 'It's the way Hercule Poirot and Miss Marple would have done it. And if that method was good enough for them then it is most certainly good enough for you.'

'Do you remember seeing film of Beslan?' Ceyda Ümit said to the plump, middle-aged man at her side.

'Was that where Chechen terrorists took over a school somewhere in Russia?' Burak Fisekçi asked.

'Yes.' Ceyda looked around the ballroom with wide, frightened 1920s-style eyes. There were, she counted, eight black-clad masked men silently watching their every move. 'They were Muslim fundamentalists.'

'Do you think that these people might be fundamentalists too?'

'I don't know,' she said. 'But whoever they are, I wasn't expecting them. I didn't sign up for this, Burak Bey.'

'None of us did,' he said. And then he smiled at her. 'If I'd known this was going to happen I would never have asked you and your friends to come and perform for us tonight, Ceyda.'

'And Söner is *dead*. How can that be?' she said. 'He was supposed to be the victim in the drama, yes, but not in real life.'

'Why was he the victim in your murder mystery entertainment?' Burak Fisekçi asked.

'No one told you?'

'No. Once we'd set the basic plot, it was decided that it was best that only the actors, you, knew all the details, in case I inadvertently gave something away. Remember?'

'Yes, sort of. I . . . I killed young Yusuf Effendi because he was blackmailing me,' she said. 'I'd been having an affair with Signor Garibaldi which Yusuf got to know about.'

Burak raised a small smile. 'How exotic.'

'Well, it would have been.' She looked around the room and then she said, 'Alp is a long time.' She frowned.

'He's with Dr Sarkissian and his brother and the policemen. I shouldn't worry.'

'He's also with more of these *people*,' Ceyda said. 'Burak Bey, can you think of a reason, any reason, why this is happening to us?'

'I can't.' He took one of her small, dry hands in one of his large, damp mitts and he smiled at her again. 'But I'm sure it will all be all right in the end. I'm sure it will.'

Ceyda forced herself to raise a smile. She'd known Burak Bey all her life and had always found him truthful and reliable. So his words were a comfort even though she knew that there was no way even Burak Fisekçi could predict what was going to happen.

Bowstrings had got the gig through Ceyda Ümit.

'Burak Fisekçi, my assistant, lives in the same apartment block as Ceyda Ümit's family,' Krikor Sarkissian told Çetin İkmen. 'When we were first considering the idea of a murder mystery event, Burak told me that he knew a young girl who was part of a theatrical troupe. They came along to the clinic. They had some good ideas and, more crucially, they'd already performed a murder mystery event at the Four Seasons. That had been very successful. I thought it would be nice to give a group of young actors a chance – not to mention some money.'

'Whose idea was it to have a murder mystery evening?' İkmen asked. The fact that the guests had been too absorbed in the fictional mystery to notice anything that might have been going awry in real life could point to some sort of connection between the play and subsequent events. But then it might not. İkmen hadn't noticed anything suspicious, with the exception of the strange man who had visited the concierge earlier. He wondered if that concierge was still in the hotel or had already gone home.

'We had a brainstorming session,' Krikor Sarkissian said. 'We do that a lot when we have a problem.'

'We?'

'Myself, Burak, our nurses, Selma Hanım, our receptionist. It was a long time ago, Çetin, eighteen months or so.'

'Do you remember who came up with the idea for a murder mystery evening?'

'We all did really,' Krikor said. 'My first thought on it was to just have a straightforward dinner somewhere with maybe some circus acts performing after the meal. We talked for hours. But because Burak knew Ceyda and her actor friends and what they did, the murder mystery evening was ultimately his idea.'

'Are any of the other participants in that meeting here tonight?'

'No, Selma Hanım didn't want to come and our nursing staff has completely changed since that time.'

'Did anyone take any notes during the meeting?' İkmen asked.

'Burak always takes notes during meetings, that is part of his function. Although I doubt very much whether he'll have those notes on him tonight.'

İkmen looked at their captors. 'I don't suppose it will be possible to leave the hotel to search for evidence, will it?'

No one spoke until the leader said, 'What do you think, Çetin Bey?'

İkmen looked him in the eyes. 'What do I think? I don't know. But I can say what worries me.'

'And what is that?' the leader asked.

'What worries me most is if Inspector Süleyman and I successfully identify who killed Söner Erkan but you choose to disagree with us.'

The eyes underneath the balaclava helmet crinkled a little as the leader's brows came together. 'But why would I do that?'

Out of the corner of his eye, İkmen saw Süleyman move a few centimetres to his left, closer to the telephone.

'Because you want to kill us,' İkmen said.

Now the eyes relaxed. 'And why would I want to do that, Inspector İkmen?'

'I have no idea,' İkmen replied. 'So far, sir, you and your colleagues represent something that is outside my experience.' Then he looked down at his notes. 'I'd like to see the crime scene,' he said. 'My first view of it was truncated by your invasion or whatever one might call it.'

'If you wish to see the crime scene again,' the leader said, 'then that can be arranged. Mr Söner Erkan hasn't gone anywhere.'

* * *

It took Ersu Bey just over a minute to realise that he was not the only man in the fridge. There was an attractive woman in her thirties and a very tall and glamorous figure who had the breasts of a woman and the feet and throat of a man. A transsexual. Ersu Bey didn't know how to feel. On one level he was repulsed while on the other he was grateful for the company of anyone in that awful, cold and confined space. However what the real woman said to him was disturbing.

'It seems some people, we don't know who, have taken over the hotel,' she said. 'We know they're armed and we suspect they've killed but—'

'Who *are* you?' Ersu Bey said. 'What are you doing here?'

The transsexual, who had one heavily lacquered fingernail keeping the door open just a crack, hissed, 'Keep it down! They'll hear you!'

Ayşe Farsakoğlu put her hand in her pocket but didn't find her police badge. She shrugged. 'I'm a police officer,' she whispered. 'My name is Sergeant Ayşe Farsakoğlu.' Then she pointed at the transsexual. 'She is Nar. I can't explain exactly who she is, it would take too long. Who are you?'

'Me?'

'Sssh!' Nar hissed again. 'Keep it down, I said!'

'I am Ersu Nadir,' he whispered. 'I am the maître d'hôtel. Why are you and this, er, person in my refrigerator?'

'Why were you locked in your own refrigerator, Ersu Bey?' Ayşe said.

'I asked—'

'It doesn't matter who asked what or why!' Ayşe was exasperated. She hadn't expected to find herself hiding in a fridge, never mind a fridge occupied by a man she got the impression was something of a martinet. 'At the moment one of the gunmen is outside the kitchen door having a smoke,' she said. 'When he comes back in and returns to the kitchen, maybe we can move out into the hotel. It depends what he and his colleagues do. Who locked you in here?'

'I've no idea.' He still didn't know whether to believe her story about being a police officer, but if she and the transsexual were going to get him out of the fridge, did it really matter too much? Not that he *really* cared . . . 'I was putting butter away and then the door closed. I didn't see who did it. Some of our kitchen staff are not as bright as they might be. Tonight they're mainly casuals.'

'You don't think that you were locked in deliberately?'

'Who knows?'

'He's coming back!' Nar took her index finger out of the crack in the door and replaced it with her little finger. The corridor from the kitchen to the back door was dingy and she wanted to cut down any light coming from the fridge as much as possible. Fortunately the fridge door opened towards the inner door of the hotel, so with any luck the man would only see the light from the crack if he looked back before he went into the kitchen. None of them breathed as they heard his footsteps pass along the corridor outside.

Chapter 11

Arto Sarkissian hadn't had any latex gloves on him when he came to the Pera Palas and so he asked the anonymous men if one of them might bring him some washing-up gloves from the hotel kitchens. The leader duly called someone and after about ten minutes a pair of yellow plastic gloves were delivered to room 411. Getting the gloves was one thing but using them was quite another. Compared to the thin latex gloves he generally used in his work, these were horribly unwieldy.

Arto examined what was a very deep wound in Söner Erkan's throat. There were other wounds to his chest but they were not, he believed, the cause of the young man's death. Like Çetin İkmen, Arto Sarkissian believed that it was the thrust to the neck that had killed him.

'Looks like a straight blade severed the carotid artery,' he said.

'Was I right? Was he still alive when it happened?' İkmen asked.

'Oh, yes,' the pathologist said.

'What about the other wounds?'

'Window dressing.'

'Meaning?'

'Either the assailant wanted to mislead us with the chest wounds for some reason, or he or she attacked the corpse post mortem, maybe because they didn't realise he was already dead.' Arto Sarkissian looked at the masked leader and said, 'Can we look for the murder weapon?'

'Of course.'

İkmen, Arto Sarkissian and Mehmet Süleyman began to search the room. Apparently only one pair of gloves had been found in the kitchen and so İkmen and Süleyman were reduced to wrapping handkerchiefs around their hands as they opened drawers and looked underneath the bed and in the bathroom. With luck, at some point in the future, a properly appointed police team would gain access to 411 to conduct a systematic search. But for the moment they just had to do what they could. In terms of fingerprints and/or footprints, only those of Lale Aktar were obvious. Her shoes were distinctive. Little, high-heeled Jimmy Choos which had left bloody stiletto and pointed toe marks across the bedroom floor and out into the corridor. But they found no weapon.

Arto Sarkissian looked down at the body again. 'I think he was lying on the bed on his back when he was stabbed,' he said.

Çetin İkmen frowned. 'But Mrs Aktar turned him on to his back.'

'Did she?'

'She saw an apparently lifeless body on her bed and wanted to see who it was,' İkmen said. 'He was on his stomach and so she turned him over. As a writer of crime fiction one would have thought she should have known better but . . .'

'So the killer must have killed him and then rolled him on to to his stomach,' Arto said. 'Odd. As for Mrs Aktar, she is neither a police officer nor a pathologist. Intellectually she may know that tampering with a crime scene is wrong, but on the level of instinct she may well react quite differently. Which indeed she did.' He looked at the leader and he said, 'Is the murder weapon in this room?'

There was a pause and then the man said, 'It's in this hotel – probably.'

The pathologist sighed. 'I don't suppose you could be more specific?'

'Now where would the fun be in that?' the leader said.

İkmen, who found the presence of the camera on one of the men's helmets sinister and disturbing, said, 'Nothing juicy to film if you tell us too much, eh?'

But no one answered him. Arto Sarkissian looked back at the dead man on the bed again and then down at the floor.

* * *

There had been a telephone call, some activity in the kitchen and then two of the men had left to go somewhere else while the other one went upstairs to the lavatory. When he left, he locked the door from the kitchen into the hotel.

Ayşe, Nar and Ersu Nadir tiptoed out of the fridge and entered a world of tiles, cookers and bains-maries.

'So what now?' Nar said to Ayşe as she waved her mobile phone in the air. 'What are we supposed to do locked in another fucking room?'

Ayşe took the slim iPhone out of Nar's hand and said, 'We need to get help. In some form.'

Back in the fridge she'd been itching to phone the station, but now she wasn't so sure. If the full weight of the İstanbul police force came down on these people, whoever they were, it could end badly. Sieges often did. But she was aware that she had to phone someone because they needed help. Apart from the small penknife Nar always carried to frighten away violent punters, they were unarmed. Ayşe called İzzet. If she could explain the situation to him then maybe he could at least try to control what might become a dangerously violent response. She had no idea who these heavily armed people were or what they wanted. Negotiation rather than force seemed to Ayşe to be the way forward, but she couldn't do it. She, like the maître d'hôtel and Nar, was entirely at the mercy of whoever these people were.

The phone went straight to voicemail which meant that İzzet was probably in the shower. Even when he slept he always left his phone on but in the shower he insisted upon being on his own.

She left a message. 'İzzet, it's me,' she said. 'Call me back on this number as soon as you can.'

He'd be alarmed that she was calling from an unrecognised phone but then maybe that would make him ring back more quickly. 'I need to keep your phone,' she said to Nar.

Nar shrugged. 'OK. But that didn't sound exactly urgent to me.'

Ayşe ignored her. 'I'll put it on silent vibrate. Are you expecting any calls?'

Nar raised an eyebrow.

'OK, I won't ask.' Ayşe put the phone in her pocket. Then she turned towards Ersu Bey. 'Now you need to tell me everything you can about this murder mystery evening,' she said.

'We have to weigh up the need to find the murder weapon against the value it will have for us when coming to a decision about this event,' Süleyman said. 'The concierge told us there are one hundred and fifteen rooms in this hotel and that is quite apart from the public rooms, the kitchens and the linen cupboards. It could take us days. We only have hours.'

One o'clock was looming already and Çetin İkmen and Arto Sarkissian were as well aware of the passage of time as Mehmet Süleyman. 'I think we need to get back downstairs and question everyone we haven't spoken to yet who knew Söner Erkan,' Süleyman continued. 'Somebody killed him for a reason.'

'Unless this lot did it,' İkmen said as he looked across room 411 at the four heavily armed men who were watching them. He said to them, 'You set this up, didn't you?'

None of them said a word.

'You must have done. You did. Whoever killed Söner Erkan is in league with you. He or she has to be.' He shrugged. 'You know.'

'Yes, we do,' the leader said. Even through the thick wool of his balaclava helmet, his voice was, if not cultured, then assured. He wasn't just some street thug. 'But the boy died for a reason quite separate from our involvement. I give you my word of honour on that point.'

İkmen laughed. 'And that's supposed to reassure me?'

'Söner Erkan died because someone in this hotel had a problem with him,' the leader said. 'Someone wanted him out of the way for a reason which has nothing to do with me or my team.'

'But you knew it was going to happen, didn't you?'

The leader did not reply.

İkmen turned back to face Süleyman and Arto

Sarkissian. 'Whoever killed Erkan knows this team and so he or she knew that all this was going to happen,' he said.

'But if we don't know who these people are, how can we even begin to find a connection between them and the people downstairs?' Arto said.

İkmen lowered his voice. 'There has to be some sort of link between one or more of the guests or the hotel staff and these people.'

'Yes, but what?'

'I don't know!'

'Isn't there some sort of police mythology that states that whoever finds a dead body is the one most likely to be its killer?' Arto said.

For a moment they all became silent and then İkmen said, 'There is some truth in that, Arto, yes.' He waited to see whether Süleyman, a man clearly attracted to Lale Aktar, would jump in with a robust rebuttal. But he didn't. 'Mrs Aktar is a very successful and wealthy novelist,' İkmen continued. 'She is married to an equally successful and wealthy man who is nevertheless thirty years her senior.'

'Söner Erkan was over ten years younger than Mrs Aktar,' Süleyman said. 'What would she want with a boy?'

İkmen gave him the kind of look that needed no explanation.

'All right, why *this* boy then?' Süleyman asked.

'Beyond the fact that he had the face of an angel and the body of a Greek god?' Arto Sarkissian said.

İkmen smiled. 'I think we should get back downstairs now,' he said. He turned to their captors, 'We're leaving.'

'Very well.'

İkmen began to walk towards the vestibule, but just before he left the bedroom he stopped. To his left was a large photograph of Agatha Christie. He looked up at it and then he smiled. 'I know that you both wrote and lived mystery, Mrs Christie,' he said. 'If there is such a thing as the afterlife, I'd be obliged if you'd come through and send us some of your inspiration now.'

One of the masked men laughed. Arto Sarkissian turned back to look at him with some disapproval, but as he did so he found himself looking at the body on the bed once again. Then he looked at the blood on the walls and Lale Aktar's footprints on the floor.

The old man took one of Krikor Sarkissian's hands in his and said, 'I don't know why I'm here.'

'Because you've been selected to stay with us?' Krikor asked.

'Yes. Why?' Hovsep Pars said. 'The policemen I can understand. You, Krikor, because this was your event, and Mrs Aktar is a crime writer. But me? I am an old man. What possible use can I be to you or to anyone? What is the significance of me?'

Krikor shrugged. 'I don't know, my friend.'

The old man shook his head. 'A lifetime of trouble and now this! You know, sometimes, Krikor, I wonder whether my family is cursed.'

'No, it's—'

'The tragedy of my sister and her husband? Of young Avram? My fiancée Nargiz dead before I could marry her? And my parents . . .'

'Your parents?' Krikor knew quite a lot about the Pars family but he had always believed that Hovsep's parents had been very fortunate people. They had certainly always been rich.

Hovsep lowered his voice so that neither their captors nor Lale Aktar could hear him. 'My mother's family came from Anatolia, the city of Diyarbakır,' he said. 'She left in nineteen fifteen . . . just her, alone . . . you know . . .'

'Yes,' Krikor cut in quickly. The events of 1915 had always been difficult for both Armenians and Turks. The Ottoman Empire had been at war with, amongst other nations, the Russians at the time. And the Russians had promised the Armenians their own homeland if they fought for them. Atrocities had been committed on all sides but questions still remained over the role and the fate of the Armenian population of Anatolia in 1915.

Some people had accused the Turks of genocide, others said that what had happened were individual acts of revenge or self-defence.

'My parents did not have a normal marriage,' the old man said. 'Because of my mother's . . . because of those formative experiences . . . She had my sister and myself very quickly after she married but I never knew my parents to share a room. My mother was . . .'

'So many Anatolians were traumatised at the end of that war,' Krikor said. 'Especially the women.'

As Turkish, Russian, Kurdish and Armenian forces had raged across Anatolia during the Great War, casualties had been massive. Even non-combatants like women and children had suffered terribly. Some women had been raped by soldiers of the enemy as well as by their own troops. The madness of war had overwhelmed everything and everyone in its path.

'Only the women and the children were innocent in that insanity,' Krikor said. 'But Hovsep, you are not cursed. There's no such thing.'

The old man smiled. 'You are a man of science, Krikor. Your life is ruled by logic.'

'It's a way of coping.' He smiled. 'And I believe it to be the truth. Forgive me, Hovsep, but curses and bad luck and everything like that make no sense to me.'

'And yet your old friend Çetin İkmen, the son of a

witch, is a man whose opinion you and Arto lay great store by.'

'True. But his mother, our Auntie Ayşe, she was, well, she was an extraordinary woman. Maybe my logical atheism can't explain her. But Çetin, whether or not he has second sight or magic or whatever you wish to call it, is a clever man with a keen sense of justice and I trust him.'

'Do you?' And then Hovsep Pars's face changed. It became something bitter that Krikor Sarkissian didn't like. 'You trust a man who was not brave enough to kill the creature who murdered our Avram, who caused my own sister and her husband to take their own lives? Clever your İkmen may be, Krikor, but I would question his keen sense of justice. If there had been a scrap of justice in his soul he would have let that creature die when he had the chance.'

Arto Sarkissian had estimated the time of Söner Erkan's death to be within two hours of his examination of the corpse. The young man had been seen alive half an hour at the most before Lale Aktar had found him in her hotel room.

'In the script, Söner, the young Prince Yusuf, was going to be found in the old wooden lift,' Ceyda Ümit told İkmen and Süleyman.

Kenan Oz, who had played the Armenian Avram Bey,

said, 'Ceyda, the princess, she killed him because he was blackmailing her over an affair she'd had years ago with her Italian tutor.'

'Signor Garibaldi?'

'Yeah, or Metin Martini, which is his real name,' Kenan said. 'His dad really is Italian but his mum's Turkish.'

'So the body . . .'

'We were all based on the fourth floor,' Kenan said. 'We were going to put some fake blood on Söner's shirt and then he was going to get into the lift and go down to the ground floor where you, the guests, would "discover" him.'

'What time was this?' İkmen asked.

'Eleven,' Ceyda said.

'I knocked on Söner's hotel room door at ten forty-five or thereabouts,' Kenan said. 'But he didn't answer. I looked for him. I went to Ceyda's room, Alp's, Deniz's—'

'Deniz?'

'She plays Sofia, the Greek housekeeper. But I couldn't find him.'

'You had no idea he was in Mrs Aktar's room?' Süleyman asked.

'No. Why would I?'

'Söner Erkan had no connection to Mrs Aktar, as far as you are aware?'

'No.'

'No,' Ceyda echoed her colleague. 'Söner was . . .' She looked up at Kenan before she carried on. 'Söner was a pain, to be totally truthful. He was rich and spoilt and I never ever saw him with a girl, much less a sophisticated woman. He could only buy people, you know. And yet he was hopeless with money. Always borrowing from other people. You, Kenan, even paid his rent, didn't you?'

'Once.'

They'd heard much of this before from Ceyda's boyfriend, Alp.

'But obviously you weren't with Söner Erkan all the time,' İkmen said.

'No.' Ceyda looked at Kenan again. 'But I don't know what he used to do outside of university and Bowstrings, do you?'

Kenan shrugged. 'No.'

'But he did get involved in the development of the script for this event?' İkmen asked.

'Oh, yes,' Ceyda said. 'We all got involved in that.'

'So you came to group decisions about who did what, why and when?'

'Mostly, yes, sometimes together with the client,' Kenan said.

'Dr Krikor Sarkissian.'

'At the beginning,' Ceyda said. 'But he's so busy, he

handed it over to his assistant, Burak Bey. Burak Bey also liaised with the hotel.'

'Do you know who Burak Bey liaised with in the hotel?' İkmen asked.

'No,' Ceyda said. 'I imagine it must have been the general manager or someone like that. We saw the concierge once when we came to rehearse last month and we met the maître d'hôtel only when we arrived today. But I can't remember his name. I think he went hours ago, though.'

Chapter 12

Discovering what really happened to people when they were held captive was not something that the brothers Sarkissian had ever really given a great deal of thought to. They were both doctors and so they knew, to some extent, how stress could affect a biological system like the human body, but now they found themselves in the midst of this phenomenon. There was rather less crying than either of them had expected, but there were more people who needed to go to the toilet – badly.

Rather than try to deal with a ballroom that looked and smelt like the Augean Stables, the gunmen accompanied the two doctors and those they were ministering to downstairs to the toilets. Some people were sick, others had diarrhoea while others just felt cold and shivery, and a couple of the men complained of chest pains. One particularly elderly man had to be helped to the toilets by both of them and it was at this point that Arto took the opportunity to seek his brother's counsel.

'Krikor!' he hissed as they pulled the man into the cubicle and sat him down on the toilet.

'What?'

'If someone had been stabbed in the throat, severing the carotid artery, they'd bleed a lot.'

'Like a sheep at bayram, yes.'

'But on a bed with a thick mattress, would the blood pool on the floor?'

Krikor told the old man that they'd be outside the cubicle if he needed them. Arto came out and they shut the door behind them. In front of them was a man with a Kalashnikov. With his eyes, Arto Sarkissian begged his brother for an answer. But Krikor couldn't reply because the armed man was just too close to them. They all waited in silence until the old man had managed to relieve himself to his own satisfaction and only then could the two Armenians go back in.

'Well?'

'If the mattress is covered with some sort of waterproof protector and if the bedclothes are thin, it's possible,' Krikor said. 'If not . . .'

'That's what I thought,' Arto whispered. 'Thank you.'

That Ayşe was somewhat prone to stomach upsets was something that İzzet was going to have to get accustomed to once they were married. Very often when they went out to eat she would have to stop because she felt unwell and either had to go to the lavatory or go home. He imagined it was probably some sort of nervous complaint. It had certainly got a lot worse since they'd started preparing for their wedding. As Ali Farsakoğlu had said, it was most likely pre-nuptial nerves.

İzzet had drunk more rakı than he should have done and so he'd stayed rather longer in the shower than he usually did. He didn't want to wake up just as he was about to go to bed but he didn't want to be horribly hung over in the morning either. So he'd had a nice long, hot shower. Now he was out he dried himself, put his pyjamas on and then lit up a cigarette. He was actually in bed by the time he switched his phone back on again.

He only had one text, from his son in İzmir, and a voice message from a number that he didn't recognise. For a moment he thought he might just delete the voice message as it was probably a wrong number. But then he thought better of it. He found himself listening to Ayşe's voice. She sounded in control of herself but only just and so he did what she'd requested and he phoned her back.

But there was no reply.

* * *

'The maître d'? He's called Ersu Bey,' Burak Fisekçi told Çetin İkmen. 'But he's gone. Went off after the meal. I think I may have even seen him go when I was on my way to the toilet, just before all this hell broke loose.'

Krikor Sarkissian's assistant came from one of those Armenian families who had converted to Islam several generations before. But they still rarely married out and Burak's mother, as well as his father, had been a converted Armenian too. In spite of his ungainly appearance, Çetin İkmen had always wondered whether it was lack of eligible Muslim Armenian ladies in İstanbul that was the reason behind Burak's single status.

'You helped to develop this murder mystery play with the actors, I understand,' İkmen said.

Light shining through the patterned ceiling domes of the Kubbeli Saloon dappled Burak Fisekçi's sallow face with tiny spots of bluish light. It made his large features appear unpleasantly mottled.

'Yes,' Burak replied. 'Although not to any great extent. I made suggestions but I was not privy to the proposed climax of the mystery.'

'Do you remember what they were? The details you were involved with?'

'Not really.' He smiled. 'About trivial things. Early plot points. How the actors should comport themselves in period costume. I studied history at university . . .'

'Yes.' Çetin İkmen had known Burak Fisekçi for over ten years, ever since he'd come to work for Krikor Sarkissian. A well-educated man, he had a degree in history from Boğaziçi University.

'Ceyda and the other youngsters did most of the work. They're very clever,' he said. 'They kept a lot of things close to their chests.'

İkmen looked down at his notes. 'Mmm.'

Krikor Sarkissian had told İkmen where Burak lived and it was in the same apartment block as Ceyda Ümit.

'Did you deliberately set out to get your neighbours' daughter and her theatrical troupe this job, Mr Fisekçi?' İkmen asked.

'No. Not really. But once Dr Sarkissian had decided that he wanted some sort of entertainment, I did remember what Cengiz Ümit, Ceyda's father, had told me about her little company. Of course Dr Sarkissian had the final say.'

'But you introduced the Bowstrings to him?'

'Yes.' He shrugged. 'Why not?'

'Why not indeed.' İkmen smiled. 'Burak Bey, do you have any idea who might have wanted to kill Söner Erkan?'

'None at all.'

'He could, I understand, be a somewhat challenging young man.'

'As you say, Çetin Bey, he was young. It is in the nature of young men to be challenging and problematic.'

'But not all young men.' İkmen smiled again. 'I didn't know you when you were the same age as Mr Erkan but I did first meet you when you were in your twenties, Burak Bey. You were far from challenging. In fact I remember being struck by just how mature your attitude was for such a young person.'

'I think Söner Erkan maybe suffered from a lack of parental control, or rather guidance,' Burak said.

This mirrored what Ceyda, Alp and others had told İkmen. 'Rich boy playing at life and messing it up,' he said. 'Yes, I've come across a few of those in my time.' He looked across the room at old Hovsep Pars who nodded his head. 'They can be dangerous.'

'Not in this case, though.'

İkmen narrowed his eyes. 'I don't know about that, Burak Bey,' he said. 'Söner Erkan was murdered for a reason. Maybe he threatened someone who killed him in an act of self-defence. Maybe he was blackmailing someone or had committed an act of cruelty or violence against an individual who took revenge upon him. Not all victims are blameless innocents. Far from it.'

* * *

'Allah!'

The man dropped to the floor, hitting his head on the hard, cold tiles. As he fell he made a sound like a goat grunting.

Nar, who had delivered the blow to his head with a copper-bottomed saucepan, bent down to look into his eyes and said, 'Have I killed him?'

Ayşe Farsakoğlu, mobile phone in one hand, took the man's wrist in her other hand. 'No,' she said. Then she lifted one of his eyelids and looked at his eye. 'But he's out for now.'

'What are we going to do with him?'

The phone Ayşe had borrowed from Nar had just started vibrating when the man had suddenly walked back into the kitchen. None of them had heard him coming. Ayşe, the phone almost at her ear, had looked straight into his eyes, while Ersu Bey had just stood as if frozen to the spot. Luckily Nar, whom the masked man hadn't seen, managed to get behind him and smash him on the head with a saucepan. Ersu Bey picked up the man's Kalashnikov rifle and with ex-military efficiency checked it over to see whether it was locked. Ayşe looked at the phone again which had now stopped vibrating. She brought up the missed calls directory and said, 'That was İzzet. I'll have to call him back.'

'Yes, but what are we going to do with *him*?' Nar

repeated, pointing at the man on the floor. 'He's one of *them* and so I think it's safe to assume that if he doesn't go back to wherever he's supposed to be, they'll come down here and look for him. What are we going to do?'

'We could put him in the fridge,' Ersu Bey said.

'Yes, but they'll still come down here looking for him,' Nar said. She put her hands up to her head in frustration. 'What was I thinking!'

'You were thinking he'd seen us and he had a gun,' Ayşe said. 'You did the right thing.'

'But now we have a problem!'

Ayşe just wanted to call İzzet back but Nar was right, the man she'd knocked out was a problem. They couldn't just leave him in the middle of the kitchen floor. Even if no one came looking for him, eventually he would come round. 'All right, let's put him in the fridge,' she said. 'No one will be able to hear him in there.'

Ersu put his arms underneath the man's armpits and began to drag him towards the corridor where the fridges and freezers were. About halfway across the floor, the man began to make groggy, groaning noises. At one point he lifted his head, although his eyes were closed.

When Ersu reached the fridge they had all been in together earlier he called out for someone to open the door. Nar obliged while Ayşe, frowning now, followed Ersu Bey into the fridge. With one last mighty tug, Ersu Bey pulled the man to the back of the fridge and then flopped him down on the floor. Wiping his sweating brow with his hand he said, 'That wasn't easy.'

'No.'

Ersu laid Ayşe and Nar's coats over the man then stepped over his body and walked out of the fridge to join Nar in the corridor. He was getting used to her now – sort of. It was at the very least reassuring that she still had all the power and aggression of a man. It made Ersu feel a little less isolated.

'Sergeant Farsakoğlu,' Nar said. The policewoman was still in the fridge, still staring at the body. She looked rooted to the spot. The body groaned again. 'Ayşe Hanım!'

Ayşe turned. She narrowed her eyes. 'How tall are you, Nar?' she asked.

'Tall?' She shrugged. One hundred and ninety-three centimetres when I was measured to do my military service. Why?'

Ayşe looked back at the man on the floor again and said, 'He must be at least a hundred and ninety. Nar . . .'

Realisation came quickly. 'Oh, I don't think so, no,' the transsexual said.

Ayşe smiled at her. 'You'd be—'

'Oh, please don't tell me it's my patriotic duty!' Nar said.

Ersu Bey, confused, said, 'What's going on?'

'What's going on? I want Nar to put this man's clothes on and find out what's happening in this hotel,' Ayşe said. 'Stuck down here we don't stand a chance of finding anything out.'

'So call your Sergeant Melik back then!' Nar said. 'Get your colleagues in here and—'

'The more my colleagues know about this situation before they come in here, the better,' Ayşe said. 'The more intelligence we can give them prior to any action they may take, the more likely it is that we all get out of here alive. Nar, you are the only person here who can fit into this man's clothes.'

'But we don't know his name or—'

'Hüseyin Hikmet.' Ersu Bey held up an ATM card that he'd found in the pocket of the unconscious man's trousers.

'If that's his card,' Nar said. She took a deep breath, exhaled and then stood in silence for a moment. Hüseyin Hikmet, or whoever he was, made more grunting noises.

'It will be a risk but I know you can handle a gun,' Ayşe said as she put a hand on Nar's shoulder. 'And I know you're not stupid.'

Nar looked down at Ayşe and shook her head. 'Ayşe

Hanım,' she said, 'I've got breasts. What can I say? I've got breasts that cost me a lot of money and I'm wearing false eyelashes and make-up.'

'Your make-up can be removed,' Ayşe said. She glanced quickly across at Ersu Bey who was looking down at the floor in a very pointed fashion. His ears, if not his face, were red with embarrassment.

'But what about my nails!' Nar held her hands up. Her nails were long, bright blue and dusted with glitter. 'What am I supposed to do about these? Rip them off?'

Ayşe could see that the nails were a problem. Even cut right down they would still be blue and glittery. For a moment she felt she'd lost the argument. But then Ersu Bey unexpectedly made a suggestion.

'We use acetone to remove blemishes from our china,' he said. 'There's at least one bottle of it underneath the sinks. Isn't acetone what is used to take off nail varnish?'

Time was moving on and even if Inspectors İkmen and Süleyman came to a conclusion about who the murderer might be soon, they could still be wrong. There were a lot of 'red herrings' – that was what the famous British crime writers called false leads. And İkmen and Süleyman only had one shot at the puzzle. After that they were out of ammunition.

But what if they did actually solve the mystery of who killed Söner Erkan? Well, that had all been taken account of in the plan. That was no more of a problem than if they got it wrong. It was just that if they did get it wrong, that would be a lot more satisfying.

Chapter 13

'I hated the sight of him.'

Just to be sure, İkmen asked, 'Söner Erkan?'

'He was a little prick!' Metin Martini, the half-Italian boy who had played the dashing Dr Enzo Garibaldi, was very sure of his feelings. 'Whatever he said went, because his mummy and daddy gave Bowstrings some money to get started. Or rather they gave their ill-gotten gains to Lions in Iron Cages.'

İkmen frowned.

'Lions in Iron Cages was the original name of Bowstrings,' the young man said. 'Alp came up with it and we all thought it was brilliant.'

'Is this a reference to the "Lion in an Iron Cage" poem?' İkmen said.

'Yes. By Nazim Hikmet, our greatest poet. He likens the lion in the cage to the untameable and uncrushable spirit of freedom. He went to prison for saying things like that. Well, Söner's parents didn't like that. They wanted something Ottoman. Arseholes!'

Out of the corner of his eye, İkmen saw the 'Ottoman' Mehmet Süleyman smile. 'So what did they say?' İkmen asked.

Metin Martini shrugged. 'I dunno. We get this job with Dr Sarkissian and the next thing I know we're not Lions any more but bloody Bowstrings!'

'At the suggestion of Söner Erkan's parents?'

'Söner told us,' he said. 'He and Alp went to a meeting with Dr Sarkissian, we got the gig, and then suddenly it's like, "We're Bowstrings now!" I was, like, *No!* But then he's all, "This is just the way it is!" and Alp doesn't say a word. We were going to be a political company, you know? There are things going on in this country that need to be challenged. I accept we needed to do this kind of gig to get some money together but me and Alp and Ceyda, we had plans.'

'Could Dr Sarkissian and not Söner Erkan's parents have made the suggestion to change the company's name?'

'Why would he do that?'

İkmen didn't know. Nazim Hikmet's work had remained contentious since his death back in the 1960s right up to his official rehabilitation by the state in 2009. It was possible that Krikor Sarkissian didn't want his charity event to be associated with the work of a long-dead communist but it wasn't that likely.

'Söner's father owns a construction company,' Metin

said. 'He was just like a builder out in Anatolia until he started doing "good works".'

'What good works?'

'Putting mosques back together in Bosnia after the war.' Metin pulled a face. 'Not exactly putting food on people's tables or giving them hospitals, but he did the whole good religious man thing and so he got in with a load of people who like all that. They put work his way.'

İkmen hadn't got the impression that Söner Erkan's family were religious people. The boy himself appeared to have been very far away from being a modest Muslim lad.

'I shouldn't be saying any of this to you, I suppose, in case you're one of them too.' Metin Martini looked down his long nose at İkmen.

'One of whom?' İkmen asked.

The boy waved a hand in the air and said, 'Religious people.'

'I have nothing to do with any organisation either secular or religious,' İkmen said. 'I serve my country, Mr Martini. That's all. And at the moment my only concern is to discover who killed Söner Erkan and why. If my colleague and I can't do that, then we have a very serious situation on our hands.'

'They'll kill us.'

İkmen looked over at the masked men who were watching him and said, 'So they say.'

Metin Martini, following İkmen and Süleyman's example, lit a cigarette. 'Well, I didn't kill Söner, Inspector,' he said. 'I hated him and I'll be honest, I wished him dead more than once, but I didn't kill him. Why would I serve prison time for that arsehole?'

'Any idea who might have killed him?' Süleyman asked.

'No.' He shrugged again. 'Söner was an annoying nonentity, nothing more. None of us liked him.'

'Did anyone dislike him more than perhaps the rest?'

Metin thought for a moment and then he said, 'He tried it on with Esma. She was horrified.'

İkmen looked down at his notebook and said, 'Esma is . . .'

'She played the American governess, Sarah,' Metin said.

She was the tall, blonde girl.

'Do you have any idea what happened when Söner "tried it on" with Esma, Metin?'

'She told him to fuck off,' he said. 'Probably called him a little creep into the bargain.'

İkmen looked at Süleyman who raised his eyebrows and said, 'So are you having a relationship with Esma yourself?'

'Me?' He laughed. 'No!'

'You make it sound as if the idea of that is either ridiculous or appalling to you,' Süleyman said.

The boy averted his eyes, then he said, 'I like Esma, don't get me wrong, but . . . Esma?' He leaned forward then and looked Süleyman straight in the eye. 'I like European girls, you know? Italians, Spaniards. I can't do with all this Turkish stuff where you don't know whether a girl is going to put out or not. It's bullshit.'

Metin Martini was a very forthright young man and so İkmen thought he'd try to shock him. 'You want to know if a girl is going to let you fuck her?'

Hovsep Pars gasped audibly.

Metin Martini was completely unmoved. 'Yes,' he said. 'That's it in a nutshell.'

İzzet rang Ayşe's mobile and home landline once each but nobody answered either of them. Perhaps she had been calling from her brother's phone. He called that number again but no one answered. İzzet wondered what to do. If she didn't want to speak to him, why had she called?

The past few months hadn't been easy. After the euphoria of their engagement had passed, the reality of the wedding hit and, with it, a host of problems. Money was only one of them. İzzet wanted his children from his first marriage to come to his wedding but their mother was not keen for them to come without her. Theoretically his daughter was too young to travel on her own but he knew that his ex-wife was also making mischief. Then there was his great-aunt Lutza, the last surviving sibling of his grandfather, Fortune. İzzet hadn't told Ayşe anything about her. He certainly hadn't told her that Aunt Lutza was, as his grandfather had been, a Jew. In itself it didn't matter, Ayşe wasn't the sort of woman who indulged in mindless prejudices. But the fact that he had concealed it from her would make her angry. İzzet himself didn't know why he'd done it.

He wasn't a 'full' Turk, he couldn't marry her in opulent, Ottoman splendour, he was rather less attractive than George Clooney. But so what? She was marrying him because she wanted to. Or did she? He looked down at the phone in his hands and contemplated the biggest obstacle to his happiness. Mehmet Süleyman.

She still had feelings for him, İzzet knew that. Every time she looked at him, it was as clear as day. Ayşe thought that İzzet couldn't see but he could. It was what all the 'wedding nerves' had been about. She was nervous because she didn't know whether she was doing the right thing by marrying him. And yet İzzet knew that if he challenged her about it she would deny everything. She was totally committed to their marriage but was that as a way of escape more than anything else? Did she want to run away from her own foolish passion for a man who was fickle and unreliable? And did he want to take her on under those circumstances? Or was it now far too late in the day to change his mind? After all, he had known about Ayşe and her boss for a very long time and for the last few months he had continually talked himself into believing that it didn't matter.

Esma cried. She shook too. She was so frightened of what was happening, her whole body was cold with terror and her hands were blue. But she hadn't hated Söner Erkan, or so she said. She'd found him silly, sometimes annoying and not very talented, but she hadn't hated him even after he had tried, and failed, to chat her up. He hadn't, she claimed, even attempted to borrow any money from her.

'It makes you realise just how much we rely upon forensic evidence these days,' İkmen said to Süleyman and Arto Sarkissian as they conferred about the people they'd interviewed so far.

Süleyman was only half listening. He still wanted to get as close to the telephone in the Kubbeli Saloon as he could. It was unlikely any of them would be able to plug 155 into it and then leave the handset off the hook without being seen – their captors were watching them all the time – but they had to try.

'We only have our naked eyes and ears to work with and it just isn't enough,' İkmen continued. 'I for one feel inadequate in the extreme.'

'Only Mrs Aktar has any visible bloodstains on her

clothes,' Arto said. 'Although . . .' He bit his lip, deep in thought, before he spoke again. 'I consulted my brother about the footprints in room four eleven.'

'Mrs Aktar's?'

'Yes.' He blinked through his spectacles, his eyes were tired. 'They worried me.'

'In what way?' İkmen asked.

For just a moment their captors talked among themselves and Süleyman was able to inspect the telephone and the wire going into it. He clicked his tongue impatiently.

İkmen looked at him. 'Wires cut?'

Tight-lipped, Süleyman said, 'Yes.'

İkmen turned back to Arto Sarkissian. 'In what way?' he repeated.

The Armenian sighed. 'The bed the boy was found on has a very deep mattress and a lot of thick covers, especially now in the winter,' he said. 'Blood spatter on the headboard and even Mrs Aktar's handprints on the wall I can understand. When she rolled him over she would have got blood on her dress. But even a severed carotid artery will not produce enough blood to soak through all those bedclothes, then the mattress and on to the floor.'

'What if the mattress has a protector on it?' Süleyman asked.

'Mmm, Krikor brought that up.'

'It's likely. This is a hotel,' İkmen said. 'And accidents do happen.'

'But I don't remember seeing a pool of blood on the floor and so I fail to see how Mrs Aktar could have managed to get blood on her shoes,' Arto said. Then he added, 'Unless she climbed on to the bed for some reason.'

Lale Aktar was only just over the other side of the Kubbeli Saloon and so İkmen lowered his voice. 'So are you saying that you suspect Mrs Aktar, Arto?'

He shrugged. 'I don't know. But as it stands I can't see why she should have had any blood on her shoes if she just went into that room, discovered the body, rolled it over and ran out again.'

'Do you want to go and have a look at the room again?' İkmen asked.

'I think we have to, don't you?'

The only people that Nar recognised when she entered the Kubbeli Saloon were the police officers, İkmen and Süleyman. But they, of course, didn't recognise her. It had been a very long time since Nar had either dressed as a man or carried a gun and it felt really odd. The roughness of the balaclava helmet against her face wasn't pleasant either. She'd had to take her make-up and false eyelashes off with kitchen washing-up liquid which had left her skin feeling as if it had been scrubbed with a house broom. If she did manage to survive the night, her skin would need some serious pampering.

No one spoke a word to her, but not far from her about six men and one, to Nar, very obvious woman were saying that 'they' wanted to go 'upstairs' again. The thickset man who appeared to be their leader looked at his watch and then said, 'That works.' He pointed to three figures, one of which was Nar, and said, 'You take them.' He didn't address anybody by name and communication between all these people was clearly kept to a minimum. The man standing next to Nar tapped her elbow to move her towards the police officers. She wondered if either İkmen or Süleyman would recognise her just by her eyes. Probably not. They didn't know her that well, she'd made sure of that.

'Dr Sarkissian has to come too,' İkmen said to the group leader.

The thickset man shrugged. Nar noticed that the man next to her was wearing a helmet that had a camera fitted to it. That was odd and, she felt, a little bit kinky. She knew men who liked to film things that other, sick people would pay to watch.

Her colleagues, the police officers, some fat Armenian doctor she didn't know and Nar herself began to walk towards the sweeping Pera Palas staircase. When and how she was going to be able to transmit who she was to the officers she didn't know. Sergeant Farsakoğlu had been a bit vague about what was going to happen next. All she'd said was that Nar should find out as much as she could and make contact with İkmen and Süleyman if she could. In the meantime, the sergeant was going to call İzzet Melik. Nar had heard on the grapevine that Ayşe Farsakoğlu was due to marry that dour old maganda. Unbelievable! Everyone knew she was still in love with Mehmet Süleyman.

She walked upstairs directly behind Çetin İkmen, listening to the sound of his cigaretty, laboured breathing. What was she doing helping the police and putting her life at risk like this? What had they ever done for her? What had anyone? Her father had deserted her by dying just after she was born and so as soon as she could walk she'd had to look after her mother who was disabled by arthritis. A hideous spell in the army as her former male self, Semih, had been followed by the death of her mother and then a merciful flight from her village to İstanbul. There she'd become Nar and had quickly established herself as champion and protector of a whole sisterhood of younger, smaller and less feisty transsexuals. She'd also started hormone therapy and had breast augmentation. Squashed down underneath the clothes she'd taken off the unconscious man in the fridge, her boobs felt distinctly uncomfortable.

Floor two became floor three and Nar wondered what would have happened if she'd just walked away from

Ayşe Farsakoğlu. In spite of the sight of an apparently dead man in the Pera Palas bar, she could have left Ayşe and just gone about her business. Even after they found that rather odd man in the fridge, she could have upped and left. But Nar knew full well why she hadn't. All her life had been spent looking after women. Disabled women, women who had been men, she even helped the old woman who lived in the apartment next to hers with her shopping. She was a knight in shining armour in a partially female body. She just couldn't help herself.

'You need to get out of there!' İzzet said into his mobile phone. He was trying to get dressed at the same time and was struggling to put his shirt on using only one hand.

'I can't do that,' Ayşe Farsakoğlu replied. Her voice was calm and a little bit echoey. But then she was, she said, in the kitchens of the Pera Palas Hotel. How she'd got there and why had not been discussed.

'Ayşe, I'm reporting this,' İzzet said.

'We don't know who these people are,' Ayşe replied. 'Not yet. Just give me time to—'

'I can't do that. You know I can't do that. Get yourself and the maître d' out. I'm not asking you.'

He heard her voice rise into barely controlled anger. 'And leave Nar in here on her own? No way! She's amongst whoever these people are and she's armed. She can try to find out who they are and she can hopefully make contact with the inspectors and Dr Sarkissian. And İzzet, until I can at least try to determine who we are dealing with I do not want our colleagues coming in here guns blazing like a bunch of Sylvester Stallone clones!'

'You don't—'

'I have every right to tell you and anyone else what to do!' Ayşe said. 'I'm here, you're not. Speak to Ardıç. He's not a fool!'

'And I am?'

Why had she even been in the vicinity of the Pera Palas? What had she been doing? Had she been hanging around on the off chance of catching a glimpse of Mehmet Süleyman in a tuxedo? Every one of İzzet's fears and suspicions about his fiancée and his boss crashed through the defences he normally erected against such things.

'Ardıç knows the meaning of restraint,' Ayşe said. 'İzzet, we could be dealing with anything. These people could have a bomb, for all we know. They are heavily armed and this hotel is full of people.'

He stopped himself alluding to Mehmet Süleyman. He said, 'What do you need?'

'I need you to tell Ardıç,' she said. 'And I need some time before the troops come blasting in.'

'How much time?' His heart was hammering against

the side of his chest and he could hear it making his voice waver.

He heard her pause to think, then she said, 'I'll call you in thirty minutes.'

'And if I don't hear from you?'

'Then you call me,' she said. 'And if that doesn't work out then it will be up to you. But this has to be controlled, İzzet, it has to be.'

Then she cut the connection, leaving him both anxious for her safety and furiously angry. Quite how a transsexual hooker had become involved he couldn't begin to imagine.

Chapter 14

The mattress did have a protective cover but there definitely wasn't any blood on the floor. It had soaked into the bedclothes, the pillows and the victim's clothing and been absorbed. Having established this, İkmen asked the masked men if they would bring Lale Aktar back again. One went, leaving two watching them like a pair of wall-eyed ghouls. Both tall and slim, had they not been armed İkmen and Süleyman could at least have had a shot at taking them on. But they had Kalashnikovs, the favoured weapon of the terrorist. The man on the right, with the helmet camera, continued to film. The police officers and the doctor waited for Lale Aktar to be brought to them in silence.

When she came in, she looked confused. 'What's going on?' she asked. The blood had all but dried on her once golden sheath dress and was making it stick to her naked body beneath.

'Can you show us what you did when you found Söner Erkan's body?' İkmen asked.

'Show you? I told you what happened,' she said.

'You said that you moved the body, in order to see its face,' Arto said. 'Can you just show us how you did that?' He looked down at Söner Erkan's body. 'You don't have to touch him, just . . .'

She moved round to the side of the bed furthest away from the door and nearest to the window. 'I pulled him this way,' she said and mimed turning the body over and towards her.

'You went round to the far side of the bed?' İkmen asked. 'You're sure?'

'Yes.'

'Why did you do that?'

'Why? I don't know,' she said. 'Why not?'

'Because it's further away from the door and the bathroom,' İkmen said. 'You could see there was a body on your bed when you came out of your bathroom. Why go round the bed to look at it?'

She shrugged. 'I don't know. I don't know!' She walked back towards the door.

'You pulled him towards yourself and that was when you got the blood down your dress?' Arto asked.

'Yes,' she said. 'As I pulled him towards me, he sort of fell against me and his blood ran down my dress. I put a hand out against the wall to steady myself because of the shock.'

They all looked down at the body for a few seconds.

No one mentioned shoes or footprints. Then İkmen said, 'You didn't climb on to the bed to turn him over?'

She looked appalled. 'No!'

After Lale Aktar had left, Çetin İkmen expressed a desire to use the lavatory. One of their guards stepped forward to go and watch over him while he used the facilities.

Everyone was looking at everyone else and Ceyda knew what they were thinking because she was thinking it too. *Where were you just before the men in the black masks arrived?*

If the policemen, the doctors, the writer, and the old Armenian man didn't solve the mystery of who killed Söner soon, they were all going to die. And nobody was going to come. As far as the world outside was concerned, the hotel was closed for a private function and whatever was going to happen would be over by the time the sun rose in the morning. But then surely all these people around her, not to mention the police officers, wouldn't go down without a fight?

Ceyda looked up at Burak Fisekçi who smiled at her. He'd told her he'd left to go to the toilet just before the men in black arrived. Ceyda herself didn't have a clue about where anyone on the ground floor had been. She'd been on the fourth floor but she hadn't heard Söner scream. If he'd screamed.

'Do you think that we're going to get out of here, Burak Bey?' she asked. They, like most of the people in the ballroom, were sitting on the floor, being watched by men with guns.

Burak Bey smiled. 'How would I ever be able to face your father if anything happened to you, Ceyda?' he said.

'So you think that we'll make it then?'

'We are in Allah's hands.'

'The policemen will get it right, won't they?'

He didn't say yes or no, he couldn't. No one knew what was going to happen and that was why a lot of the people in the ballroom were crying. Then she felt one of Burak Bey's hands on her knee and she looked up at him and smiled.

'You'll be all right, Ceyda,' he said. 'You will.'

'I hope so,' she said. But then her face clouded. 'You know, Burak Bey, there is one thing that I didn't tell the police about Söner.'

'What was that, Ceyda?'

She averted her eyes. 'Oh, you know,' she said. 'I think I need to tell them, Burak Bey.'

İkmen's eyes were everywhere. He'd already looked in the one cupboard that was in the bathroom. Now he was peeing, he was intent upon the area around the toilet. He was also very aware that one of the masked men was looking at him. When he came still closer, Çetin İkmen began to sweat. He hated being watched in the toilets at the station where he knew everybody, but here, with these people, he was very unhappy. However, if he concentrated on what he was looking for . . .

'Sergeant Farsakoğlu says hello.'

İkmen froze.

'Carry on peeing,' the man behind him said.

'Who are you?' His voice wavered. He was in an unfamiliar bathroom, with a gunman at his back and his penis in his hands. Vulnerable was not a big enough word to cover the way he felt.

'I know your cousin, Samsun,' Nar said. 'I'm like Samsun.'

İkmen made as if to look round but Nar stopped him. 'Eyes front, Inspector,' she said. 'I'm strictly in man mode at the moment. Now what's going on here?'

It could so easily be some sort of sick trap but because this person had mentioned Samsun, İkmen went along with it. 'These people, I don't know who they are, are holding us hostage. If Süleyman and myself don't deduce correctly who killed that boy lying on the bed, they'll kill us all. It's some deranged game to them. We've got until sunrise, seven twenty. Where's Sergeant Farsakoğlu?'

'In the hotel kitchen.'

'How—'

'Don't ask. But they don't know she's there. They don't know the man who used to wear this gear before me is down there too. In the fridge.'

İkmen smiled.

One of the masked men back in the bedroom called out. 'Hasn't he finished?'

'His bladder's weird,' Nar shot back. 'Middle-aged man stuff.'

İkmen stifled an urge to snap.

'The sergeant has called this incident in,' Nar said.

İkmen stopped peeing and zipped up his fly. 'They mustn't come in heavy-handed,' he said. 'They'll kill us all.'

'She knows that. How many of them are there, do you know?'

İkmen turned to face Nar. There was no way of telling that he was in fact, at least in part, a she. 'I thought there were ten but now there seem to be more like fifteen,' he said.

'Come on!' the other masked man in the bedroom shouted.

Nar raised a hand in salute. İkmen noticed that some of its fingers showed traces of blue nail polish. 'OK!' Nar replied and she pushed İkmen forward. Then she said to him, 'I'm going to find a reason to get back to the kitchens and tell the sergeant I've made contact.

Like you, Çetin Bey, I did my army service. I know exactly how to use this weapon.'

The more Krikor Sarkissian looked at his guest list, the more disquieted he became. Lale Aktar had suggested that maybe one or more of his guests was working with the gunmen, that this person or persons had somehow let them in. But Krikor was much more inclined to believe that if they did indeed have any fifth columnists amongst their number, they were members of the hotel staff. Each guest either had some sort of longstanding connection to his addiction centre project or had been hand-picked by himself or Burak as a representative of another philanthropic or ethically aware financial organisation. Then again, anyone could be corrupted or persuaded to do terrible things if enough money was involved. And it would depend also on why this was happening.

Everyone was terrified. He could hear some of them crying in the ballroom as he sat, impotently, in the Kubbeli Saloon. At one point he thought he heard Caroun's voice.

'I need a drink.' Hovsep Pars broke into Krikor's thoughts. 'A rakı or maybe absinthe if they have it.'

Krikor looked at the old man and said, 'There's nothing left.'

'There's a bar just through there.' Hovsep pointed

a crooked finger at the door to his left. 'I'm an old, dying man and I feel the cold. I need alcohol.' Then he leaned in so that only Krikor could hear him. 'And if they deny me it then we'll know that they're Islamic fundamentalists.'

Krikor wasn't so sure about that but he called one of the masked men over and asked him if his friend could have a drink from the bar. At first the man was obstructive. 'No!' he said. 'Enough alcohol has been splashed around here tonight!'

But Krikor pleaded with him. 'If you don't want to get it for him, I'll do it,' he said. 'Come with me into the bar and I'll get it.'

The man thought for a moment. Hovsep Pars gave Krikor a meaningful look. In his mind this proved that the gang were most definitely Muslim fundamentalists.

Eventually the man said, 'OK,' and he stood aside while Krikor stood up and then walked behind him.

'Make it a large one,' Hovsep Pars said as he watched Krikor Sarkissian go.

The Pera Palas Hotel bar was softly lit. Dominated by tones of wine, dark wood and maroon, it was not easy to make out fine details, especially at night. But Krikor could see that the bodies of the four people the gunmen had already killed had been removed. There was blood on the carpet, which made an unpleasant squelching noise as he walked towards the service area.

The last time he'd got a drink from this room, champagne, he'd been laughing.

The masked man followed him over to the optics and Krikor looked to see what was available.

'Just pour something and let's go,' the man said impatiently.

Krikor shot him a glare he hoped was sufficiently vicious. 'I'm not getting him anything he doesn't like,' he said. 'He wants absinthe.'

The man regarded him with what Krikor interpreted as disgust. 'It's all alcohol.'

'There's alcohol and alcohol,' Krikor said. 'But then I can tell that you're clearly not a drinker.'

'No.' But he didn't expand as to why that might be and Krikor didn't ask. Behind the bar he found some very impressive whiskies, both Scottish and Irish, several brands of rakı, four different types of vodka, one gin—

'Come on!'

He was looking for green, a green bottle . . . Ah, absinthe. He took hold of a long, thin, emerald-coloured bottle and poured a generous measure into a highball glass. Poor Hovsep Pars was dying, a big drink was the least he was due. As he poured he said, 'I see you've removed the bodies of the people you killed.'

He'd only really known one of them, the woman,

who had been an ardent spokesperson in favour of prison reform and the decriminalisation of addiction. She, like Krikor, had been passionate in her belief that prison was not the right place for people with problems of substance abuse. He was sorry that she was dead. He was also sorry that the men he didn't know, but had wanted to get to know, men with money who had been invited by Burak, were dead too. Now he would never know them and he felt responsible for their deaths. He walked back into the Kubbeli Saloon with the highball glass which he gave to Hovsep Pars.

'Here.'

The old man smiled. 'Thank you.'

The gunman looked at them both with disgust. Krikor took a tissue out of his pocket and began to wipe blood from the soles of his shoes.

Ayşe Farsakoğlu paced the kitchen floor like a caged cat. It was coming up to the half hour mark and she wanted to know what, if anything, Nar had discovered. She was also anxious to know whether Nar's disguise had worked.

'It doesn't make the time pass any quicker, you know,' Ersu Bey said. He was sitting on a bain-marie, smoking a cigarette, using a saucer as an ashtray. He felt awful abusing hotel crockery in this way but he needed a smoke.

'What doesn't?'

'Walking up and down.'

Ayşe stopped. 'I know that,' she said. 'But I have to do something.'

'Then conserve your energy,' Ersu Bey said. 'It's what you have to do when you go into the armed forces. Your friend knows. He, she or whatever it is was in the army.'

He was the type of man Ayşe didn't like. A preening, macho idiot, the sort people called a 'maganda', an intolerant man of the street. She'd thought that İzzet was one of those until she'd got to know him better.

Footsteps on the stairs outside the kitchen made both of them dive for the floor and Ersu Bey put his cigarette out.

'I've made contact,' a familiar voice said. As quickly as they'd hit the floor, Ayşe and Ersu Bey stood up. When Nar took her balaclava helmet off, her hair looked an absolute fright. Bleached to the point of no return, it stuck out at all angles from her head and looked not unlike a small bale of hay.

'With whom?' Ayşe asked.

'Çetin İkmen,' Nar said. 'Him and Mehmet Süleyman and a doctor, a fat man.'

'Dr Sarkissian.' She put a hand up to her chest. Well, at least they were still alive. She smiled.

'They don't know who the gunmen are,' Nar continued. 'No idea. But they're making them play a sort of murder game.'

Ayşe frowned.

'A young boy has been killed and İkmen and Süleyman have to work out who did it.'

'Well, didn't these gunmen—'

'No. But if İkmen and Süleyman don't manage to solve the mystery, or if they get the identity of the killer wrong, the gunmen have said they'll kill everyone in the hotel.'

Ayşe put her arms around her own shoulders because now she felt cold.

'I'd better get back,' Nar said. 'I told them I was going to the toilet. What are you going to say to Sergeant Melik?'

'Do you know how long they've got to solve this crime?' Ayşe asked as she twirled Nar's phone over and over in her hands.

'Until sunrise which'll be seven twenty, İkmen says.'

Ersu Bey frowned. 'But the morning shift will come on before that, at six,' he said. 'I was due to come on then myself.'

Nar shrugged. 'I'll go back, see what else I can find out.'

'You don't have to go back, you know,' Ayşe said, 'I can call and—'

'No.' Nar shook her head. 'I'm inside now. I might not like it, but I'm inside and I've got a weapon which I know how to use.' She put her balaclava helmet back on.

Chapter 15

The leader said that the young lady wanted to see İkmen alone. That wasn't possible but İkmen did manage to arrange for Ceyda Ümit to talk to him with just one masked guard in attendance. They talked out by the lift.

The girl spoke with her eyes fixed on the floor at her feet. 'I slept with Söner Erkan,' she said. 'I didn't tell you because I didn't want anyone to know. I especially don't want Alp to know.'

'Because you love him?' İkmen asked.

'Yes.'

'So why, if you love Alp, did you sleep with Söner?'

'Because he made me.'

'He made you?'

Now she looked up, into İkmen's eyes. 'Söner was bad with money,' she said, 'but he always managed to buy what he wanted – one way or another.'

'And how did he buy you, Ceyda?'

'He said that if I didn't sleep with him he'd get his parents to withdraw their funding from Bowstrings.'

'And you didn't tell him to do it and be damned?' İkmen asked.

She looked down at the floor again. 'I know you'll think I'm a stupid, wicked girl, Inspector . . .'

'I think nothing of the sort.'

'In the theatre is where Alp wants to be,' she said. 'Professionally. It means a lot to him. He doesn't come from a rich family and he sees acting and directing as a way out.'

'So you had sex with Söner to keep Alp's dreams alive?'

'Yes.' She pulled a face and wrinkled her nose. 'It was disgusting! He was a good-looking boy but he was like some sort of slobbering animal!'

İkmen put a hand on her shoulder.

'But I swear I didn't kill him,' Ceyda said.

'Weren't you afraid that he might ask you to go to bed with him again? Maybe threaten to tell Alp if you didn't?'

'Yes, of course. But that still doesn't mean that I killed him,' she said. 'I'm sorry I didn't tell you about this before, Inspector, but just the thought of Alp finding out . . .' She began to cry. 'Once it was over I just put it out of my mind. It was the only way that I could live with it!'

İkmen took her gently in his arms and let her cry against his chest.

* * *

Commissioner Ardıç looked across at the front of the Pera Palas Hotel from the doorway of something that advertised itself as a pub. With the exception of a lack of door staff either inside or outside the hotel, the Pera Palas looked very normal.

Ardıç puffed on his cigar and turned to İzzet Melik. 'No idea about affiliation?'

'Sergeant Farsakoğlu said not,' İzzet replied. 'They just want the murder of some boy "solved". Apart from that there haven't been any demands. They're masked and so there's no way to find out who they are from their appearance. It's some sort of game.'

'Mmm.' Ardıç rubbed his chin. He had one police and one special operations military team at his disposal. His dilemma was how to deploy them and when. As well as Sergeant Farsakoğlu inside the hotel kitchens, there was also apparently a civilian who had infiltrated the masked hostage-takers. In addition there was a hotel employee who, at any minute, should be coming out through the back entrance to the hotel.

Both İzzet and Ayşe Farsakoğlu had decided that it would be best if Ersu Nadir left the building and assisted the police directly. He knew the hotel and its layout well and could advise Ardıç and the military team. The back door into the kitchen remained unlocked, providing Ersu Bey with a means of escape and Ayşe with a possible route out if things went wrong. When Nar went back upstairs, she left the door from the kitchen into the hotel's Agatha Restaurant open. This gave Ayşe access to the rest of the hotel which, to İzzet's horror, she intended to exploit. Ardıç, however, was pleased about this. If a trained police officer could get behind a civilian who apparently had a gun then maybe between them they could unravel the mystery of the team of masked assailants. He had no idea, and İzzet didn't tell him, just who and what the civilian was.

A uniformed officer in a stab vest ran from behind the right-hand side of the hotel with his arm round another figure which was limping slightly as it ran. As they got closer, İzzet and Ardıç could see that it was a man in a dark, tailcoat suit, aged fifty or so. He looked pale and drained and Ardıç immediately took him through into the pub, whose owners had put the premises at the disposal of the police and Special Forces teams.

Ardıç sat down at one of the tables and motioned for Ersu to take a seat opposite him. İzzet Melik went to the bar where the somewhat bleary-eyed owner was dispensing coffee and tea. In order not to alert anyone glancing out of the windows of the Pera Palas, the pub was in darkness and the heavily armed officers moved quietly and spoke in low tones.

Ardıç fixed his eyes on Ersu Nadir. 'Tell me about it,' he said.

Ersu Bey began where he became locked in the fridge

and explained how he had been rescued by Ayşe Farsakoğlu and a transsexual.

'She, he is called Nar,' he said. 'I've no idea why, er, she was with Sergeant Farsakoğlu and I've no idea why Sergeant Farsakoğlu was in the hotel herself.'

İzzet Melik put a cup of coffee down in front of the maître d'. He knew, or thought that he knew, why Ayşe had been at the Pera Palas Hotel. It made his face fall into a scowl which did not go unnoticed by Ersu Nadir.

'Is everything all right, Sergeant?' he asked.

Ardıç, who was still recovering from the news that the civilian on the inside of the hotel was a very tall transsexual, said, 'Oh, don't mind Melik, Ersu Bey, he always looks like that. So now let me get this right. Sergeant Farsakoğlu is unarmed while this, this . . .'

'Nar. She has the Kalashnikov we took from the man she smashed over the head.'

'What did this man the transsexual hit look like?' Ardıç asked.

'Tall, in his thirties, I'd say,' Ersu said. 'We found an ATM card on him but no actual identity card.'

'What name was on the ATM card?'

'Hüseyin Hikmet,' he said. 'Once we'd taken his clothes off, we wrapped him up in some coats and left him in the fridge. He was groaning by that time and we couldn't . . .'

'I understand.' Ardıç smiled. Then he looked at İzzet

Melik. 'Look up the name Hüseyin Hikmet, tall, thirties,' he said. 'The name isn't familiar to me and it could well be bogus but let's run it.'

'Yes, sir.' İzzet walked over to the tables that had been given over to three laptop computer systems.

'Now you need to come and speak to Commander İpek,' Ardıç said to Ersu Bey. 'He's in charge of the military. He'll want to hear everything you know about the layout and security arrangements for the hotel.'

Ersu Bey stood up. Then he said, 'Oh, and there's something else you should know too.'

'Oh?' Ardıç said.

'The gunmen have told your Inspector İkmen that he has until sunrise, seven twenty, this morning to solve the murder. But if these terrorists intend to get out of the hotel without being detected then they'll have to leave before six a.m. because that's when the morning shift arrives.'

In all probability emboldened by the notion that one person with a gun, plus Ayşe Farsakoğlu, was in the hotel, İkmen told the leader that he and the other people in the investigative group needed some time on their own. 'I know you can't leave us,' he said. 'I know you won't. But if you can move back so that you're not sitting on our laps, that would be helpful. We need to talk about what we've discovered so far.'

'We're not stopping you, Inspector.'

'I want some privacy.' İkmen stared into the eyes which were blue and cold and appeared to have nothing behind them. 'I'm assuming that you want us to solve this crime to save you the bother of having to kill so many of us.'

The leader did not reply.

'Or maybe not,' İkmen said. 'All I'm asking is that while we talk, you and your people stay at the margins of the room to give us room to breathe.'

'The Kubbeli Saloon has a very high ceiling . . .'

'I'm talking in psychological terms!' İkmen said, exasperated now as well as very tired. 'I am not, as you may have gathered, a marble and chandelier type of person. I generally do my thinking and have my discussions in rooms that you could fit into this one about ten times over.' To calm his nerves he lit a cigarette. The hard blue eyes blinked in disgust. 'Now I'm going to pull some chairs round that table there, all right?' İkmen pointed to the large table in the middle of the room that in more normal times held plates and cake stands loaded with tiny sandwiches and delicious pastries.

The leader shrugged.

'I'll take that as a yes,' İkmen said.

Like the kitchens, the Agatha Restaurant was in the basement. As Ayşe moved through it she noticed that there was a window in one wall that allowed diners with a particular interest in food and food preparation to see what was happening in the kitchen. She found it a bit weird. Ayşe moved quickly through the Agatha and out on to the stairwell. In the middle of the well was the shaft for the old wooden lift – the first and oldest elevator in the city. Just one floor above her were the rooms in which Süleyman and the others were being held. She could hear a low hum of voices above her head. But down in the basement was where the toilets were too and so any ascent of the staircase would have to be attempted with care. At any moment someone could walk down the stairs and see her.

With Nar on the inside, Ayşe simply wanted to observe. Ersu Bey was out of the hotel now and giving as much information as he could to Ardıç. But if she could augment this with her own, more up-to-date observations, then all the better. And she did want to see Süleyman if she could.

Slowly, her ears straining for any sound, Ayşe began to ascend. Ardıç had called her when Ersu Bey had arrived and told her that as far as he could tell there was no one on either the concierge or the reception desks in the front lobby. The front doors could be operated electronically from inside the hotel. If she could get into the lobby she could, if necessary, do this. But she had to get up to the ground floor first. She put a hand on the banister that ran around the barrier that enclosed the lift shaft. Above she heard voices more distinctly now. She couldn't make out words but she could hear the sharp edge of panic in their tones and the unmistakable sound of weeping.

Now alone for the first time since she'd become involved with this situation, she tried to find reasons for what was happening. The gunmen were playing what was effectively a game with all these people, some of whom were police. The rewards would have to be considerable to be worth such a high-risk strategy. But what rewards? And who was providing them?

'Nobody really liked Söner Erkan, as far as I can see,' Süleyman said. 'The leader of the company, Alp, found him dictatorial, a financial drain and arrogant.'

'That just about goes for all the people involved in Bowstrings,' Arto Sarkissian said.

'And I've just discovered something else,' Cetin İkmen said.

'What's that?'

'Ceyda Ümit, Alp's girlfriend, slept with Söner,' he said. 'She says that Söner coerced her into it by threatening to get his parents to withdraw their funding for Bowstrings. Alp, according to Ceyda, doesn't know.'

'She thinks.'

'Exactly.'

'Then there's the discovery of the body,' Krikor said.

'I think that maybe you should talk about that without me,' Lale Aktar said.

Süleyman frowned. 'No,' he said. 'You were there, you—'

'I've told you everything I did, everything I know,' she said. 'I can't do any more. You need to talk about the scene on your own and I need to go to the lavatory.'

İkmen remembered that Lale Aktar had a period. He smiled. 'All right.'

She called one of the masked men over and asked to be taken down to the toilets. She stood up, put her handbag on her chair and left with him. For a moment, İkmen stared at the bag and then he said, 'Söner Erkan also "tried it on", as Metin Martini put it, with another member of the company, Esma. But unlike Ceyda she was not vulnerable and she rejected him.' He turned to Krikor Sarkissian, while at the same time keeping half an eye on their captors. 'We know why you engaged the Bowstrings, Krikor,' he said. 'Basically via Burak Fisekçi. But did you make them change their name?'

'Change their name? Oh, you mean from "Lions in Iron Cages"? I'd almost forgotten about that. No,' he said. 'That was a decision they made.'

'They?'

'Alp and Söner, as far as I know,' he said. 'They came

to see me and said that they'd thought about the name and decided it was too political. How and why they came up with Bowstrings, I don't know. I accepted it because I thought that it was really quite good.'

'Very Ottoman,' Hovsep Pars said. He was rather more relaxed since he'd been drinking his absinthe.

'Metin Martini reckons that Söner's parents made them change it,' İkmen said.

He looked at their captors again and saw that, while they were still watching them, they were having their own conversation too and the leader was actually on his phone. He took his chance and lowered his voice, 'Listen and don't react,' he said. 'One of the gunmen is on our side and there's a police officer in the building too.' He looked at Süleyman. 'Sergeant Farsakoğlu.'

'Ayşe!'

'Keep your voice down! Our police colleagues outside know and they are working with Sergeant Farsakoğlu who has apparently impressed upon them the need for restraint.'

'How do you know this?' Süleyman asked.

'You know when I went to the bathroom in room four eleven? The man who took me is working with Ayşe. I don't know why or how and . . . Yes, bathroom, I have to tell you about bathrooms . . .'

'What are you talking about?' They all looked up as the leader came towards them. 'No whispering!'

For a moment, until he walked away again, they all sat in silence. Then İkmen said to Süleyman, 'We should see Alp again.'

'Agreed.'

'Well, I think we're getting too involved in details.' They all looked at Krikor Sarkissian. 'We have very limited time to come to a decision and we only have one shot at it.'

'Which is exactly why we have to get it right,' İkmen said. 'And that involves looking into details.'

'But it's taking so much time!'

İkmen lowered his voice. 'Krikor, did you actually hear what I was saying a few moments ago?'

'Yes, I did.'

'Then you'll know that—'

'*I* know precisely who did it!'

Hovsep Pars, and his absinthe glass, were sitting at the head of the table nearest the door. All the other men at the table looked at him.

'Muhammed Ersoy!' the old man said with a smile. 'He killed the young prince. He killed everyone!'

Muhammed Ersoy, the man who had killed his nephew and who, Hovsep believed, was responsible for all his family's ills. None of them spoke. Ersoy had been in psychiatric hospitals and prisons for over a decade. As the old man began to laugh, all the other men tried not to look at him. Çetin İkmen fixed his gaze just above

Hovsep Pars's head, on a point just in front of the old wooden lift. It was as he was doing this that he saw the figure of a familiar woman run past the opening. Ayşe Farsakoğlu.

Chapter 16

Tick-tock went the clock in what could have been an annoying fashion, but wasn't. What would be, would be. Kismet – except that in this case fate was being given a helping hand.

But the excitement of finding out who İkmen and Süleyman were going to accuse was growing and it was exquisite. It was just past two fifteen and the policemen and their little band of others were lost in a maze of dead ends, details and the madness of old Hovsep Pars. It was going to be a lot of fun finding out whether they would manage to identify who in their midst had been telling little lies.

'That was Söner, Inspector,' Alp said. 'He came to me and said we couldn't use the name "Lions in Iron Cages" any more.'

'Did he say why?' Süleyman asked.

'No.'

'This wasn't some edict from his parents?'

'I've no idea,' Alp said. 'He didn't say. It's possible.'

'So what happened?'

'Söner just told me we were changing the name before one of the early meetings with Dr Sarkissian and his team,' Alp said. 'No one seemed to be too bothered by it. In fact, Burak Bey said that he actually liked it better.'

'Thank you, Alp,' Süleyman said. He walked back through the ranks of the anxious guests. Now that he knew that Ayşe Farsakoğlu was somewhere in the hotel, he looked for her everywhere. But he didn't see her.

He passed in front of the door to the bar where a small group of masked men were talking in low tones among themselves. One of them laughed. How could they do that! There were dead bodies in that bar although he couldn't actually see them. Whoever was laughing was probably the kind of sociopath who could kill and then go off, have a laugh and eat a full meal. Süleyman had met a few and that was what sociopaths did.

The most prominent one he'd ever come across had been the man Hovsep Pars had named, Muhammed Ersoy. He'd killed his own younger brother and his lover, Hovsep Pars's nephew, Avram Avedykian. Unable to carry on after their son's death, both Sevan Avedykian and his wife Akabi had committed suicide.

Hovsep Pars, Akabi's only sibling, saw the aristocratic Muhammed Ersoy as the Devil. Everything bad in life he attributed to that man and he still bitterly resented Çetin İkmen for having helped to save his life. Süleyman shot Ersoy to stop him from killing Arto Sarkissian. Ersoy could have died but İkmen had been determined that he stand trial for his crimes. And he had done. Death would have been an easy and, for Ersoy, very desirable way out.

Süleyman walked back into the Kubbeli Saloon and made his way over to Çetin İkmen and Krikor Sarkissian who were murmuring together. Then the doctor rubbed what looked like a bloodied tissue on the bottom of his shoe and held it up to İkmen's nose. 'Do you see what I mean?' he said.

İkmen, frowning, nodded his head.

Süleyman sat down between Krikor Sarkissian and Lale Aktar. 'Alp says that Söner chose the new name for the troupe,' he said. 'He's no idea whether this was done under pressure from Söner's parents or not.' Then he asked İkmen, 'What are you doing?'

'I think we need to speak to our captors,' İkmen said. 'We need to know whether or not actively misleading us is permissible in this game of theirs.'

Ayşe Farsakoğlu had managed to get herself underneath the hotel concierge's desk. If she put her head out from behind the left-hand side, she could see the front entrance to the hotel, the metal detector arch and the electronic control panel. She called Ardiç to tell him where she was and that İkmen and Süleyman were alive and appeared to be unharmed. It was two forty-five. According to Ersu Bey, the day staff didn't come on until six and so this gave Ardiç and the police and military teams a clear two hours before they had to prepare to storm the building.

Now that she was in the hotel lobby, Ayşe found herself at a loss as to what she could do. Every so often masked men passed through the area and so getting to the front door would be difficult. Even if she did make it to the front door, what could she do then? She couldn't get anybody out, they were all under guard. Only Nar could possibly be spirited away but Ayşe didn't know where she was. If only she'd brought her phone with her! If she'd done that she'd be able to speak to Nar. As it was, Nar was alone and basically clueless. Ayşe heard footsteps and ducked as far as she could underneath the desk.

She heard a male voice say, 'They've just found out.' Then a silent pause. 'Yes.'

He had to be on the phone.

Then he said, 'Really well. *Really* well. Good.'

She heard him walk somewhere across the marble floor until the sound of his footsteps disappeared. Ayşe put her head around the side of the desk again and looked at the front door. İzzet, Ardıç and the others were based at that bar opposite. She couldn't see them or even really the front of the building but she knew it was there. She also knew that they probably already had officers actually outside the hotel and they had to have closed the road. Soon, surely, the gunmen would realise that they couldn't keep everyone captive in the hotel without the outside world noticing. Unless of course a siege was what they wanted . . .

'Where are they?' İkmen asked the leader.

'Where are who?'

Everyone except Hovsep Pars was standing, Süleyman directly behind İkmen, the two doctors and Lale Aktar behind them. The lights from the Kubbeli Saloon's Christmas tree lit up what looked like amusement in the leader's eyes.

'The people you "killed",' İkmen said.

'I imagine they're dead,' the leader replied. 'Don't you?'

'Frankly, no,' İkmen said.

'And why is that?'

'Because earlier, as you know, Dr Krikor Sarkissian went into the bar where you placed the bodies, in order to get a drink for Hovsep Bey,' İkmen said. 'The carpet was covered in blood.'

'It would be.'

'Some of which Dr Sarkissian got on his shoes.'

'Yes?'

'Or rather he would have done, had the substance on the carpet been blood,' İkmen said. 'But what oozed up on to Dr Sarkissian's shoes wasn't blood.'

'Wasn't it?'

'You know full well it wasn't,' İkmen said. He maintained control of his voice but with some difficulty. He was furious. 'It is some sort of red liquid. Fake, theatrical blood, I imagine, although I don't have a lot of experience of that so I can't say for certain what it is. But it isn't real blood. Both Dr Sarkissian and myself have had enough contact with that over the years to know exactly what it feels, smells and tastes like. What's on his shoes isn't blood.'

There was a pause and then İkmen said, 'You want us to tell you who killed Söner Erkan and yet you are misleading us and concealing information from us. How can we have even a fighting chance if you do that? If you want to kill us all anyway, why not just get on and do it?'

Another pause, a longer one.

'I'm led to the conclusion that the people you "shot" are still alive,' İkmen went on. 'Where are they? Are they now wearing the uniform you all wear? I thought that maybe you were bringing more people in from outside to swell your numbers when I noticed there were more of you earlier. But that isn't the case, is it? You already had people on the inside. I was going to ask why you aren't playing fair with us, but I think I know the answer to that question anyway.' He took a step forward, towards the leader. All around them, the sound of Kalashnikovs being prepared for firing made the two doctors and the crime writer move a few steps back. 'So shoot me.' İkmen shrugged. 'You're going to do it anyway.'

Süleyman put a hand on İkmen's shoulder. 'Çetin . . .'

Ignoring him, İkmen continued, 'But you'll get caught. Not by me, I know. But if you think that what is going on here won't eventually attract attention, then you're living in a fantasy. You're not going to get away with this!' He laughed. 'Kill us all now and you might just get away . . .' From somewhere behind him, somebody gasped. 'Leave it and you don't stand a hope.' Yet another pause came and went while he looked into the still, amused eyes of the leader. 'But you won't do that, will you?' he said. 'Because this is a game. It's a game you refuse to play in a fair and equitable way, but it's still a game.'

'You should use your time to try and solve the puzzle you have been set,' the leader said.

'Should I?' İkmen scowled. Then he took yet another step forward. This time the muzzle of a gun came between him and the leader. 'What if I just reached over and pulled your mask down and looked at your face?' he said.

The Kalashnikov dug into İkmen's chest.

Süleyman said again, 'Çetin.'

İkmen smiled. He put one finger on the muzzle of the rifle and said, 'Oh, don't worry, Mehmet, my friend, I'm not going to do anything rash.' Then looking steadily into the leader's eyes he said, 'But you should know that we are not fools. Have your fun with us, we can't stop you doing that, but don't underestimate us. Underestimate my intelligence, and you will make me very angry.'

They were getting what people in American cop films would call 'tooled up'. In other words, they were selecting weapons, checking them and positioning them on belts, straps, inside jackets and in holsters on their legs. Ersu Nadir remembered this kind of activity from his time in the army. When he and his soldier brothers had gone out on patrol, they'd prepared themselves in a similar fashion.

Some members of the Special Forces team had already been deployed outside the hotel and, with the help of Sergeant Farsakoğlu inside, it had been decided to attempt to infiltrate the building via the kitchens at some point. But the heavily mustachioed police sergeant, who was apparently her fiancée, was almost wearing the floor of the pub out as he paced back and forth in a state of high anxiety. The overweight police commissioner pointedly ignored him. As far as Ersu could tell, there were no immediate plans to storm the hotel but he could also understand İzzet Melik's state of mind. Ayşe Farsakoğlu was the woman he intended to marry and so of course he didn't want her to take any risks.

The commissioner came and sat down opposite Ersu, slopping some of his coffee as he moved behind the table. He said, 'Now, Ersu Bey, about this man Hüseyin Hikmet . . .'

'The one that Nar hit over the head.'

'Yes. You told us he was tall and in his thirties, but is there anything else you can tell us about him?'

'But you have his ATM card, his name, surely—'

'Ersu Bey, it is a common name,' Ardıç said. 'The more we can narrow the field, the better. Did you perhaps recognise him as someone who had worked on a casual basis at the hotel before?'

'No,' Ersu said. 'But then people come and go all the time.'

'Was there anything distinguishing about this man? Something like a mole on his face or a scar?'

Ersu Bey replayed in his mind what he recalled of Nar hitting the man over the head and then the three of them putting him in the fridge and undressing him. He'd just been a rather tall, dark, ordinary-looking thirty-something man, quite hairy on his body, and well muscled without looking as if he was a bodybuilder. He'd struck Ersu Bey as the sort of man who had continued to keep fit after his discharge from army service. Not unlike himself in that respect. But had he possessed any distinguishing marks or scars?

People got all sorts of scuffs, abrasions and dents when they did their military service. He himself had a slightly misshapen right calf where he'd broken it when on patrol that day he'd fallen into a cistern just outside the city of Mardin. On bad days he limped.

Ersu Bey closed his eyes. Sometimes, cutting out distractions in the present allowed the memory to have more of a fighting chance to find what was only barely noticed in the past. Sergeant Farsakoğlu, the transsexual and Ersu had pulled the man's clothes off roughly. Aware that any one of his colleagues could come down the corridor at any moment, they'd done what they'd had to do quickly. Nar had chirruped on about how Turkish men always wore vests because they were all basically mummy's boys. But beyond that . . .

And then, finally, he remembered.

He looked at Ardıç and said, 'He'd lost his little finger. On his left hand. There was just a stump.'

* * *

Nar was very aware of the fact that all of these masked gunmen called each other on their mobile phones. She'd searched Hüseyin Hikmet's pockets to try and find his phone but his jumpsuit was heavy and had pockets all over the place and it was only when her right leg appeared to break out into 'When I'm Gone' by Eminem that she discovered the small zip-up pocket just under the knee. She was in the toilet.

'I need you in the ballroom,' a man's voice said.

'OK.' She knew she had to keep all her responses short and sweet. Her voice had been affected by hormone treatment; even without that, she didn't necessarily sound like Hüseyin Hikmet, the man in the fridge.

'Where are you?' the voice asked.

'I'm in the . . .' Turkish men could be very coy about toilets. 'Downstairs,' she said.

He got the code. 'All right,' he said. 'But don't be long.'

Nar stared down at the phone for a few seconds. Then she came out of the toilet cubicle and, looking about to make sure that she was alone, she called her own number.

After a short pause, Ayşe Farsakoğlu answered. 'Who is this?' she whispered.

'It's me, Nar.'

'Nar? But you haven't got a phone, I've got your—'

'Ayşe Hanım, listen,' Nar said. They didn't have time for details. 'Keep this number and call me on it. Where are you?'

But Ayşe hesitated. It was then that Nar thought that maybe the policewoman feared some sort of trap.

'My leg rang and I found the phone in a small pocket underneath my knee,' Nar said.

There was another short pause and then Ayşe said, 'I'm in the front lobby but I'm moving out soon. Do you know who these people are yet?'

'No,' Nar said. 'But I do know that something very strange is going on.'

'Yes, Nar,' Ayşe said. 'I think I've worked that out!'

'No.' Nar looked nervously at the door into the toilets. 'İkmen had a stand-up row with whoever leads this bunch,' she said. 'You know where we saw that dead body in the bar?'

'How can I ever forget?' Ayşe whispered.

'One of those doctors discovered that all that blood was fake,' Nar said.

'Fake?'

'As in the blood you see on TV. İkmen reckons that this game they're being forced to play is being loaded against them.'

'So the man we saw dead in the bar wasn't dead?' Ayşe said.

'Maybe,' Nar said. But then the toilet door opened and she ended the call and put the phone back into the pocket just below her knee.

Chapter 17

All of the actors had been up on the fourth floor of the hotel when Söner Erkan was murdered. Not only was the company staying on that floor, they were all supposed to be there at that time in order to enact the fake killing that was to have provided the highlight of the murder mystery evening. Apart from Lale Aktar, who had found the body, Burak Fisekçi who had been in the lavatory, and the hotel concierge who had been at his post, everybody else's whereabouts had still to be established.

Now Krikor Sarkissian, armed with a guest list, performed a roll call of everyone in the ballroom. He asked them to say where they had been just before Lale Aktar came downstairs with blood on her dress. As they gave their answers he watched them and those around them for any sign they might be lying. The roll call also allowed him to determine who the guests who had supposedly been shot really were.

Once he had completed this task he went back into

the Kubbeli Saloon and sat down next to his brother between İkmen and Süleyman. Hovsep Pars, Lale Aktar and Arto Sarkissian spoke quietly to each other on one side. With his pen, Krikor pointed to each name unaccounted for on his list.

'Aysel Ökte is a great believer in the decriminalisation of addiction and in prison reform,' he said. 'I know her quite well. She came to the clinic for meetings often. But then there are these three.' He pointed to three men's names on different parts of the list. 'Raşit Demir, Yiannis Istefanopoulos and Haluk Mert.'

'Is Mert something to do with the family Mert who run that chain of fitness clubs or whatever one calls such things?' İkmen said.

'Maybe. Aren't they quite well-connected?'

Süleyman, who had been leaning over and frowning at the list, said, 'All three of those men are well-connected – and the woman. Aysel Ökte is a descendant of Hüsnü Paşa who was one of Sultan Vehdettin's most trusted servants. The Mert family have served both the Ottoman Empire and then the Republic for decades as members of the military elite.'

İkmen and Krikor Sarkissian looked at each other. It wasn't always a boon to have someone on hand whose family had been royalty, but sometimes it was invaluable.

'Raşit Demir also comes from a good family. I know

that because I went to the Lycée with his older brother,' Süleyman said. 'I think they were regional governors during the Empire. As for Mr Istefanopoulos, well, he's a Fener Greek, a Byzantine. It doesn't get more ancient and venerable than that.'

'So you think they set out to kill people of quality?' Krikor asked.

'If they did then they missed one,' İkmen said as he looked across at Süleyman. 'And anyway, do we know that they're actually dead? No, we don't. Their bodies have disappeared, there was fake blood where their bodies had been and now we have more masked men, which may or may not be connected to these people. So if you didn't know Demir, Mert and Istefanopoulos, who invited them, Krikor?'

He shrugged. 'Well, I did,' he said. 'In concert with my team. We compiled the guest list together. We went through all the prominent or influential or just plain rich people we knew and we invited them. Aysel, for example, has been involved with prisoners and their families for years, first in the old Bayrampaşa Prison and now in Silivri. She's also, I believe, been involved in some of the regional prisons too: Kayseri, İzmir spring to mind.'

'Why were Demir, Mert and Istefanopoulos put on the list?' İkmen asked. 'What good works did they do?'

'I can't remember,' Krikor said. 'But Burak might.'

Süleyman, who had been lost in thought, said, 'If I remember correctly, Raşit Demir became a psycho-analyst.'

'As in Freud? Oedipus complex?' İkmen asked.

'Yes.'

'Mmm. Not a therapy I usually give much credence to,' Krikor said, 'but clearly someone on the team must have. We'll have to talk to Burak. Inspector Süleyman, I don't suppose you know what Mert and Istefanopoulos do?'

'They're both in business,' Süleyman said. 'Like Inspector İkmen said, I think that Mert is something to do with health clubs. I do know they're both rich and I also know that it's said they don't like each other, but I don't know why.'

'They must have been invited because of their wealth,' Krikor said. 'I'll speak to Burak.'

But neither Krikor Sarkissian nor either of the police officers moved. They were being very closely watched and listened to by their captors. Were they smiling underneath those balaclava helmets? Or were they worried that, with time ticking on, their captives were moving ever closer to some sort of solution? İkmen for one did not feel that the latter was even on the cards. Although he hardly dared to admit it to himself, he was pinning his hopes on some sort of intervention via Ayşe Farsakoğlu. By this time she had certainly alerted Ardıç which meant that there was probably a squad of police officers outside the hotel, if not a detachment of Special Forces. But what would, realistically, happen if they stormed the hotel? The masked men were heavily armed. He thought about that for a few moments and then the words, *Are they?* came quite unbidden into his mind.

What Ardıç had decided posed Ayşe Farsakoğlu with both a problem and a feeling of relief. Hiding out in the Pera Palas wasn't doing any of the people who were being held hostage any good and, as Ardıç said, if they could get someone in who could do something constructive, all the better. The lock on the back door into the kitchen had now been broken and, as far as she could tell, nobody was in the basement at the moment, unless they were in the toilets. Her biggest problem was getting Nar to meet her down there. Special Forces officers were moving in and the plan was for one of them to take Nar's place. This would get the two women out and also allow infiltration of the masked assailants by a highly trained officer wearing a microphone. It would give the police the eye on the inside that they needed. They also planned to bring out the man she, Nar and Ersu Bey had bundled into the fridge.

But so far the text Ayşe had sent to Nar had not

elicited a reply, in all probability because she was unable to respond. She could not, after all, just answer a text if she was in full view of her colleagues.

But Ayşe couldn't afford to just wait. She had to get out from behind the concierge's desk, down the stairs to the basement and into the kitchens. Since she'd left the kitchen herself, she'd only seen people go down to the basement to go to the toilet. She knew this because either she'd seen masked men take guests down or gang members had gone down alone and then returned. But had she seen *all* of them go and then return? And if lone gunmen went down to the basement, were they really just going to the toilet or were they doing something else – like going to the kitchens? She couldn't be sure. But she'd sent a text to Ardıç telling him she was making for the kitchens. She had to do it soon. Time was passing and an intervention needed to be effected before the gunmen made good on their threat to kill all of their hostages.

'I want to go . . . sir,' İzzet Melik added the last word grudgingly. Ardıç was being obstructive inasmuch as he was not letting İzzet do what he wanted.

The commissioner puffed on his cigar and then sighed. 'Two Special Forces officers are going in,' he said. 'Two young, very highly trained, very fit, very fast, completely ruthless men. Now, Sergeant Melik, if you can tell me what you possess in common with these men, I will let you go. And before you tell me that you're highly trained, yes, you are, but not like them and you know it.'

There was no arguing with anything his superior had said. But that didn't stop İzzet from wanting to go into the hotel with the Special Forces officers anyway. Ayşe was in there and he wanted to be the one to get her out.

Ardıç, who knew human nature better than even he cared to acknowledge, said, 'This bears out everything I have ever believed about relationships between police officers. They are wrong. You want to rescue your fiancée but it just isn't appropriate in this situation. Do you understand?'

Of course he did. Melik put his head down. 'Yes, sir.'

'You have to trust that Sergeant Farsakoğlu knows what she's doing,' Ardıç said. 'I do.'

İzzet looked up at him. A contradictory beast, Ardıç was both a traditionalist and a liberal, a man of religious faith who also believed passionately in the necessity for secular authority. He could be misogynistic and his tolerance for people who lived 'alternative' lifestyles was low, but there were always exceptions to his 'rules' and he was the first to admit it.

'Sergeant Farsakoğlu is one of our best officers,' Ardıç continued. 'Without her intervention we wouldn't have known anything about this situation.'

That was true. Although why she'd been at the Pera Palas at all still bothered İzzet.

'We all have our jobs to do, Melik,' Ardıç said, 'and yours, this time like my own, is to wait.' He looked over into a corner of the room where two young men were putting on Kevlar vests and slotting weapons into their boots and round their waists. 'Quite apart from Sergeant Farsakoğlu, we need to get Hüseyin Hikmet out,' Ardıç continued. 'We need to talk to him and we have to get someone on the inside who can actually provide us with some intelligence.'

Not talking to what was actually a woman at her side was no easy task. Dressed all in black as anonymously as Nar herself, she nevertheless looked undoubtedly woman-shaped. She also wanted to talk.

In a way Nar wanted to talk too. The woman was clearly part of the gang and if she could talk to her then she might be able to find out who these people were. But the woman just wanted to gossip.

'Do you see that girl over there?' she said to Nar as she pointed towards a young woman sitting at a table, idly smoking a cigarette. 'That's Senay Tuna. You know who her daddy is? A proper spoilt little madam!'

Nar didn't know who Senay Tuna was, much less her father, and so she said nothing. That had to be better than saying the wrong thing. Her other fear was that this woman would pick up the girly tones in her voice and start to become suspicious. There was only one woman in this crew, as far as Nar knew, and there certainly wasn't one as tall as she was.

She'd had a text which may or may not be from Sergeant Farsakoğlu. She'd felt the phone vibrate against her calf. But she hadn't been able to do anything about it. She'd been ordered to keep guard over the guests with this woman and that was where she had to stay.

In the middle of the room, she could see Inspector İkmen and one of his Armenian doctor friends talking to a man who, to Nar, looked a bit sweaty and slug-like. She couldn't hear what was being said but the woman beside her had to comment. 'Look at them!' she sneered. 'Useless! They're never going to solve it.' Then her eyes slid across to a woman dressed entirely in green. 'Oh, I do like that gown,' she said. 'That's *very* nice.'

Nar had observed that the gunmen didn't seem to approve of alcohol. They didn't want their hostages to drink and they were very vocal about it. Only the men she'd seen down in the kitchens had smoked and no one had eaten anything that Nar had noticed. Of course they didn't want anyone to see their faces but there was something else too. There was a sort of a puritanism about them which could point towards Islamic fundamentalism. But she hadn't heard any of them say anything of a religious nature and this woman at her side was very interested in what was an extremely revealing gown.

Was the woman's chat all just smoke and mirrors? But if that was the case, why was she doing it with a 'man' she thought was one of her own? Nar began to become very paranoid that maybe the woman had tumbled that she was not who she appeared to be and she began to sweat. That text was really worrying her too. Who had sent it? What was it about? And was it important?

'I don't like sequins on a gown, I think they look common,' the woman at Nar's side said as she watched a lady whose dress was covered in sequins pour herself a glass of water. 'The only sparkly things any woman should wear are diamonds.'

Ayşe Farsakoğlu stood outside the fridge she had once hidden inside and waited. Her heart was still thudding painfully inside her chest after the precarious journey she'd made from the hotel lobby down to where she was now. Guests, escorted by gunmen, had been in and out of the toilets almost all the time. They felt sick or they had diarrhoea, mainly because they were frightened. Ayşe couldn't blame them for that, but it had made her progress difficult. Now she was waiting for the two

Special Forces officers. One of them would help her take the gunman she'd put in the fridge out and the other would, hopefully, take over from Nar. If Nar made an appearance.

Ayşe looked back into the kitchens to see whether Nar was coming and it was in that moment that two men silently appeared at her side. She hadn't heard the back door open, or feet on the floor or anything. To stop herself from audibly gasping, Ayşe put her hand over her mouth. One of the men looked first at her and then at what she imagined was an image of her face on his phone and said, 'Sergeant, where's your insider?'

'Nar? I don't know,' Ayşe whispered. 'I sent her a text.'

'So she may be unable to get away.'

'Or she's been exposed as an impostor,' Ayşe said. It didn't bear thinking about but she still had to say it. It was, after all, a real possibility.

The other man, young and good-looking and grave, just like his colleague, said, 'Was the man in the fridge unconscious when you left him?'

Ayşe thought back to the limp body she had watched Ersu drag into the fridge. 'He grunted,' she said, 'when we put him in. We covered him with our coats.'

'So he could be awake or waking up.'

'He could be, yes,' she said. He could also, Ayşe

knew, and in spite of the grunting, be dead. She hoped he wasn't.

One of the men looked at his watch, at his partner and then he said, 'OK, let's do this.' He pushed the fridge door handle down while the other man stood across the corridor with his gun pointed out in front of him. Light burst into the corridor from the fridge and all three of them looked inside. The man was exactly where Ayşe and the others had left him, on the floor, covered up with coats. Maybe he was dead, after all. But as the officer who wasn't wielding a gun went inside, she heard the man on the floor very softly mutter, 'Allah!' She was relieved.

'Do you want me to help . . .' Ayşe let her offer die as she watched the officer lift the man up and sling him across his back as if he weighed nothing. He walked out of the fridge and closed the door behind him. He looked at his colleague. 'I'll take this one and the sergeant out,' he said.

'OK. I'll stay here.'

Ayşe looked back towards the kitchen again but she still couldn't see Nar.

'I'll wait,' the officer said. 'You have to go now, Sergeant.'

Ayşe bit her lip. She didn't want to leave the hotel without Nar.

'I—'

'You can't do any more here,' the officer said. 'Go now.'

He was not to be argued with. His voice as well as his body told her to go. And so Ayşe reluctantly left the hotel with the other officer and the man who could, possibly, tell them who the gunmen in the Pera Palas were.

Now that they were all being watched so closely, Çetin İkmen didn't feel able to say what was on his mind, even to Süleyman. The atmosphere in the Kubbeli Saloon was getting more and more claustrophobic, more and more unbearable. Did these gunmen have any interest in them working this out or not? Logically, if the four people their captors had shot hadn't really been shot at all, then those who had fired at them had to have been using blanks. No other explanation was possible. And whilst İkmen knew that it would be rash to assume that just because one or two people were carrying blanks, everyone else was as well, it had to be possible that at least some of them were. What if they were all actually being held hostage by unarmed men?

According to Krikor Sarkissian's assistant, Burak Fisekçi, the clinic's receptionist, Selma Hanım, knew Yiannis Istefanopoulos in some capacity and so he was her suggestion. Krikor knew Aysel Ökte, but neither he nor Burak could remember suggesting either Mert or Demir. Their names had probably originated with one or more of Krikor's nurses.

İkmen knew that he was moving away from the central issue and he had to get back to that. Who had killed Söner Erkan? He looked around the Kubbeli Saloon and into the ballroom and realised that he didn't have the first idea. No one who knew the boy seemed to have liked him, Lale Aktar had found him, but who else could have killed him and why? None of those who had been out of the ballroom when the boy was murdered had any sort of connection to Söner Erkan except for Burak Fisekçi. But his connection, via Krikor Sarkissian, was only slight. Could a clue possibly exist in the fictional scenario the Bowstrings were to have enacted?

The young prince (Söner) was blackmailing his sister-in-law (Ceyda) over an affair she had once had with the Italian Garibaldi (Metin Martini). He wanted to be paid off not to tell his sister-in-law's husband, the prince (Alp), about the affair. But rather than pay the young prince, his sister-in-law had killed him. İkmen sighed. If there was anything there, he couldn't see it. He was tired and stressed and in an ideal world he needed some space to wander about and think. But they wouldn't let him go anywhere on his own. Escorted he could go to the toilet or up to room 411 again, but they weren't going to allow him to go anywhere else. Or rather he thought that they probably wouldn't. What if he was wrong?

He looked up and caught the leader's eye.

'I want to go for a walk, I need to think,' he said. 'Can someone take me for a walk?'

The man thought for a moment and then he said, 'In order to be fair, I suppose I have to agree to that, yes.' He beckoned one of his men over to him.

İkmen inclined his head in thanks.

Süleyman, who was sitting beside him, said, 'I'll come with you.'

But İkmen put a restraining hand on his arm. 'No, Mehmet, thank you,' he said. 'I need to be as alone as I can be. I need to think.'

'I can understand that, Inspector,' Lale Aktar said. 'Sometimes the solitary path is the best, especially when you're trying to solve a problem.'

One of the gunmen came over to İkmen and said, 'Where do you want to go for this walk?'

He sounded annoyed. Not a person, İkmen imagined, who walked for pleasure. But at least he wasn't the man with the camera on his helmet.

'I want to go up to the fourth floor and walk round and round the central space and contemplate the nothingness above and below,' İkmen said. Above the Kubbeli Saloon was a vast space around which were suspended the floors of the hotel in rising galleries. Above that was the massive glass roof. It was a lot of thinking space.

'Why the fourth floor?' the gunman asked.

But before İkmen could answer, the leader said, 'So that he can smoke with a clear conscience.'

İkmen smiled. 'Ah, I see you know me very well,' he said.

As usual, climbing four flights of stairs wore Çetin İkmen out and he had to spend a few moments when he reached the top of the last flight standing still and catching his breath. His legs as well as his lungs didn't like such exercise any more. In fact, they hadn't liked it for years. Çetin İkmen had been unfit for ever.

But walking on flat surfaces was OK and so he did that. Round and round the gallery, always feeling a little queasy whenever he reached the door of room 411. The masked man watched him with his Kalashnikov always ready in his hands. At a distance he didn't look so much frightening as absurd. İkmen almost laughed. He lit a cigarette. But then he realised that he didn't have an ashtray and so he riffled in his jacket pocket for the empty cufflink box he knew was in there and he took the lid off and used that. Just after he passed the door of room 411 for the third time, a masked figure came out of one of the rooms much further down towards the lift. He or she was carrying something. It was something that İkmen recognised and which, if it was what he thought it was, made him sweat with fear. It provoked a whole sequence of terrible memories of appalling events.

Chapter 18

Hüseyin Hikmet, or whoever the man was, refused to speak except to say that 'Allah is great!' They'd thrown everything they knew about the situation at him – and that included the intelligence about the fake blood that Ayşe Farsakoğlu had given them. Now they wanted to progress to harsher measures. Ardıç and the Special Forces commander, İpek, were conferring about it behind the bar.

Ayşe Farsakoğlu, looking over at the heated discussion between the two men, said, 'I expect they want to smash up what remains of his fingers.' Just as Ersu Nadir had told them, Hüseyin Hikmet had only four fingers on his left hand.

'Yes.' But İzzet Melik was hardly listening. With one arm round her shoulders and a protective hand on her arm, he wasn't letting her move or even really breathe without him.

'It'll do them no good,' Ayşe continued. 'He's clearly a religious fanatic. He's made a decision not to speak and even if they beat words out of him, they won't be able to be sure that he's telling the truth.' Her eyes filled with tears. 'Allah, what if these people are al Qaeda – or worse!'

But İzzet Melik ignored that remark. He had other issues on his mind. 'What were you doing at the Pera Palas, Ayşe?' His words were almost as much of a shock to him as they were to her. Their tone, which was calm, was also surprising.

She looked at him. 'What?'

'The Pera Palas,' he said. 'Why were you there? You went home.'

'My stomach felt bad,' she said, 'so I went for a walk.'

'What made you walk to the Pera Palas?' he asked.

İzzet had not been with the department when the original owner of the golden samovar Ayşe had seen being taken into the hotel had killed his brother and his lover. She and others had told him various things about the case over the years but it wasn't in his blood, like it was in hers – and Süleyman's. 'You may not have noticed but when we passed the Pera Palas earlier on this evening someone got out of a car with a samovar,' she said.

İzzet shrugged. 'Yes, I did notice but so what?'

'I recognised it,' Ayşe said. 'I'm sure of it. It was the gold samovar that Dr Krikor Sarkissian used to own.

The one he was given by the murderer Muhammed Ersoy—'

'Muhammed Ersoy?' It was Commissioner Ardıç's voice that interrupted her. Ayşe looked over at him.

'What has the name of that bastard got to do with anything?' he asked her.

'I saw a samovar, gold, like the one that Ersoy gave to Dr Krikor Sarkissian going into the hotel earlier, when I was passing the Pera Palas with Sergeant Melik,' she said.

Commander İpek, somewhat nonplussed at having his conversation with Ardıç suddenly cut short, said, 'Commissioner, what is this about?'

But Ardıç ignored him. 'Why didn't you tell someone about this before?' he said to Ayşe.

His fiancée now, apparently, under attack, İzzet pulled Ayşe close to him again.

'Because sure as I *felt*, I accept that I could be wrong,' she said. 'And anyway, Dr Sarkissian sold it on years ago.'

'Be that as it may,' Ardıç said, 'it clearly worried you or you wouldn't be talking about it now. Did you go back to the hotel later because of it?'

'Yes.' But she blushed. That was not of course the only reason she'd gone back to the Pera Palas.

'Did you see this samovar when you were in the hotel?'

'No, sir.'

'So this could be irrelevant?'

'Yes, sir.'

Ardıç, under the gaze of the confused and offended Commander İpek, frowned and sucked on his teeth. Only Ayşe knew what he was thinking because that was what she was thinking too. Anything to do with Muhammed Ersoy, even an inanimate object, had a resonance that, at the very least, had to be attended to.

Ardıç walked over to a constable who was sitting at one of the laptop computers that had been set up in the bar and said, 'Look it up. Google it or whatever it is you do.'

'Google what, sir?'

'Gold Turkish samovar and Muhammed Ersoy,' he said. 'Try and find out who owns it now.'

When Çetin İkmen was not around, conversation among the rest of the group who were supposed to be solving the mystery of Söner Erkan's death descended into gossip. The two doctors fretted about the state of health of their friends and colleagues in the ballroom, Hovsep Pars was drunk and Lale Aktar appeared to have slipped into a fitful sleep. Only Mehmet Süleyman retained a firm grip on the awful reality of the situation, which was that if they didn't find the person responsible for Söner's death, they were all going to die. Probably.

He looked at the masked men who were guarding them and wondered how many of them were guests who had been 'shot' earlier. How many of these people carried real ammunition and how many blanks? He also pondered on the fact that one of them was actually someone that Ayşe Farsakoğlu had sent in. Which one was it?

Lale Aktar stirred in her sleep and then opened her eyes. She looked at him and smiled.

'Are you OK?' he asked.

She sat upright and said, 'I could do with a freshen up.'

She wanted to go to the toilet. Süleyman called one of their captors over, who got another masked man from the ballroom to take her downstairs. When she'd gone, Süleyman found himself staring at her handbag, which was made, in part, from ostrich feathers. It was fascinating the way the individual fronds of feather moved very gently in the air-conditioned breeze. He was starting to fixate on irrelevances. He was exhausted. He shook himself awake. Hovsep Pars, watching him, laughed. 'You're beginning to drift,' he said. 'You should have a drink, Inspector.'

'Wouldn't that make me even more sleepy?' Süleyman asked.

The old man said, 'Maybe. But what does it matter if it does?'

Arto Sarkissian, who was sitting next to Hovsep Pars, put a hand on his leg and said, 'We must try to remain positive.'

He laughed. 'Positive? We're all going to be slaughtered by lunatics.'

'Not necessarily.'

'But then Armenians have been slaughtered by all sorts of people, why not lunatics?' Hovsep Pars said.

And then Çetin İkmen and his guard walked back into the Kubbeli Saloon. When they saw him, all the others became silent, even Hovsep Pars. He had the look of a man who had just seen an atrocity so terrible he might never recover.

Lale Aktar stood in front of the long row of stylish sinks in the toilet and she began to speak. 'Now—'

'Be quiet!' Nar held up a hand to silence her, while she read the text that Ayşe Farsakoğlu had sent her earlier. This was the first opportunity she'd had to read it. Someone had come to take her place. A soldier. Was he still in the kitchen?

'Now look—'

'No, you look,' Nar said as she put her phone back into her pocket. She checked to make sure that no one else was in the toilets and then she lifted up her balaclava helmet. Lale Aktar's eyes widened.

'I've come to get you out of here,' Nar said. 'Or rather I'm here to . . .' She found that she couldn't begin to explain what she was doing. 'Look,' she said as she replaced her mask, 'to get you out of here I need to go.'

'Go?'

'Someone's come to take my place – from outside – and . . . Look, I have to go but I may be back.' She began to walk back towards the toilet door. 'But I might come back as someone else,' she said.

And then she left. Her last view of Lale Aktar was of a woman who was both confused and possibly a little bit outraged too.

Nar ran through the Agatha Restaurant and into the kitchen. There was no one there. She began to search around the cookers, the sinks, the cupboards – anywhere her replacement might be hiding. After all, if he was a soldier then he'd know not to immediately reveal himself to just anyone who came into the kitchen. She had to be careful too but, hot from the anxiety she'd experienced over the last couple of hours as well as stifled by the balaclava and the jumpsuit, Nar pulled the helmet off and fanned her face with her hand.

She walked out of the kitchen and down the corridor

that led towards the back door when suddenly a hand reached around the side of her head and came to rest across her mouth.

It wasn't often that Çetin İkmen didn't know what to do but now was one of those times. Should he confront the gunmen about the golden samovar or not? What if it wasn't the samovar formerly owned by Muhammed Ersoy but just some gold-coloured thing that had no meaning? He could ask Krikor Sarkissian about it but he really didn't want to do that in front of the gunmen. So he wrote him a note. They'd allowed him his notebook and so he wrote 'To whom did you sell the samovar Muhammed Ersoy gave you?'

Krikor looked down at what he had written and frowned.

'Write it down,' İkmen told him.

Still confused, Krikor nevertheless began to write. Long experience with Çetin İkmen had taught him that he very rarely did anything, however weird, without a good reason.

İkmen looked at what Krikor had written and then asked, 'Russian?'

'Yes,' Krikor said.

'Did he take it back to Russia?'

'Yes.'

'Mmm.' Çetin İkmen lit a cigarette and then passed his notebook to Süleyman.

The leader, who had been watching, said, 'What are you doing?'

'When I was walking, I had some thoughts,' İkmen said. 'I wrote them down. Now I'm showing them to my colleagues.'

'Why don't you just tell them?'

İkmen looked into his eyes and said, 'Because I've already written them down. Why should I now repeat them?'

'Because you don't want us to hear what you're saying?'

'Maybe,' İkmen replied.

The leader's eyes narrowed. 'And if I want to see what you've written down?'

'Then do so.' İkmen shrugged. Süleyman, who had read what he had written, went cold.

The leader looked at the man standing next to him, the man with the camera, laughed and then walked to the back of the room. The cameraman carried on filming.

After a short, tense pause, Süleyman turned to İkmen. 'Why the interest in that?' he asked him.

'Because I think I saw it here,' İkmen replied.

'In the hotel?' Krikor Sarkissian wiped a hand across his face nervously. 'That can't be possible.'

Arto said, 'What are you talking about?'

Süleyman passed him İkmen's notebook. The cameraman snorted in amusement. Arto cleared his throat and then gave the notebook back to İkmen. Hovsep Pars, who had fallen asleep, snuffled gently.

'But if it is here and it is in fact what we think it is, then what does it mean?' Süleyman asked. 'What relevance does it have to the death of Söner Erkan?'

'Maybe none at all,' İkmen said. 'But earlier this evening I saw a man, who later got a taxi to Yeniköy, deliver something to the concierge's desk. I didn't see what it was, but the whole situation gave me a bad feeling. Maybe that was because the delivery was the article in question – not that I actually saw it then.'

'And because the deliverer was going to Yeniköy . . .'

Muhammed Ersoy, the murderous one-time owner of the samovar, had lived in Yeniköy.

'Maybe you're putting two and two together and making five,' Arto said to İkmen. 'Can't you speak to the concierge?'

'Wrong concierge,' İkmen said. 'This one must have come on duty sometime after I witnessed that scene in the reception area.'

'And yet when it comes to . . .' Süleyman eyed the cameraman and then said, 'We all know how delicate this particular subject is. We have no idea what, if anything, our captors may know about it. But none of us trusts them.'

'We never did. Did we?'

'No, but after the fake blood . . .'

They heard footsteps coming from over by the lift. Hovsep Pars apparently woke up and said, just as if he had been awake all through their conversation and had seen İkmen's notebook, 'Mrs Aktar comes back to us. I don't think there is any need to tell her about the Devil, do you? Women should be protected against such evil.'

'Who is Nikolai Nikolaevitch Toplovski?' Ardıç asked the young man at his side staring at the computer screen.

'An oligarch,' the constable said. 'It says here he's big in Vladimir Putin's party.'

'Well, any oligarch that isn't is abroad, in prison or dead, as far as I can tell,' Ardıç said. 'So this Toplovski has the golden samovar, does he?'

'He had it,' the constable said. 'Then he sold it in late two thousand and nine.'

'Where?'

'Moscow.'

'To whom?'

The constable scrolled down the screen and said, 'I'm just trying to . . .'

'We don't have much time,' Ardıç said as he shifted his large stomach uncomfortably. The chairs in the pub were spindly and hard and he just couldn't get comfortable.

Ayşe Farsakoğlu, looking on with İzzet Melik, wanted to tell her superior that the poor constable could only work as fast as he could translate the information on the screen from English into Turkish. He had spent much of his life in England where his Turkish parents still owned a restaurant but it still wasn't easy.

The constable touched the screen with one finger and said, 'Bought by a company called Fener Maritime Sigorta.' He looked up. 'So, Turkish!'

'They must have really wanted it to go to Moscow,' Ardıç said.

'Maybe, but then perhaps they just placed their bids by telephone, sir,' the constable said. 'Or online.'

'Mmm.' It wasn't easy for Ardıç to not look sour when certain modern ways of doing things were mentioned. Bidding in an auction 'online' seemed very, very strange. How could anyone bid for anything they hadn't actually seen in the flesh, as it were.

'Fener Maritime Sigorta are based in Maslak,' the constable said. It was logical that an insurance company would have its headquarters in one of the bright, shiny new business districts of İstanbul.

'Look up the name of the managing director,' Ardıç said. 'I need a telephone number or an address or both.'

'Yes, sir.' The young man began to do those things on the computer that Ardıç was in the habit of describing as 'arcane' and so the commissioner stood up and walked away.

Ayşe Farsakoğlu left İzzet Melik to stand beside Ardıç. She said, 'Sir, this samovar thing could be meaningless.'

He looked at her with red, watery eyes and said, 'If it was meaningful enough to make you walk back to the Pera Palas and look through the windows then it is not something I intend to leave uninvestigated. And anyway, it concerns Ersoy. You and I both remember that, don't we, Sergeant?' Then he waved her away. 'I must try and explain this to Commander İpek. I do believe he thinks we may all have gone mad.'

Ayşe returned to İzzet who was staring at her with unusually emotionless eyes. 'But you didn't just go back because of the samovar, did you?' he said.

She didn't reply. She made an attempt to walk past him but İzzet caught her arm. 'It was to see *him*, wasn't it?' he said. 'Because *he's* still in your head.' He lowered his voice. 'Look me in the eye and tell me that it isn't so, Ayşe.'

She raised her head and looked at him but she couldn't speak. Tears gathered at the corners of her eyes and she felt a tenderness for him that made her put a hand up to his cheek. But he pushed her away.

'You can't tell me that I'm wrong, can you?' İzzet whispered. 'Because I'm not. Are you still in love with him or is he just a fantasy that you can't get over?'

Again, Ayşe had nothing to say. She didn't know. Mehmet Süleyman was not a man she liked, but did she love him? Or did she just obsess about him because of who he was and what he looked like? Or was it perhaps that he represented all the aspirations she'd had as a girl about being loved by a tall, dark, exciting man?

'I won't stand for it,' İzzet said into her ear. Some of their fellow officers as well as a few of the Special Forces men were looking at them now. It wasn't comfortable.

'İzzet, I—'

'Commissioner, I've got a name and a district,' the constable at the computer said.

Ardıç lumbered over and stood behind the young man. Ayşe and İzzet separated, both trying to concentrate on things other than their own feelings.

'The managing director of Fener Maritime lives in Yeniköy,' the constable said. 'His name is Yiannis Istefanopoulos.'

The name meant nothing to anyone. But Ardıç told İzzet Melik to get in his car and drive to Yeniköy while officers back at the station identified his actual address and telephone number. If nothing else, Mr Istefanopoulos would need to check and see whether his gold samovar was where he usually kept it.

Chapter 19

Even though it was cold, Nar felt so much better wearing her thin, satin dress than she had done in that heavy jumpsuit. It was the dead time of night, almost 4 a.m., and she was with a Special Forces officer who looked about half her age. They kept low as they ran underneath the hotel's windows, Nar scanning the area continuously for her discarded shoes. They were fake Jimmy Choos and she loved them. What she wasn't quite so keen on was the idea of being 'debriefed'. The officer who had changed places with her in the kitchen had passed her on to this kid who had told her that she had to be debriefed about her time in the hotel.

There was a lot to tell but really Nar had to get back to work. Even at 4 a.m. there were still punters on the streets and, apart from anything else, the other girls would be wondering where she'd got to. But she had no choice in the matter. This kid was taking her to Sergeant Farsakoğlu and her superiors and that was that. As they passed underneath the windows of the bar, she was tempted to look in and see if that dead body that had started this whole adventure off was still there. But she resisted the urge. She still looked for her shoes but she didn't find them. Nar eventually came to the conclusion that some thieving bastard must have picked them up and taken them home.

When she finally reached the pub opposite the Pera Palas (where she sometimes took the odd drink or two) Nar immediately recognised the man they all knew as Hüseyin Hikmet. Not that he recognised her. He just looked horrified. Nar said to him, 'Oh, grow up. You know that given half a chance you would.'

'So you are Nar.'

She turned and saw a fat man smoking a cigar standing behind her.

'I am Commissioner Ardıç,' he said. 'We have a lot to thank you for and, I am afraid, a lot of questions to ask you.'

Over Ardıç's shoulder, Nar saw Ayşe Farsakoğlu and smiled, but the policewoman did not smile back. In fact she looked as if she was about to cry. Nar extended her hand to Ardıç, which he, rather haltingly, shook. 'No problem,' Nar said. 'Only two conditions.'

'Conditions?'

'This is a bar, so I'd like a vodka and Fanta, and I want to be able to smoke in here,' she said.

Ardıç put his cigar into his mouth and puffed. Then

he took it out and said to one of the police officers across the room, 'Yıldız, will you get this lady a vodka and Fanta now.'

Nar smiled. 'Thank you,' she said.

'You're welcome.' Ardıç guided Nar over to a table by one of the windows overlooking the Pera Palas and introduced her to a thin, fit-looking man in his fifties. This was Commander İpek. He looked more than a little stunned, but Nar smiled at him anyway, even though he visibly cringed.

Once her vodka and Fanta had arrived, Nar took a very long slug, lit up a cigarette and then said, 'So what do you want to know?'

'Firstly, Nar,' Ardıç said, 'I'd like to know whether at any time while you were in the hotel you heard anyone say the name Muhammed Ersoy?'

Nar thought. It was a name she knew, although she didn't know where from. She was pretty sure it wasn't from the Pera Palas. 'No,' she said. 'Why?'

'You sure?'

'Yes.'

'Mmm. Not important at the moment,' Ardıç said. 'Now what about this fake blood?'

'Those people, the . . . the gunmen, and woman, were supposed to have killed some of the guests when they first arrived,' Nar said. 'Before I got in there. But then later your Inspector İkmen got really angry with the leader about the fact that the blood that was supposed to have come from the victims was fake.'

'Do you know how Inspector İkmen knew about this?'

'There's a couple of doctors with him. One of them told him.'

'And did you see the gunman's response?' Commander İpek asked.

'Yes.'

'What was it?'

Nar took another gulp from her glass, dragged on her cigarette and said, 'Nothing. Didn't say a thing. Although I can tell you that the Kalashnikov I had was loaded with real ammunition, not blanks. I did my military service. I know these things.'

'But the gunman wasn't disturbed.'

'Nah! But then they're all the same, aren't they, that type?' Nar said.

'What type?'

'Puritans,' she said.

'What do you mean by puritans?' Ardıç asked. 'Do you mean religious fundamentalists?' Hüseyin Hikmet seemed to be one of those.

It was a question that Nar had been asking herself the whole time she was with the gunmen. On the one hand they had discouraged the guests from drinking alcohol. With the exception of one young man she'd seen in the kitchen when she and Ayşe had first got in there, they didn't smoke, and none of the gang had, while she had been looking at them, eaten or drunk anything. On the other hand, they hadn't made any religious or nationalistic pronouncements and the woman she had shared guard duty with in the ballroom had actively admired some of the female guests' clothes. She had also said that a woman should only wear diamonds.

'To be honest, I don't know,' Nar said. She relayed her thoughts and observations.

There was a pause.

Then Commander İpek turned to Commissioner Ardıç and said, 'Do you know what this reminds me of?'

'No. What does it remind you of?'

Commander İpek bit his bottom lip and then he said, 'That film. The one where people in an office block are taken hostage but what it is really all about is a robbery. It's American, quite old—'

'*Die Hard*,' Nar said. 'I loved that film! Although I didn't like the bit where Bruce Willis cut his feet open on all that glass, that was horrible.'

'It was based upon a misdirection, a crime committed to cover another crime.'

'A robbery,' Ardıç said. 'Mmm.' Then he looked at Nar again and said, 'Did you, during your travels around that hotel, ever see a golden samovar?'

Nar frowned. 'A golden samovar? What, you mean made of actual gold?'

'Yes.'

She shook her head. 'No,' she said. 'I'd remember that if I'd seen it.' Then she laughed. 'I might even have had it away myself!'

Mehmet Süleyman watched Lale Aktar go with one of the gunmen. Down to the toilets again. The stress was making her feel sick. He turned to İkmen. 'We need some sort of break,' he said.

Usually during the course of an investigation they had access to a range of media, forensic evidence and the benefit of being able to converse freely. They also had time. But not here.

'The only person we can definitively place at the scene is Lale Aktar,' İkmen said. 'But I am extremely wary of pointing the finger at her because she is far too obvious a choice. This is, after all, a game to these people. And besides, if Lale Aktar did kill Söner Erkan, we have to accept that she is one of these people.'

'You don't think she is?'

'I didn't say that. She's not being entirely straight with us, I feel,' İkmen said. 'But I don't think she killed the boy.'

'Unless it's a double bluff.' Süleyman turned away briefly and then said to the cameraman whose head was almost in his face, 'Can you back off!'

The man pulled away. Süleyman shook his head in frustration.

'I'm going to interview all those people who were out of the ballroom when Mrs Aktar found the body,' İkmen said.

'The actors.'

'No, not the actors,' İkmen said. He picked up Krikor Sarkissian's guest list from the table and looked at it. 'Anyone who isn't an actor.'

'Hoping to find what?' Arto Sarkissian said.

'I don't know,' İkmen replied.

'But if Lale Aktar didn't kill Söner Erkan and she didn't see anyone else in her room . . .' Arto continued.

'The room was dark,' Süleyman said.

'And we only have Mrs Aktar's word that she didn't see anyone in her room,' İkmen said.

'I still can't work out how she got blood on her shoes,' Arto said.

'Yes, blood does seem to be a bit of a problem for Mrs Aktar all round.'

Everyone except Hovsep Pars looked at İkmen.

Süleyman frowned. 'Meaning?'

'Meaning that I need to talk to quite a few people in a short space of time and then I need to speak to Mrs Aktar,' İkmen answered obscurely.

* * *

İzzet Melik got back into his car and picked up his mobile phone. The pretty Bosphorus village of Yeniköy was peaceful and most of the houses were dark, with the exception of the massive yalı he had just been inside.

He called Ardıç. 'Yiannis Istefanopoulos is not at home in Yeniköy,' he said. 'I've just spoken to his housekeeper and I've had a look around the place too.'

'Do you know where he is?' Ardıç asked.

'According to the housekeeper, he's at a function at the Pera Palas Hotel,' İzzet said.

He heard Ardıç draw in a deep breath. 'So both Istefanopoulos and his samovar are in the hotel.'

'Potentially, yes.'

'All right.' Ardıç cut the connection.

İzzet turned the key in the ignition and put the car into first gear. Then he stopped. He couldn't really see to drive properly because his eyes were so full of tears. He had so wanted to marry Ayşe! He had so looked forward to it! But if she was still in love with Mehmet Süleyman then it was all over. It had to be. He couldn't share Ayşe with anyone.

The Pera Palas Hotel concierge, Saffet Güler, had been behind his desk in reception when Söner Erkan was murdered. The first thing he'd known about it was when he saw Lale Aktar running down the stairs into the

Kubbeli Saloon covered in blood. He'd taken over from the previous concierge at 10 p.m. But he didn't know anything about any golden samovar.

'Do you keep records of deliveries made to guests?' İkmen asked.

'Of course,' Saffet Güler said. 'And whenever I come on shift I always check to see whether there are any outstanding deliveries either to guests or to hotel staff.'

'You check on computer?'

'Yes,' he said.

'I need to see your system,' İkmen said.

The leader of the gunmen approached them. 'I'll take you out to the lobby,' he said.

İkmen, Güler and the gunman left the Kubbeli Saloon.

Having questioned and then dispensed with Rauf Özal, the car dealer from Nişantaşı, who had been having an unauthorised cigarette in the Patisserie de Pera – from where he claimed to have seen Saffet Güler the concierge – Süleyman and the Sarkissians were now interrogating a friend. David Bonomo was a secretary at the office of the Chief Rabbi of İstanbul. He was someone they had all known for many years.

'There's no polite way of putting this,' David said as he looked up at the man with the camera on his helmet. 'I have irritable bowel syndrome. Usually I take a dose of anti-diarrhoea medication before I go out to eat, but this time . . .' He shrugged. 'While that poor boy was dying upstairs, I was down in the toilet thinking I was dying.'

Krikor Sarkissian shook his head impatiently. 'You should get that attended to,' he said. 'You can't go on like that. You've had it for years!'

David Bonomo ignored him. Krikor meant well but he didn't know much, if anything, about his affliction. 'I was completely oblivious to anything except my own discomfort,' Bonomo said to Süleyman. 'By the time I got out of the toilet the whole place was awash with masked men. I wasn't even around when Mrs Aktar came down the stairs covered in blood.' He looked over at her, but Lale Aktar was asleep. Whispering, he said, 'She doesn't look well.'

'No.' Süleyman looked at the novelist, slumped in a chair beside an equally unconscious Hovsep Pars. It was clear that writing novels about crime in no way prepared one for the real thing. Süleyman now felt a little bit ashamed of the fact that when the murder mystery evening had started he had been so anxious to beat her.

'David, did you see or hear anyone else in the toilet when you were in there?' Krikor Sarkissian asked.

David Bonomo thought. He was a spare, hawk-like man who always looked up when he was seriously considering something. 'Mmm,' he said. He looked down again. 'I don't remember having any company in there. But, as I said before, I was in something of a state.'

'You think that would prevent you from being aware of other people around you?'

David Bonomo looked up again. 'Well . . .'

'Forgive me if I'm wrong.' Arto Sarkissian leaned forward in his chair and folded his arms across his chest. 'But I would, probably in my ignorance, imagine that if one was suffering from gastric "issues", shall we say, one would be acutely aware of, and nervous about, other people being in one's immediate vicinity. One would want not just a cubicle but a whole toilet block to oneself – I imagine.'

David Bonomo nodded. 'There is some truth in that, Arto,' he said. 'A lot of truth.' He looked up at the ceiling again. 'And actually, in spite of being in some pain, I was quite relaxed – in a way,' he said.

'Does that mean that you were probably alone, David?' Süleyman asked.

'Probably. I couldn't swear to it. But that does seem likely.'

'And you definitely did not see my assistant Burak?' Krikor said.

'No.'

Krikor Sarkissian looked at Mehmet Süleyman. They both knew what the other one was thinking. Eventually it was Krikor who broke the silence. 'So,' he said, 'shall I go and speak to Burak?'

But then Çetin İkmen returned with the hotel concierge. The policeman looked at them all and said, 'The man who Saffet Bey here came in to replace, the concierge known as Ali Yalçın, left no record of anyone delivering anything. My question, gentlemen, and lady, is did he just forget or was he working with whoever these people are?'

Chapter 20

All they could hear were people's voices but they were muffled and diffuse. The officer inside the hotel hadn't actually managed to engage the gunmen in anything like a conversation. They'd told him to go places and he'd gone, to do things and he'd done them. He had made contact with the novelist Lale Aktar and she had said that, somehow, she would let İkmen know that Nar was out and he was in.

Ardıç and Commander İpek sat beside the technician listening in to the officer's microphone, both looking very subdued. But neither of them spoke. Everyone in the pub was quiet now. Even Nar had stopped trying to flirt because time was moving on and everyone knew that it was also running out. İzzet Melik, recently returned from Yeniköy, was careful not to sit or stand anywhere near his fiancée. Ayşe Farsakoğlu was angry and upset and he didn't know how any of this was making him feel about her.

Ardıç looked at the technician who shook his head.

Ardıç sighed and then stood up. Everybody looked at him. He cleared his throat.

'It is our understanding that Inspectors İkmen and Süleyman have until sunrise to find out who killed a young man in one of the hotel bedrooms,' he said. 'However, Ersu Bey, the hotel maître d', has told us that if the gunmen want to get out of the Pera Palas unchallenged they will have to do that before six a.m. when the day shift arrive. Now we don't think that anyone witnessed this killing, our officers have no access to forensic or outside help of any sort and if they don't get it right they will be killed. It is now,' he squinted down at his watch, 'four thirty and so time is short. Unless İkmen and Süleyman have access to information that can conclusively prove that a particular person has unequivocally killed that boy then whatever name they eventually give to their captors will be a gamble. I have the utmost faith in my officers but with all due respect to them, as things stand it cannot be anything but a gamble. Further, this "game" these people are playing may well mean that even if our officers do get it right, they might be killed anyway. At some point, we think, they will spring it on İkmen and Süleyman that they will have to have their answer before six a.m. These are unknown and therefore unpredictable people and even though we may like to think that maybe they are not as heavily armed as they seem, we have to assume that they are lethal. I had a discussion with Commander İpek earlier about how we might proceed if we got to this stage, effectively no further forward than we were before the Special Forces officer went in, and we decided then that we would have to prepare to storm the building.'

Everyone looked grave.

İpek, standing as well now, said, 'We have the building surrounded. Now we need to begin a slow process of infiltration. Provided the gunmen are still unaware of the fact that the kitchen door is open, we will proceed through that entrance. The aim is to strategically position a small group of six Special Forces officers in the Pera Palas in order to facilitate entry for the main force which will be deployed on my command. These officers will identify key operatives within the terrorist organisation and prepare to eliminate them once the operation begins. From Sergeant Farsakoğlu we have learned that the gunmen have been sighted in the kitchen. We have also learned that getting from the kitchen up the stairs and into the main public areas of the hotel without being seen is not easy. Floor plans of the hotel have been emailed to us by the managing director of the Pera Palas and we have the expertise of Ersu Bey to guide us. But this is all the information we have. Our man on the inside has been given uninterrupted guard duty in the ballroom away from what we imagine is the central command of a leader-type figure and his entourage, who have taken up positions in the Kubbeli Saloon with the police officers.' İpek looked over at his own men and said, 'I'm going to choose six of you – now.'

Çetin İkmen looked first at the sleeping figure of Hovsep Pars and then at Lale Aktar. Awake now, she smiled at him and he smiled back. Only then did he turn his attention to Burak Fisekçi. 'Burak Bey,' he said as the Armenian sat down opposite him, 'we're still trying to accurately place everyone in the hotel at the time of young Söner Erkan's death. You said you were in the toilets downstairs.'

'Yes.'

'Do you remember, Burak Bey, whether you were alone?'

'Alone in the toilets?' He looked away, averting his eyes from İkmen. Then he said, 'I can't be certain but I think that someone was in one of the cubicles. But I don't know who.'

If Burak Fisekçi was telling the truth then that was almost certainly David Bonomo. But then why wouldn't Burak Fisekçi be telling the truth?

'Burak Bey, can you tell me anything about the four people who were killed earlier on this evening?' İkmen said. Then he looked down at his notebook and read their names. 'Yiannis Istefanopoulos, Aysel Ökte . . .'

'You've asked me this before,' Burak said. 'And I told you then—'

'Just think again,' İkmen said. 'All of our lives could depend upon it.'

'Yes, I know, but I've—'

'Please listen. Yiannis Istefanopoulos, Aysel Ökte, Raşit Demir . . .'

'Huh!' It was a sound that signified disgust, but it didn't come from Burak Fisekçi. A now wakeful Hovsep Pars exclaimed, 'That fool!'

İkmen turned to him and said, 'Why is Raşit Demir a fool, Hovsep Bey?'

'Because he talks to the Devil,' Hovsep Pars said. 'He goes into Silivri Prison and he attempts to reason with the unreasonable.'

Muhammed Ersoy. Again. Aysel Ökte had a connection with Silivri too. Did she, somehow, know its most famous prisoner? Was that the connection between these supposedly murdered people? Muhammed Ersoy? But it couldn't be because if that was indeed the case, why hadn't Hovsep Pars been shot too? As the uncle of Muhammed Ersoy's murdered lover, he had the closest connection to the man he called the Devil of anyone in the hotel, as far as İkmen could tell.

'He calls himself a psychiatrist or some such,' the old Armenian continued. 'He goes into prisons and tries to understand people who are easy to understand. Then he writes academic papers about it.'

Of course, Raşit Demir was a psychoanalyst.

'What's to understand?' Hovsep Pars said. 'Evil is evil. There is nothing to be gained by speaking to evil people. They should be shot or hanged, like they were in the old days.'

When Burak Fisekçi went back into the ballroom he made straight for Ceyda Ümit. Holding her boyfriend Alp's hand, she let go of it when she saw Burak and she smiled.

'Come and sit with us, Burak Bey,' she said as she put a chair beside her own and patted the seat. She'd always liked Burak Bey. When his elderly mother, Siroun Hanım, had still been alive, she had sometimes come into the Ümits' apartment and spent time with Ceyda's grandmother Edibe. Sometimes Burak Bey would join them. Ceyda could still remember, as an infant, crawling around underneath the table while her grandmother, Siroun Hanım, Burak Bey and the old kapıcı of the building played bridge when her parents were both out with their friends every Thursday in the bars and restaurants of Çiçek Pasaj. Ceyda had never known life without Burak Bey and so to her he represented a stability she felt she really needed in such a perilous situation.

'What are the police doing?' she asked anxiously as Burak sat down beside her.

'Asking questions.'

'They've been asking questions for hours,' Alp said. Then he turned away, shaking his head impatiently. It was all getting to him. It was all getting to everyone. As the time when the policemen had to name their suspect grew closer, everyone in the ballroom became quieter, more tense and, in some cases, lacking in any sort of hope or faith.

Burak took one of Ceyda's hands in his. 'You have to trust,' he said.

'Trust what?'

'Whatever you like,' he said. 'The police, Allah, your friends, even me if you like, Ceyda.'

'And what good will uninformed, blind trust do for her?' Alp was looking at Burak Bey again. Both his words and his demeanour were challenging and Ceyda felt embarrassed.

'Alp!'

But Burak Bey just smiled and squeezed her hand. 'Alp is anxious, as we all are,' he said. 'Tensions can run high.'

'On the verge of death they tend to,' Alp put in quickly.

Burak Bey ignored him. 'You will be all right, Ceyda,' he said.

She knew he was just saying what she wanted to hear

in exactly the same way he'd done when she'd been a child. But Ceyda appreciated it. Alp's negativity didn't really achieve anything, but it was a manifestation of how frightened he was. They had all been shocked by Söner's death – that had been bad enough – but this!

Burak Bey was older and more accustomed to life. He made Ceyda feel safe in a way that could only be bettered by her own father. But then Burak Bey had always been like a very attentive uncle to her.

In response to a warm smile from Lale Aktar, İkmen went over and sat down next to her. The time had finally arrived when he could have that little chat he wanted to have with her. It wasn't going to be easy. The leader and the man with the camera on his helmet were watching them and the subject he had to raise with Lale Aktar was delicate to say the least. But he sat down beside her and they exchanged a few pleasantries before he launched into what he knew was bringing a visible blush to his otherwise very pale cheeks.

'Mrs Aktar,' he said, 'may I ask you about something?'

'All our lives are in your hands, Inspector, you may ask me anything,' she said.

'Mmm. I'm glad you feel that way,' İkmen said. 'Because, madam, it is about an issue that pertains specifically to women . . .'

'Oh, then I must be an expert!' she smiled again.

'Yes. Indeed.' He was finding this very hard. Even with Fatma he found talking about women's things very difficult. With his daughters it had been well nigh impossible. He'd managed, once, to talk about, well, *sex* to Ayşe Farsakoğlu. But that had been in an extreme situation years ago when she'd put herself at risk from a sexually sadistic man. This wasn't anywhere near as weird as that. In fact this wasn't weird at all. It was quite natural.

Lale Aktar looked at him. 'Inspector?'

İkmen knew that he just had to launch into it. He took a deep breath and then he said, 'Well, madam, it's about your, your menstrual . . . er, your period . . .'

Lale Aktar furrowed her brow. İkmen saw the two masked men look at him very intently.

'Yes, it's . . .'

The masked man with the camera in his helmet turned away. Clearly even with his face covered he was embarrassed. İkmen felt his own face burn.

'What do you want to know about my period, Inspector?' Lale Aktar said. She looked slightly amused – probably by his old-fashioned awkwardness.

Well, Çetin İkmen wanted to say, *I'd really like to know why it is that after going back to your room to get a clean sanitary towel when you found the body of Söner Erkan, you haven't, seemingly, changed your sanitary protection since. Every time you've been to the lavatory you've left your handbag, which would logically contain things like sanitary towels, behind on a chair or a table. Also I didn't actually discover any sanitary towels in your bathroom. I find it odd. Could you please explain it to me?*

But he couldn't say that. He just said, 'Um.'

Lale Aktar frowned and said again, 'What do you want to know, Inspector İkmen?'

He opened his mouth to just say it when he, and everyone else, was distracted by the sound of a gunshot. It seemed to have come from the direction of the bar.

The technician took his headphones off and threw them on to the table in front of him, his face contorted in an expression of pain. Commissioner Ardıç, concerned, said, 'What's the matter? What's happened?'

The technician shook his head. 'There was a crack,' he said. He put the headphones back on but all he could make out was silence. He took the headphones off again.

'Well?'

Over behind the bar, six Special Forces men were arming themselves prior to their infiltration mission. For a moment they stopped and listened to what was being said.

'It could have been a gunshot or maybe the mic has been knocked out,' the technician said. He shook his head impatiently. 'I don't know.'

'They could've killed our man.'

'Possibly.'

Commander İpek told his men to step up and get ready to go. Then he said to Ardıç, 'If they did discover our man and kill him, we need to get in there now.'

Ardıç nodded. 'Agreed.'

Ayşe Farsakoğlu, who had been listening with increasing anxiety to what had just happened, came forward and said to Ardıç, 'Sir, we mustn't just go in and put the hostages at risk!'

Behind her, İzzet Melik looked at her with a mixture of pain and loathing on his face.

Commander İpek answered her. 'We will stick to the plan, Sergeant,' he said. 'My men will enter via the kitchens and assess the situation before any major assault is made upon the building. But if the Pera Palas day shift is due to come on at six, we have only just over an hour to free those hostages. Remember, this is a game these people are playing. We have to be cleverer at that game than they are – if we can.' Then he looked over at his six hand-picked men who were now ready and he said, 'All right now, go.'

Chapter 21

They dragged the body into the Kubbeli Saloon and laid it down in front of Çetin İkmen, Mehmet Süleyman and the others. Inside the ballroom other guests, who didn't know what was going on but were frightened by the sound of gunfire, sobbed and screamed. The body wasn't wearing its balaclava helmet any more and so İkmen could see its face. It was clearly a man, as opposed to a transgendered person, which was, in a way, a relief. But why had the gunmen killed one of their own?

Lale Aktar put her hands on İkmen's arm and hid her head behind his shoulder.

Süleyman said, 'What's this?'

The leader pointed his gun at the body and said, 'This is one of yours.'

'I don't know him!' Süleyman said.

'He came to try and rescue you,' the leader said. The cameraman beside him leaned close into the dead man's face. 'But then you had to know that.'

'We didn't,' İkmen said.

Lale Aktar began to cry. İkmen tried to push down his fear. If this man had indeed come to rescue them, then where was the transsexual and how much longer could she keep her identity a secret from these people? In addition, how many more rescuers were in the hotel and did this mean that the place was about to be stormed? He looked at Süleyman, who was sweating. They both knew how sieges went. Negotiation with terrorists was not, usually, what the Turkish authorities did.

'I don't care what you say,' the leader said. 'Your time is up.'

'What do you mean?' İkmen said.

'You have ten minutes to tell me who you think killed the young prince and why,' the leader said.

Krikor Sarkissian, who had come forward to check for a pulse in the dead man's neck, said, 'But you told us we have until sunrise!'

The leader shrugged. 'That was then,' he said. 'Now we are apparently under attack from outside. You have ten minutes. That's it.'

Then leaving just the man with the camera plus one other to cover them all, he walked through to the ball-room. He shut the door behind him.

Commander İpek's six men ran silently through the hotel kitchens and then set off up the stairs and into the main body of the building.

They had all been allocated to different positions on the ground and first floors of the hotel. These could, according to the building's floor plans and the information they had been given by the maître d' and Sergeant Farsakoğlu, give them either visual, aural or strategic access to the masked gunmen and their hostages. Two of the men positioned themselves in the reception area – one behind the concierge's desk, the other in the Patisserie de Pera. Two more made their way up to the first floor, while the final pair hunkered down beside the old wooden lift. This latter pair could see into the Kubbeli Saloon where they both quickly identified two gunmen and six civilians. The door between the Kubbeli Saloon and the ballroom was closed. Officers outside the hotel reported that the gunmen had closed all the gaps in the ballroom curtains some minutes ago.

'We have to make a decision,' Süleyman said to Çetin İkmen. 'Who do you think killed Söner Erkan?'

İkmen looked at the two remaining masked men in the Kubbeli Saloon. Could he, Süleyman and the two doctors overpower them? He kept his eye on them and said, 'We don't know what will happen to whoever we name.'

'Everyone will die if we don't name anyone,' Arto Sarkissian said.

'That's what we *think*.'

'Çetin, it's utilitarianism at its most basic,' Krikor Sarkissian said. 'The sacrifice of one for the greater good of the many.'

İkmen looked at him with horror. 'You can't believe in that, Krikor! Surely!'

'Of course I don't!' Krikor Sarkissian said. 'But what else do you suggest, Çetin? The rescue plan from the outside has clearly run into trouble . . .'

'We should have a secret ballot.' They'd all thought that Hovsep Pars had gone to sleep again. 'Well, why not?' the old man continued. 'Can any of you think of a better idea? Inspector İkmen, tell me, do you or Inspector Süleyman have a suspect in mind?'

İkmen wanted to say something about not having been able to 'complete my investigations', but that was never going to happen anyway. He had hoped that somehow the situation would have been brought under control by this time but that hadn't happened either and, he had to assume, it never would. So who, realistically, was in the frame?

Anyone who was on the fourth floor at the time of the murder, which meant all of the actors, plus Burak Fisekçi, David Bonomo and Lale Aktar. The hotel concierge and the Nişantaşı car dealer had effectively provided alibis for each other. None of his fellow actors had liked Söner Erkan, but had they disliked him enough to kill him? David Bonomo was a quiet family man who worked for the Chief Rabbi and, as far as İkmen could tell, had no connection with Söner Erkan. Burak Fisekçi knew him via his neighbour Ceyda Ümit and through working with him on the murder mystery project. Was it possible he had come to hate the boy enough in that time to want to kill him? And what of Lale Aktar? She'd found the boy's body – apparently.

Of course the missing link in all of this was the connection between whoever had killed the boy and the gunmen. That had to exist. Without that, coming to any sort of reasonable conclusion was impossible.

Cetin İkmen looked into the camera on the gunman's helmet and said, 'This task is completely impossible and you know it.'

And then he remembered the conversation he'd been trying to have with Lale Aktar when the supposed infiltrator had been shot. He still needed to have that conversation and now he felt he could do that without the embarrassment he had experienced earlier. If they were all going to die anyway, there was no place for prudishness.

He turned to Lale Aktar and he said, 'Mrs Aktar, are you having a period or are you not?'

All the men around him gasped at the baldness of his words. Lale Aktar herself looked appalled. Turkish men didn't talk about such things, at least not in public. It wasn't done.

There was a moment of horrified silence. And then Krikor Sarkissian looked at the novelist, frowned, and said, 'But Lale, my dear, you had a hysterectomy last year.'

Commissioner Ardıç looked at his watch and said, 'If these people are serious about their intentions then İkmen and Süleyman have just over five minutes to come up with the name of the murderer of this Söner Erkan.'

The men already positioned inside the Pera Palas had relayed what they had heard and observed to Commander İpek who, along with his remaining troops, was preparing himself for a firefight inside the hotel. The management of the Pera Palas had been informed, and although naturally fearful for the integrity of their beautiful historic building, they knew that lives had to be put in front of crystal chandeliers and marble flooring.

'All that is irrelevant now,' İpek said. 'We're going in.'

'But what if it's just some sort of huge bluff?'

Ardıç and İpek turned and looked at Ayşe Farsakoğlu. Her face was grey and she looked, suddenly, like the middle-aged woman she actually was. But then Ardıç, at least, knew that facing the prospect of losing a person one is in love with can make time take flight.

'We can't take that risk, Sergeant,' he said to her. Then he looked at İpek. 'We must commit our men to your care, Commander, and to the will of Allah.'

Commander İpek bowed his head. 'Of course,' he said. And then without another word, he and his men left the bar and ran across the road towards the Pera Palas Hotel.

Ardıç, observing that Sergeant Farsakoğlu was alone in the centre of the room, went over to İzzet Melik and whispered, 'Be with her.'

'Sir?'

Ardıç took him to one side. 'I know there are effectively three of you in this relationship you have with Farsakoğlu,' he said.

Melik was shocked both by the fact that Ardıç knew and that he was speaking about such a personal thing.

'So that is how it is,' Ardıç continued. 'Your fiancée is not sleeping with Süleyman.'

'Sir, she—'

'She is a woman of honour, trust me on this,' Ardıç said. 'But Süleyman may be about to die. You love her. You should be with her.'

They both looked across at Ayşe, who was crying. Nar was lumbering over with her arms outstretched.

Ardıç said, 'Sergeant Melik, would you really have

your fiancée comforted by a person who has multiple convictions for soliciting?'

İzzet Melik watched Nar put her arms around Ayşe and hug her. But, frozen by indecision, he just couldn't move.

'Where are we going?' İkmen asked.

The leader had rejoined the man with the camera and the other masked man and they were herding the policemen, the doctors, Lale Aktar and Hovsep Pars up the main hotel staircase.

The novelist, her face still red with fury over what Krikor Sarkissian had said, was continuing to refute his allegation. 'I did not have a hysterectomy!' she said as Krikor took her arm and led her forwards.

'Lale, my dear,' he said, 'your husband is one of my best friends. He showed me the X-ray that your surgeon took after the operation. He wanted to know my opinion of what had been done, as a doctor and a friend. The surgery appeared to me to have been performed well. Faruk was relieved.'

'I did not have any hysterectomy! I didn't!'

Krikor Sarkissian caught Çetin İkmen's eye. Lale Aktar saw it and said, 'And anyway, this is all about nothing. Whether I went to my room to get a sanitary towel or not—'

'But if you didn't go to get a sanitary towel then why

did you go to your room when you did?' İkmen asked. 'Was it to kill Söner Erkan?'

'No!'

He turned away from her and repeated his question to the leader. 'Where are we going?'

'To room four hundred and eleven,' the leader said.

And then İkmen smiled. 'Oh, but of course,' he said. 'Why didn't I think of that? A room resonant with drama.' Then he stared hard into the leader's eyes. 'What are you getting out of this? Where's the money in this?'

He received no reply. İkmen looked at Süleyman who, years of experience told him, was preparing himself to take these men on. In view of the gravity of their situation as well as the strange fact that only three of their captors were accompanying them upstairs, this wasn't such a ridiculous idea. Unless of course the help that he knew existed outside the hotel was on its way. If it was, stalling these people rather than attacking them had to be the best idea. But how were they to know which course of action to take? If they did attack their captors, the other masked individuals down in the ballroom would no doubt be alerted somehow. Then what would they do? Would they kill all the hostages in the ballroom? If only he knew why all of this was happening, he might be able to take an informed view. But he couldn't. All he did know now was that there was a strong possibility that Lale Aktar was working with these people for some reason. And then suddenly a reason came to him. Putting two and two together and maybe making five, it was just possible that Hovsep Pars wasn't such a crazy old man after all.

Chapter 22

Ceyda Ümit was cold. They'd blindfolded her, made her take off all her clothes except her underwear, and then tied her legs together with what felt like wire. Her hands were attached, behind her back, to those of the person next to her, which was Burak Fisekçi. Although accustomed to being seen in her underwear by her fellow performers in Bowstrings, she wasn't used to being seen almost naked by strangers. Through trembling lips she said to Fisekçi, 'Do you think that they're going to kill us, Burak Bey?'

He squeezed her hands with his but didn't reply.

'I wish I knew where Alp was,' Ceyda said.

The last time she'd seen him had been just before they'd blindfolded her. He'd been across the other side of the ballroom with Kenan and Metin. Had they made him take his clothes off too?

'I'm sure that Alp is OK,' Burak Fisekçi said.

'But you don't know that.'

'No, I don't but . . .'

'Burak Bey, we're going to die!' she said. And then she began to cry. She couldn't help herself. Together with Alp she had hoped to be part of a theatrical movement and hopefully a dynasty that would take the country by storm. Bowstrings had only ever been a means towards achieving a future in serious, political theatre. But now that was never going to happen because Bowstrings, albeit indirectly, was going to kill them.

Ceyda felt her tears stick her blindfold to her closed eyelids like wallpaper paste. Her nose ran with snot and she felt ugly, humiliated and sick. 'Oh, Burak Bey,' she said, 'I'm so sorry. I should be stronger than this. But I'm just not.'

Burak Fisekçi said nothing. But then after she'd been crying for some minutes, Ceyda Ümit felt Burak Bey's hands suddenly free themselves from hers and from whatever had tied them.

No one had moved Söner Erkan's body. It still lay on Agatha Christie's bed, its dead eyes seemingly fixed on nothing for all time. Çetin İkmen and Mehmet Süleyman stood on the side of the bed nearest the door, while the doctors, the old man and the novelist stood opposite, nearest the window. The gunmen ranged themselves in front of Agatha Christie's books and her portrait on the wall. İkmen looked down at the body on the bed.

The leader said, 'Well?'

İkmen looked up. 'Well what?'

'Who do you think, in your professional opinion and after your investigation, killed this man?' the leader asked.

Çetin İkmen shrugged.

'Is that it?'

There was a tense moment. The two doctors and Mehmet Süleyman visibly started to sweat. İkmen looked slowly around the room until he was looking at the leader again. He said, 'What do you want me to say? That Mrs Aktar did it?'

'I didn't kill him!' Lale Aktar said. 'I—'

'You probably watched – or helped or something,' İkmen said.

'I—'

'Oh, please save your breath, Mrs Aktar,' İkmen said. 'You lied about why you came back to this room when you "found" the body. I don't know why and quite honestly I don't much care. The fact that you made up a load of rubbish about wanting sanitary protection tells me you were not in this room with benign intent. It points my nose in the direction of you being in with these people in some way. But then I think that whoever set this up would know I'd find you out and so you're just too obvious to be our killer.'

The man with the camera looked at his watch and then nudged the leader.

'So if Mrs Aktar didn't kill Söner Erkan, who did?' the leader asked. 'You know what depends on this, don't you?'

'I do.' İkmen looked at the Sarkissian brothers, at Hovsep Pars and at Mehmet Süleyman and he said, 'Any ideas?' No one said a word. Then he looked back at the leader again and smiled. 'No,' he said. 'We have no ideas.'

He heard the three men in front of them take the safety catches off their weapons.

'I could hazard a guess, though.'

The three masked men leaned forward slightly.

'To be honest with you,' İkmen said, 'I think that Mr Pars here was probably more correct than anyone else in his assessment of this situation. Putting that together with what this poor dead boy told us all about his fictional princely life, that he was an orphan in the care of his older brother, his mother had committed suicide . . . Of course that still doesn't bring us any closer to who actually stuck a knife into his throat. But if you're looking at the concept of killing by proxy—'

'Get to the point, Inspector.'

İkmen saw Hovsep Pars nod at him. The old man said, 'So now you know.'

'Yes.'

'For sure?'

'Nothing is certain in this life, Hovsep Bey, but I have come, shall we say, via a certain golden samovar, to see the merit in your words.'

Lale Aktar, still standing beside Krikor Sarkissian, began to shake. Krikor put his arms round her but he didn't speak.

'For me, it was the intricacy of the operation, the slow planning that had to have been involved – years – and the camera,' İkmen said. 'A camera implies a watcher, either by a direct feed or later on a disk. One hears of such "facilities" in prisons, for "special" prisoners. Unofficial of course.'

'We need a name,' the leader said. 'Of the actual killer. Take a guess.'

'Take a guess?' İkmen laughed. 'You're going to kill us anyway. Except Mrs Aktar, of course.' He looked over at her. 'Why don't you go and stand with your friends, Lale Hanım?'

But the novelist neither moved nor spoke.

'All those good works you do,' İkmen said to her. 'Just like Aysel Ökte. Feeding the poor, espousing the cause of the dispossessed, visiting prisons. Couldn't visit your own father in his prison, could you? Too close to home? But then *he* was so different, wasn't he? Not like your father, not like your old husband. *He* was charming and handsome and so romantic—'

'Stop it!' she shouted. Her face screwed up with anger and tears and she screamed, 'How would someone like you ever understand?'

'Ah, so I was right,' İkmen said. 'But then I knew Mr Ersoy really quite well . . .'

The first shot, which came from somewhere below them, was followed by the sound of screaming and then more shots. Everyone in room 411 looked at the door, including the gunmen. İkmen pulled at Süleyman's sleeve and together they took their one small chance.

They were shooting the hostages! Other men in black were bursting through every door and window into the ballroom. Ceyda looked for Alp but she couldn't see him through the smoke. They'd flung tear gas into the room and everything was hazy and evil-smelling and awful. Why were they shooting the hostages? A woman in a dress that looked like one great glittering peacock feather fell to the ground clutching her stomach.

Someone had taken her blindfold off. Ceyda thought it had been Burak Bey. But when she'd looked for him he'd gone. Now frantically trying to untie the wire that held her legs together, Ceyda cried and shook and screamed whenever she saw a dark figure wearing a gas mask loom out of the smoke. If these people were the police or the army, they were making a terrible mistake.

Ceyda cut her fingers on the wire. Getting it off so that she could run was the only thing she could think about. Every part of her body trembled. She was almost naked but she didn't care, she had to get out before these people killed her. She threw the bloodied wire to one side and stood up. She couldn't see any of the figures who had been her captors anywhere. Just these 'things' in gas masks, shooting everyone.

Her eyes felt blinded by blood and pain and tears but she stumbled forward to where she thought she remembered one of the doors from the Kubbeli Saloon into the ballroom was. All around her, people screamed and fell to the floor, either because they had been shot or because they were trying not to be shot. Ceyda came to what seemed to be a wall. She felt her way along it, tripping over chairs, tables and people as she went. She wanted Alp and her parents and she wanted Söner to still be alive even though she'd hated him. If she survived she was never going to take part in a murder mystery evening ever again.

Ceyda tried to open one of her eyes but it was far too painful to do so. With a little whimper she shut it again and continued to move forward, blindly. Eventually and inevitably she fell over something and her body hit the floor full length. Ceyda thought that this was the end of her. But then she felt two arms encircle her body and lift her to her feet.

'Come with me,' she heard Burak Fisekçi say.

*   *   *

Çetin İkmen flung himself at the leader. Distracted by what was happening downstairs, the man was taken completely by surprise. While his two colleagues fired wildly at anything that moved, his Kalashnikov skittered across the floor until it landed at the feet of Arto Sarkissian. Together with his brother and Lale Aktar, Arto hit the floor. From over the other side of the bed he heard a voice shout, 'Throw it to me!'

There was blood coming from somewhere and bullets everywhere but Arto Sarkissian made himself rise on to his haunches to throw the rifle across the bed towards Mehmet Süleyman. Had the doctor known how to use it he would have done so, but his military service was a lifetime away and he hadn't touched a firearm since.

While İkmen wrestled with the unarmed leader on the floor, Süleyman shot the man without a camera on his helmet. He smashed against Agatha Christie's typewriter which had been behind him and then sank to the floor like a puppet. The cameraman looked down at İkmen struggling with his leader on the floor and trained his gun on him, but then Süleyman fired at him, missed, and the cameraman made a break for the door.

Although his first instinct was to follow the cameraman, Süleyman could see that İkmen was struggling to subdue the leader and so he ran over and smashed the man's head against the floor until he lost consciousness.

Slowly, İkmen stood up. 'I am far too old for this,' he panted.

'Hovsep Bey is hit!'

Both İkmen and Süleyman turned to see Arto Sarkissian cradling Hovsep Pars in his arms.

'Where?'

'Shoulder,' Arto replied. Krikor Sarkissian was applying compression while Lale Aktar cried into the thick velvet curtains. She seemed to be unhurt.

İkmen picked up the rifle that Süleyman had dropped on the floor.

'What are you doing?' the younger policeman asked.

'Going to get help.' İkmen moved towards the door of room 411.

'Don't you think it would be better if I—'

'Stay here and don't open this door until you hear my voice,' İkmen said. And then he opened the door, walked through it and shut it behind him. Out on the fourth-floor gallery he could hear the shooting from down in the public rooms more clearly. He also felt that itch behind the eyes that signalled the presence of tear gas.

He jogged along the gallery, looking down at the tops of the domes in the ceiling of the Kubbeli Saloon. Now he could hear screaming too. He increased his pace even though his chest was aching and the sound of his heart was deafening.

When he saw Krikor's assistant Burak Fisekçi and a half-naked girl with one hand over her face coming towards him, he was both relieved and disturbed. Burak had been one of the few people who had been out of the ballroom when Söner Erkan was killed. But he was also Krikor Sarkissian's trusted lieutenant.

'Inspector İkmen, what on earth has happened?' Burak Fisekçi said. He looked at the Kalashnikov.

İkmen said, 'They tried to kill us in room four eleven. Did you see the man with the camera on his helmet come past?'

'No.'

'Burak Bey,' the girl said, 'someone—'

İkmen should have let her speak but instead he cut her off. He had other considerations. 'Hovsep Bey has been shot,' he said. 'We need to get him out of here.'

'Of course.' Burak Fisekçi put his hands on İkmen's shoulders and smiled.

Çetin İkmen allowed himself a brief moment to draw breath. It was in this fleeting hiatus that Burak Fisekçi took hold of the much smaller and lighter man and threw him over the ornate gallery banister into the great void above the Kubbeli Saloon. As he tried to grab on to the banister, İkmen let the Kalashnikov go. He heard it clatter down on to something somewhere below him.

Chapter 23

It was odd but not entirely unexpected that Çetin İkmen's first thought upon almost being flung to his death was about earthquakes. As far as he was concerned, if an earthquake erupted while he was hanging like a rag doll from one of the joists that kept the vast space in the centre of the hotel stable, that would be just typical. It was his birthday, when awful things always happened; something even more ghastly was bound to occur soon. But then İkmen remembered something that made him think slightly differently about this. It wasn't his birthday any more. It was now 13 December and even with his heart hammering like a road drill and his chest feeling as if it had been skinned, the knowledge made him feel better.

He still thought that he was going to die but his senses began to work properly again and he heard what sounded like a struggle up on the fourth-floor gallery. He raised his head as far as he was able and he saw an arm, probably Burak's, grab hold of the half-naked girl. İkmen was just about to yell something about not throwing the poor child into the void too when he heard Burak say, 'Ceyda, it has to be this way!'

'You've killed Inspector İkmen!' he heard Ceyda Ümit say.

'He was going to mess it all up!' Burak said.

'He would have got us out of here!' the girl said.

'Yes, but not together,' Burak said. 'The only people who can do that are in room four eleven.'

'Who's in room four eleven?' Ceyda said. 'Söner! Oh, my—'

'No, my colleagues are in there,' Burak said. 'Now that the police are here, we'll need help to get out.'

'No.' There was a pause. Then the girl said, 'The police were . . .' And then she stopped again as if trying and failing to work something out in her head. 'The police were killing people, hostages . . .'

'Exactly!' Burak said. 'Now come on!'

Çetin İkmen wanted to speak. He wanted to ask the girl why she thought that the police were firing on the hostages. But he could barely breathe, much less speak.

'Burak Bey, why were the police killing the hostages?'

İkmen heard their feet running along the gallery, towards room 411 and Süleyman, the doctors, Lale Aktar, Hovsep Pars. But then the footsteps came to an abrupt stop and he heard the girl speak again. 'What do you mean, Burak Bey,' she said, 'about us having to get out together?'

* * *

The young man wearing the deep red evening gown and the sparkly shoes put his hands in the air. He could hardly see any more and his brother had already been shot, what was the point of going on?

The Special Forces officer in front of him, breathing audibly through a gas mask, pointed his gun towards a small group of other oddly attired men and a woman in the corner of the ballroom. He went without comment or complaint. It had all gone very wrong. He didn't know why. But what he was sure about was that there was never going to be any idyllic life in Bodrum for him. He sat down next to an ex-Bulgarian Mafia enforcer and kept his hands where his captors could see them.

If he personally hadn't panicked he might have got away. As soon as their leader, Nurettin, had found and killed that Special Forces officer, he should have put some time into deciding who he was going to change clothes with. As it happened he'd just grabbed the nearest body which had been a woman with a penchant for shoes that could easily double as instruments of torture. Admittedly she was a short lady, but the heels on those things were still ridiculous. He took the shoes off and considered a life in prison. He'd been in there before. That was where he'd got this job. But last time had just been for theft. This was going to be for who knew what. Terrorism? Attempted murder? Collusion with killers? Nurettin had killed that Special Forces man as well as someone called Haluk Mert and so any attempt to try and explain that nobody was supposed to die at all would be futile. And anyway, only some of the Kalashnikovs fired blanks. Not all of them, not Nurettin's and not his. And Mert had always been marked for death. That Greek man had wanted him gone for some reason.

Now that the air was clearing a bit, his eyes streamed less. He could see men who looked not unlike the way he had looked until he'd ditched his clothes in favour of a dress. They wore black and some of them stood over him and his compatriots, while others moved through the ballroom doors and into other parts of the building.

Several minutes passed and then three people arrived. A fat man with a cigar in his mouth, a middle-aged macho type, and an attractive woman who looked around in the sort of way one does when one is searching for someone or something specific.

Mehmet Süleyman had never been able to resist the sound of a woman in distress. In response to hysterical weeping and what sounded like pleading somewhere outside room 411, he went to the door and opened it. İkmen would have been furious with him but he had to do it. What he saw was Ceyda Ümit apparently fighting with Burak Fisekçi.

'I don't want you!' he heard the girl say. Burak Fisekçi

had his back to him while the girl was facing him and, as he caught her eye, he put his finger to his lips to silence her.

'Ceyda, I will look after you!' Burak Fisekçi said as he held on to her wrists and tried to pull her towards himself. 'We are meant to be together. I did this for you!'

Did what? Süleyman began to feel nauseous. He moved forward and delivered a chop with the edge of his hand to the neck of a person he'd always known as a decent man. He watched him drop unconscious to the floor. The girl, who was wearing only her underwear, ran into his arms and said, 'Burak Bey has gone mad.'

Süleyman took his jacket off and was just about to put it round the girl's shoulders when she said, 'You have to help Inspector İkmen!'

'Inspector İkmen?' He dropped his jacket on the floor. 'Where is he?'

She took hold of one of his hands and ran towards the great open space at the heart of the hotel. With his arms and legs draped either side of one of the metal joists holding the building together, İkmen looked like an array of scruffy washing – with a Kalashnikov balanced precariously on a dome just below his feet.

'Çetin!' Süleyman leaned on the banister. 'Çetin!'

'Burak Bey pushed him,' Ceyda Ümit said. 'He tried to kill him! He's gone mad. He must have done.'

But Süleyman wasn't listening. He couldn't see whether İkmen was breathing or not. He called his name once again. 'Çetin!'

This time a guttural groan came out of the body on the joist and Süleyman thanked Allah that his friend was not dead.

'We're going to get you out of there,' Süleyman said. 'Just hang on! Just . . .' He didn't have a clue how he was going to get İkmen out of this predicament and he knew İkmen would know that. 'I will get help,' he said. And then he added, stupidly, 'Stay there!'

From the void came something that sounded very much like a laugh.

The leader was coming back to consciousness. Every so often he groaned and pulled impotently against the rough selection of sheets and dressing-gown cords with which Arto Sarkissian had tied him to the bed. Together with the sound of weeping that was coming from Lale Aktar, this was the soundtrack to the Sarkissian brothers' world in room 411.

In spite of Krikor's attempts to staunch the bleeding from Hovsep Pars's shoulder, his blood continued to pour out and soak everything that was pressed against the wound. Sporadic firing could still be heard from somewhere in the hotel and now that Süleyman had gone, who knew where, they were effectively on their own.

Words were useless in a situation like this but Krikor at least had to speak in order to take his mind off the groaning of the gunman and the crying of the woman.

Inclining his head down towards the old man in his arms he said, 'He takes warfarin.'

His brother nodded. 'He's an inactive old man who has suffered much, it's not surprising he needs blood thinners,' he said. He shook his head impatiently. 'Where is Inspector Süleyman? And Çetin?'

Krikor shrugged.

'If Allah wills it they will still be alive.' Still sobbing, Lale Aktar spoke for the first time since İkmen had left room 411.

Arto, who could see her face over Hovsep Pars's one good shoulder, said, 'So now you speak, Lale Hanım.'

'I don't want Mr Pars to die,' she said.

'Don't you? Following my friend Çetin İkmen's thesis about this whole event and your place in it, I wouldn't have thought that you cared about anything or anyone except the man who has come to obsess you.'

Lale Aktar looked down at the floor.

'Muhammed Ersoy,' Arto said.

Hovsep Pars's eyes sprang open and Krikor shook his head at his brother.

But Arto smiled at the old man and said, 'Hovsep Bey understands that if that devil is indeed behind this carnage then it is our duty, to the Pars family if no one else, to punish everyone who has colluded with Ersoy. And that includes this woman.'

'Yes, but—'

'Arto is right,' the old man whispered. He patted Krikor's hand.

Arto Sarkissian looked at Lale Aktar with cold eyes. She had married one of his brother's best friends and, it seemed, she had betrayed him. 'Lale Hanım,' he began, 'what—'

'Do you know, Dr Sarkissian, what it's like to fall in love? I don't mean just having a fancy for someone, lusting after them or being captivated by their personality. Falling in love is being subsumed by another. It involves being prepared to do anything, *anything* to promote that person's happiness.'

'And that is how you feel about Ersoy?'

Her face, which had been pale, coloured slightly.

'But he's never getting out of prison,' Arto said. 'You can have no future with him. I still don't understand why you are involved with this.'

She paused. 'I wanted to please him,' she said. 'We all did, Dr Sarkissian. But Muhammed only actually loved me.'

'He told you that?'

'Yes.'

'And you believed him?'

'Yes.'

Krikor Sarkissian, his face dark with fury, said, 'Have you slept with him?'

Prison was never the same for the rich and Muhammed Ersoy had been rich.

'Yes.'

'He bought his way into your arms.'

She didn't reply. But that was how it must have been. Ersoy, even in prison, remained a man who commanded great wealth. Committed to a whole life sentence, he had somehow used his money to bribe his way to comfort and good food and to buy whoever he needed.

'Muhammed was bored,' she said. 'Not with me, with prison. This was a diversion for him.'

The camera on one of those men's helmets. Had Ersoy been watching every move or was this to be an entertainment for him later? It was certainly sick enough, whichever way it was presented.

Arto Sarkissian tried to digest what had just been said to him. 'So, by proxy, Ersoy kills us all and then you and these "others" get away with it?'

She looked him straight in the eyes. 'Oh, I never imagined I'd get clear,' she said. 'I can't speak for anyone else, but I never realistically hoped to get away, ultimately, with anything.'

'And so amusing Ersoy was the entire point?'

'Yes,' she said. 'Absolutely.'

* * *

He saw Commissioner Ardıç first. Then Ayşe Farsakoğlu flung herself into his arms. It was as much a shock – and indeed an entirely unwanted one – to him as it was to the commissioner and a smouldering İzzet Melik. He pushed her aside roughly and said to his superior, 'Sir, Inspector İkmen is suspended above the Kubbeli Saloon on a metal joist. I don't know how much longer he can hang on.'

Ardıç resisted the urge to ask why İkmen was in the predicament he was and called two Special Forces officers over and told them to go wherever Süleyman took them. Süleyman duly began to lead the officers up the staircase, still shrouded in residue from tear gas canisters. Then he turned and called down to Ardıç, 'And we need medics to go to room four eleven. A man called Hovsep Pars has been shot.' He put Ardıç and an apparently nascent domestic situation between Ayşe Farsakoğlu and İzzet Melik behind him and ran.

When he reached the fourth floor he jogged over to the banister, hoping against hope that İkmen was still managing to hold on. 'Çetin!'

This time, via what Süleyman imagined was a vast act of will, İkmen actually managed to raise his head and look at him.

'We're getting you out of there!' Süleyman said. Then he turned to the two Special Forces officers and asked them, 'How do we achieve this?'

'Do we know if he's broken any bones?' one of the officers said. 'Principally his back.'

'Well, he can move his head and he is holding on with his hands,' Süleyman said. 'I think I've seen a foot move. So no, I don't think he's broken his back.'

Both the officers looked at the figure lying on the joist, then they looked at each other and nodded. The taller of the two said just one word, 'Tightrope.'

There was a lot of shouting and what sounded like heavy machinery or something being heaved around. Loud thuds reverberated through the joist, making hanging on to it even more difficult than it already was. How he had come to land on the joist, he had no idea. He remembered that Burak Fisekçi had thrown him. But the actual fall itself was a complete blank. One moment he had been on the fourth-floor gallery and the next he had been hanging from the joist like a broken toy. But how broken?

İkmen had determined that he was probably reasonably all right by virtue of the fact that he was now actively holding on to the joist with his hands. Some ribs had certainly been broken, that was a given, but he could move his feet – although doing that hurt, and so he may have broken a leg or an ankle or possibly both. But he hadn't broken his back.

Why had Burak Fisekçi thrown him over the banister?

Ceyda Ümit had been about to tell him something regarding the man with the camera on his helmet; he'd stupidly cut her off and then Burak had hurled him into the void. Why?

A noise like a cable being unravelled tempted İkmen to try and see what was going on but he resisted it. Moving his neck in any direction hurt and he was in quite enough pain with his ribs and his legs without risking any more forays into the world of agony. Instead he focused on Burak Fisekçi.

Good and faithful Burak, dedicated assistant to Krikor Sarkissian for more years than İkmen could remember. Burak Fisekçi, Muslim Armenian, listening ear for the bad, the mad, the addicted, the friendless, Burak Fisekçi, bachelor. Was Burak Fisekçi really implicated in what had happened at the Pera Palas?

Burak had engaged the theatre company. He'd been involved in developing the ideas and the script for the murder mystery evening and he had had a big hand in inviting the guests. Could he have betrayed Krikor? Why?

Like Lale Aktar and that prison reformer Aysel Ökte, Burak sometimes went into jails. Krikor's clinic provided services to both ex-offenders and those on remand. Had Burak been to Silivri Prison and, like the novelist, met Ersoy? In all his long and varied career, Çetin İkmen had never encountered anyone like Muhammed Ersoy.

Rich, opinionated, handsome, educated and completely without conscience. He drew people to him of all races, genders and religious persuasions in a way that put Süleyman's sexual power over women not just in the shade but in darkness. He'd been sent to prison for life, his assets had passed to a distant cousin from the east and yet İkmen knew for a fact that Ersoy still lived in some comfort. Money passed from the relative to the convict although how or in what quantities, İkmen didn't know. And then what of the golden samovar? He'd seen it. He hadn't dreamed it.

Some pressure accompanied by a feeling of weight on the joist made İkmen stop thinking about Muhammed Ersoy. Although his neck was so painful that just raising it a millimetre made him feel sick, İkmen did lift his head up a little. On the joist in front of him he saw a pair of large feet in what looked like black ballet pumps.

This was no fun, looking at a toilet wall and listening to the sound of a man panting in fear. Where was İkmen? Where was that Ottoman gentleman Süleyman? And where was all the blood and the fear and the delicious hilarity?

Chapter 24

When the medical team arrived, Krikor Sarkissian chose to accompany them and their charge, Hovsep Pars, to the Taksim Hospital. Krikor knew that the old man was in the last stages of terminal cancer and so he was unlikely to survive long. But he wanted to go with him anyway. Apparently Krikor's wife Caroun was still in the ballroom, shaken, but she was alive. His brother Arto, together with Süleyman, İzzet Melik and two Special Forces officers took charge of Lale Aktar and the man who had been the apparent leader of the gunmen. He was a very pale character with reddish blond hair and an almost Nordic cast to his features. As soon as he was fully conscious, Süleyman questioned him.

'Who are you?'

He failed to reply.

'What was your purpose here tonight? Did you do this for money? Notoriety? Religion? Politics? What?'

Nothing. He just looked into Süleyman's face with his cold blue eyes and gave a Mona Lisa smile. A Special

Forces officer dragged him to his feet and, because he struggled, punched him in the stomach. Süleyman turned to Lale Aktar. Still crying, she was being handcuffed by İzzet Melik. 'And you, Lale Hanım?' Süleyman asked her. 'What about you? What about you and Muhammed Ersoy?'

While he waited for a response, Süleyman glanced up and caught the look of absolute hatred that İzzet was directing at him. Given the way that Ayşe Farsakoğlu had rushed into his arms earlier, he wondered what on earth had happened between them.

He returned his gaze to the novelist. With her hands cuffed behind her back, Lale Aktar could no longer wipe her nose and so snot ran down her face and on to her blood-soaked gown. She looked dirty, ugly and disgusting. 'Well?'

She raised her head. 'If I tell you where the golden samovar that belonged to the Ersoy family is . . .' she began.

Süleyman walked over to her and took her chin roughly between his fingers. 'I do not do deals, lady,' he said. 'You will tell me where that golden samovar is.'

'Or you'll do what?' she said.

Süleyman moved his face so close to hers that their noses almost touched. He said, 'To you? Nothing. But remember, Muhammed Ersoy is still in prison and for every guard who admires him and gives him privileges in exchange for money there will be others who would like to beat the shit out of him.'

The ballet shoes were most apt. Even though İkmen imagined that the man who was coming to get him had to be attached to a rope or line of some sort, the way those feet moved along that joist was very elegant.

A familiar voice, presumably from the fourth-floor gallery, called out to him, 'Hang on, İkmen!' Ardıç. Comforting but also irritating. What did he think he was going to do? Get up and run about?

'Yes, sir,' he mumbled. Ardıç probably didn't hear him but that hardly mattered. And then one of the ballet pumps disappeared and İkmen felt a surge of panic. Had his saviour fallen to his death among the domes of the Kubbeli Saloon?

But then he saw a shin, part of a thigh and a lean arm, a torso and finally a face in front of him. 'I'm going to put a rope over your shoulders and underneath your arms,' the young man said.

İkmen nodded his head. Somehow the young officer had lowered himself down so that he was sitting on the joist – like one of the tightrope walkers İkmen remembered seeing as a child when his mother had taken him and his brother to the old fairground in Gülhane Park. Not that the tightrope walkers had been his favourites.

He'd liked the snake pit best – mainly because he'd found it so very frightening.

The noose that was passed over his head, past his shoulders and underneath his arms was smooth and even when it touched his skin, it didn't burn.

'Now you don't have to do anything,' the young officer said. 'The noose will tighten around your chest, which will hurt, but I'll support you all the way. Is that clear?'

'Yes.'

'OK, then we're going to start now.'

Some sort of mechanical sound was accompanied by the worst chest pain Çetin İkmen had ever experienced in his life. As well as pulling him upwards, the noose crushed his already broken ribs which made his head swim with pain.

The officer, now slowly and elegantly rising on to both feet and supporting İkmen's body, said, 'Talk, Inspector, and keep talking if you can.'

He wanted to make sure that he didn't pass out. İkmen was inclined to think that he'd need some luck with that. But he managed to mumble, 'OK. So what's your name then, officer? It's all right, you don't have to answer, I'm just making noises with my mouth . . .'

He was in screaming agony, his eyes were not focused and he felt all the food he'd eaten at dinner rear up inside his stomach, but İkmen eventually stood. Supported by the Special Forces officer and attached, just like the young man, to a rope connected to a winch, he began to shuffle painfully along the joist until he was actually in the officer's arms. Then the two of them were pulled up over the void, raised and eventually deposited by the mechanical arm of the winch on to the fourth-floor gallery.

İkmen just heard Ardıç yell the word, 'Medic!' before he fainted on the floor.

'You know you should drink more,' Nar said to Ersu Nadir. She was already halfway through a bottle of vodka and several cans of Fanta lay empty on the table in front of her. 'That would help the pain in your leg.'

'I don't like to drink,' the maître d' said. 'People do stupid things when they drink. And then sometimes they become addicted. Addiction is a terrible thing.'

Nar waved a slack, dismissive hand. When all the Special Forces officers had departed, closely followed by the police officers, Nar and Ersu had been left alone with one young constable and the owner of the pub who was clearly a very generous man.

'Fucking military!' Nar continued through a miasma of cigarette smoke. 'I got shot in the thigh somewhere over towards Syria. Midyat.' She shook her head. 'Fucking Kurds! But I was lucky, the bullet just went through flesh and muscle, not bone. Not like you, Ersu Bey. But I still get pain and so I drink. Works every time. You should try it for your leg. Trust me.'

It was odd sitting with someone like Nar. Ersu Bey had heard of men who liked to sleep with transsexuals, but it was not a fancy he had ever shared. Nar was taller than he was and, by the look of her biceps, she could probably completely destroy him in an arm-wrestling bout. She was braver than he was too. If that police sergeant had asked him to go back into the hotel undercover, he didn't know what he would have done. Probably died of fright.

That said, he cared about the hotel and everyone in it. Like Nar, he'd heard the shooting and the sound of breaking glass when the Special Forces had broken in and it had horrified him. How many people were going to die? How many would be injured and how much of his beautiful hotel would be left intact when all this was over? Although he had a small flat of his own, the Pera Palas was his real home. Just after his divorce he'd been made redundant from his job at a hotel over in Sultanahmet. A period of casual and really unpleasant labour had followed and then the job at the newly refurbished Pera Palas had come up and Ersu Bey had felt his luck change. Was it going to hold now? After all this?

Nar pushed the bottle of vodka across the table at Ersu Bey. 'Oh, join me,' she said. 'Come on!'

He'd already, without thinking, downed a large glass of rakı and was feeling a little hazy but as he looked at the bottle of vodka and then at Nar he thought, why not?

He poured what had to be a triple measure of vodka into his rakı glass, topped it up with Fanta and drank. It was disgusting but he smiled anyway.

'There you go,' Nar said as she matily patted one of his knees. 'Now that is what you need for a happy life, Ersu Bey. Trust me, I may have tits, a booze problem and a few other little addictions, but I'm a veteran too.'

There were two sensations that overruled all others. Firstly the feel of the cold, early-morning wind on his face and then the bright if fuzzy goldness that was in front of his eyes. Çetin İkmen tried to sit up but found that he couldn't. Whether he was tied down in some way or just simply unable to do so, he couldn't tell. But it was impossible.

He blinked. The goldness came more into focus and he heard Süleyman say, 'You were right about the samovar, Çetin. Here it is.'

Yes! It *was* a samovar and it was gold. He thought he said, *But is it definitely the samovar that Muhammed Ersoy gave to Krikor Sarkissian?* But Süleyman just said, 'It was in room four eleven.'

İkmen didn't remember it being there. When he'd last seen the samovar it had been outside a room further along the fourth-floor gallery. But then the goldness went away, there was the sound of a door slamming and whatever he was lying on began to move.

He felt a pressure on his left arm and then he heard a man say, 'BP's ninety over sixty.'

A woman said, 'And dropping?'

The pressure on his arm started again and then it released. The man said, 'Yeah.'

'OK, let's get him in.'

And then there was a very familiar noise. It was a siren.

There was confusion. It was, Süleyman felt, a very planned chaos. There were bodies – of those who had died both before and during the firefight when the Special Forces officers had broken in. There were terrified guests, some of whom were blindfolded and some of whom were half naked. There were men and women dressed in black whose faces had once been covered by balaclava helmets, and there were people in smart evening wear who were currently in handcuffs. Apart from the gunmen who had taken İkmen, Süleyman and the others to room 411, the rest of the group had forced some of the hostages to give them their clothes. Those officers who entered via the hotel kitchens found this cohort as they attempted to make their escape. Not buying into the story that these 'hostages' were armed because they had overpowered their captors, the officers had disarmed and handcuffed some of them. But some of them had fought and now they were dead.

Süleyman looked down at the golden samovar in his hands. He noticed that a middle-aged man who was being handcuffed and searched was looking at it too. His expression was one of furious, thwarted lust. Süleyman shook his head. He remembered this artefact so well. Ten years before, Muhammed Ersoy had given it to Krikor Sarkissian at an ornate dinner in his Yeniköy palace. Ersoy had presented the samovar to Krikor's drug rehab foundation as a vehicle for raising funds for further community involvement. This had been only a matter of a fortnight at the most after Ersoy had killed his own brother and just before he killed his lover, Hovsep Pars's nephew, Avram Avedykian. Now imprisoned, his vast fortune apparently in the hands of some cousin, Muhammed Ersoy had come back to haunt those who had put him away, those who had hated him and even some who hadn't known him at all. He'd even, somehow, managed to get his old samovar back from wherever it had been after Krikor Sarkissian had sold it. It was going to be most interesting finding out just how he had managed to do all this. But then Süleyman remembered someone that he couldn't recall having seen for some time. Ceyda Ümit. When he'd rescued her from what had looked like the amorous advances of Burak Fisekçi, Ceyda had run away. But where had she run to?

* * *

He slipped out of the toilets with the camera underneath his arm. He'd discarded the helmet and the jumpsuit, which left him just in his white vest and a pair of jogging bottoms he'd put on before the operation because he was cold. He stood out and he knew it, but he had to make some sort of attempt to get away because if he didn't, apart from getting himself arrested, he'd also probably be kissing goodbye to the considerable reward he'd been counting on. If he got that, he could secure his family's future in Van as well as buying himself a really good car, like a Mitsubishi Evolution or maybe a Nissan Skyline.

But things hadn't gone to plan and so now he had to improvise. He looked into the camera and whispered, 'Now, Beyefendi, we get out of here.'

He actually managed to reach the open front door of the hotel – which was good going – before he felt a heavy, official hand fall on his shoulder.

Chapter 25

Burak Fisekçi had gone. When the Sarkissian brothers were finally relieved in room 411, there was no sign of Burak Fisekçi whom Süleyman had knocked out cold – or so he'd thought – just outside on the gallery. He looked up and then down the gallery. The winch that had finally brought İkmen to safety was still in position but no one was doing anything with it now. Süleyman ran to the banisters and looked down into the central void above the Kubbeli Saloon. Nothing.

Where had Fisekçi gone and where was Ceyda? The girl had been in her underwear and frightened and he just hoped that she was all right. Lale Aktar had apparently been taken to police headquarters, along with those people who had, so far, been identified as gunmen. This group had included three of the people who were apparently 'shot' when the building was first taken over: Yiannis Istefanopoulos, Aysel Ökte and Raşit Demir. The fourth 'victim', Haluk Mert, was really dead. Why just him?

'Oh, Allah, help me!'

The voice, which was female, came from above. Süleyman looked up and saw Ceyda Ümit's terrified face leaning over the balcony one floor above. He took the pistol he'd picked up from one of the Special Forces officers and ran up the stairs to the fifth floor. He heard the girl scream again, which was followed by the sound of running and grunting. When he reached the fifth floor, he came upon Ceyda Ümit struggling in the arms of Burak Fisekçi who had a knife.

At first he didn't see Süleyman at all.

'Ceyda, you love me!' he said. 'You know you do!'

'As a friend, yes! As my uncle. Not like . . .'

He pulled her forward and tried to kiss her. Ceyda turned her head away sharply and said, 'No!'

'Leave her alone, Burak Bey.'

The sound of another man's voice took a few seconds to penetrate Burak Fisekçi's consciousness. But when it did, he turned and looked at Süleyman while holding even more firmly on to Ceyda.

'This has got nothing to do with you,' he said to the policeman. 'Ceyda and myself have made the decision to go away together.'

'No!'

'Burak, I don't think that Ceyda has made that decision, I think that's only you,' Süleyman said.

'Oh? And what business is it of yours?' Overweight

and red-faced, Burak Fisekçi looked comically arrogant – though his intentions were far from funny. In addition, to suggest that abduction was no business of an officer of the law indicated that he had possibly lost some contact with reality – this on top of the patent absurdity of his belief that a girl like Ceyda could be in love with him.

Süleyman moved forward and Burak put the knife up to the girl's throat. 'I'll kill her!' he said.

There was a strong chance that he would. Clearly obsessed, he could reason that he'd rather no one have Ceyda if he couldn't. Burak Fisekçi had always been, in Süleyman's experience, one of those overlooked people, one of those almost sexless characters who can be easy to ignore. Was it years and years of being ignored that had made him do this now? Süleyman tried to imagine the resentment Burak had harboured; judging by the expression on his face as he held the knife up to Ceyda's neck, it was a lot.

'Burak,' he said, 'if you try and escape from this building, you are not going to make it. I don't know whether you were in any way in league with the people who took over this hotel but I can assure you that they no longer have control. We do.'

Burak Fisekçi had to know this but he still said, 'You're lying.'

'I'm not,' Süleyman said. 'Now let Ceyda go. If you

really care about her you won't want to hurt her, will you?'

Burak Bey's face went red again. 'I don't want to hurt Ceyda! I never wanted to hurt her! I did this so that no one else would hurt her, ever!'

'You did what, Burak?' Süleyman kept his pistol in plain sight but down, held beside his left leg.

'I killed the boy,' he said. He enunciated the words without any emotion whatsoever. 'If I killed the boy then I'd get enough money to give Ceyda whatever she wanted for ever. And anyway the boy was an animal! A pig!'

Süleyman imagined he knew which boy Burak was talking about but he checked it out anyway. 'You mean Söner Erkan?'

'Yes.'

'You killed Söner Erkan?'

'Yes.'

Ceyda Ümit just mouthed the word 'Allah' as tears began to fall from her eyes.

'Someone paid you to kill Söner Erkan?'

'He will,' he said. 'Muhammed Beyefendi.'

Ersoy.

'And why did Muhammed Ersoy want you to kill Söner Erkan? Did he know him?'

'No.'

Ceyda Ümit said, 'Poor Söner! Poor stupid, selfish Söner!'

'The boy's death was all just part of the game,' Burak said, 'the puzzle that Muhammed Beyefendi set you and İkmen, the Sarkissians and that silly old Armenian. He's a genius, you know, Muhammed Beyefendi.'

Süleyman, whose elder brother had been to school with – and been bullied by – Muhammed Ersoy, couldn't argue with that. Ersoy was one of the cleverest as well as probably the most malevolent person he had ever met. But none of this helped him to disarm Fisekçi.

'Burak, I have a gun . . .'

'I know. Do you think I care about that, Inspector?'

Süleyman heard a creak on the stairs behind him and hoped that whoever was at his back was also on his side. Not all of the gunmen had as yet been positively identified. But he held his ground. 'I will shoot you,' he said, 'if you harm Ceyda.'

'We could die together, Ceyda and myself,' Burak said brightly. How, in all the years that he'd known him, had Süleyman never noticed until now just how insane Burak Fisekçi was? His ex-wife the psychiatrist would have laughed herself sick at his incompetence.

The girl screamed. But Burak did not increase the pressure on the knife. This seemed to suggest that he actually wanted her to live.

'Burak, if you let Ceyda go, the three of us can all sit down and talk about this like civilised people.' Süleyman knew that he was talking nonsense and so did Burak Fisekçi, who just laughed. If he let the girl go, Süleyman would put a gun to his head and then march him downstairs to be cuffed and taken to police headquarters. There would be no little talks, no niceties. He'd be arrested, thrown into a cell and eventually sent to prison for the rest of his life. And Burak Fisekçi, who had worked with drug-dependent offenders for years, knew this.

He moved his head to one side of Ceyda's, smiled and then said, 'So, go on, shoot me.'

His head exploded in a shower of bone, blood and brains. Ceyda Ümit hit the floor while Mehmet Süleyman brought his hands up to shield his own face.

Commissioner Ardıç had insisted upon going to Silivri Prison in person. Escorted by two Special Forces officers, he made his way to Muhammed Ersoy's cell rather more rapidly than certain elements in the administration of the prison really seemed to want. The prisoner was looking at the screen of his laptop computer as Ardıç entered. He stood up. And he smiled.

'Commissioner.'

Ardıç ignored the outstretched hand and instead directed the two men with him to note what was on the computer screen, shut it down and then seize it. A mobile phone, on the table beside the laptop, was also grabbed.

'Ersoy.' He hadn't seen him for ten years. Irritatingly,

and contrary to all the fears Ersoy had had about ageing when he'd committed his first offences, he was still a very handsome and well-preserved man.

'I imagine you've come about my entertainment at the Pera Palas,' Muhammed Ersoy said.

He didn't even have the decency to try and deny it. But then why should he? He had already been given a whole life sentence. There was nothing much more that anyone could do to him.

Ardıç sat down on Ersoy's narrow if unusually comfortable prison bed. It sagged just slightly underneath his weight. 'A game is how it was described by some of whatever you call people who do your bidding.'

'Slaves.' He smiled. 'Yes, it was. Tremendous fun!' Then his face fell. 'Until the end of course but then, well, things happen, don't they, Commissioner?'

'Things apparently happen around you, Ersoy.'

'Only because I make them, Commissioner,' he said. 'It was just like Hamlet tonight! I know you weren't there, but believe me, it really was.'

'Was it indeed.'

Ersoy laughed. Then, as the two Special Forces officers unplugged his laptop, he sat down at his table again and said, 'Now, would you like to know the names of all the people here in Silivri who helped me organise tonight's entertainment?'

* * *

Süleyman was just grateful that it hadn't been him. He'd never actively liked Burak Fisekçi but he hadn't disliked him either. He would not have found shooting him easy, had he been required to do so. But a Special Forces marksman had taken him out. His had been the footsteps Süleyman had heard on the stairs behind him. Poor Ceyda Ümit was hysterical and so Süleyman picked her up and carried her down the stairs while the marksman and a fellow officer secured the scene of Burak Fisekçi's demise.

Arriving at the ground floor, Süleyman looked for Ardıç but didn't find him. Ceyda Ümit just kept on saying, 'I want Alp! I want Alp!'

But Süleyman didn't know where her boyfriend was. It was a fair assumption that he was in the ballroom but a quick scan of the area proved negative. Then he heard a voice at his shoulder. 'Alp İlhan has been taken to hospital.'

He turned and saw Ayşe Farsakoğlu at his shoulder. He gently put Ceyda Ümit's feet to the ground. 'Oh, Allah!' the girl said. 'The hospital!'

Ayşe took one of her hands. 'He's fine,' she said. 'If it's any consolation, he walked out of here with no assistance. But the doctors need to check his lungs. He was coughing badly after the tear gas.'

'He's OK? Really?'

Ayşe smiled. 'He's OK and he was asking for you,' she said. 'We'll get you to the hospital as soon as we can, Ceyda.'

Ceyda felt a bit wobbly then and so Ayşe pulled a chair out from underneath one of the tables and sat her down. The girl instantly laid her head in the smashed-up table setting and sobbed. She didn't want anybody near her or touching her, she just wanted to cry.

Süleyman looked at Ayşe and he began, 'I heard you were—'

'I saw a golden samovar being delivered to this hotel,' she said. 'It . . . resonated with me.'

'You had to see whether or not it was the samovar we all remember.'

She paused for just a moment, trying to decide whether or not she should tell him why else she had come back to the Pera Palas Hotel after her night out with her brother and İzzet. Then she said, 'Yes.'

'It was very fortunate for us that you did so.'

'Someone would have reported something, eventually,' she said.

'But by that time maybe it would have been too late.' He put a hand on her shoulder. Unfortunately, just at that moment İzzet Melik came into the ballroom. When he saw them together, he froze.

'I owe you my life,' Süleyman said to Ayşe Farsakoğlu. Neither of them saw İzzet and he didn't wait around for them to spot him. He left as quickly as he had arrived, but with tears in his eyes.

* * *

The doctor wasn't going to let him out, even with his ribs strapped up. They wanted to take his blood pressure every half hour. Apparently it was unstable, whatever that meant. A nurse came to the side of his bed, put a cuff round his bicep and took it again. When she'd finished, Çetin İkmen looked at her questioningly.

'Now it's raised,' she said in answer to his silent question.

'Is it high?'

'Raised,' she reiterated.

'So?'

'So it's going up and down all the time. We can't release you until it settles. You've broken four ribs and you've had a shock.' She put her hands on her hips. 'Can't you even *try* to relax, Inspector?'

'I might give it a go if I had a cigarette,' he said.

The nurse pulled a face. 'No chance.'

She walked away. İkmen recognised at least two of the actors from the murder mystery performance in nearby beds, as well as the hotel concierge. But Hovsep Pars was nowhere to be seen. It was infuriating for İkmen not to know what was going on. He remembered that Mehmet Süleyman had shown him Muhammed Ersoy's golden samovar. He seemed to have a recollection that Süleyman had said something about it coming from room 411. But he didn't remember it being in there when he'd searched Agatha Christie's old room.

'Çetin?'

A plump and comfortably familiar face smiled down at him.

'Arto.'

The Armenian sat down on his bed. 'I thought you'd like to know that Hovsep Bey is in surgery now,' he said.

'Let us hope . . .'

'He's already dying, Çetin,' Arto said. 'Cancer.'

İkmen looked down at the sheet that covered his body. 'I know,' he said.

'He told you?'

'Yes. He was very candid about it. Has the leader of the gang been arrested?'

'He's actually in surgery too,' Arto said. 'I think he may have a ruptured spleen.'

İkmen looked alarmed. 'Because I hit . . .'

'No, no, no. He struggled when one of the Special Forces officers was trying to cuff him,' Arto said. 'The officer punched him in the stomach.'

'I see.' İkmen changed the subject. 'How is Krikor? And Mrs Aktar?'

'Krikor's fine,' Arto said. Then he averted his eyes a little. 'Mrs Aktar has been taken into custody. She colluded with Muhammed Ersoy and whoever he employed to do his bidding. She was in love with him.'

İkmen shook his head. 'Love!'

'Given Ersoy's previous record of romantic conquest, I wouldn't be surprised if she isn't the only one to have been dazzled by Mr Ersoy,' Arto said.

'Love is wonderful but it's uncontrollable,' İkmen said.

One of the actors, the one who had played the Italian tutor, groaned.

'Have you seen Ayşe Farsakoğlu?'

'Only briefly,' Arto said. 'We have much to thank her for. Without her we'd probably all be dead by now. You know, Çetin, some of the gunmen tried to get out of the hotel dressed as hostages.'

İkmen shrugged. 'Quite a smart move.' Then he changed the subject back to his sergeant again. 'Have you thought about why Sergeant Farsakoğlu was hanging around the Pera Palas?'

'Because she'd seen the golden samovar go into the building earlier in the evening,' Arto said.

'Then why didn't she do something about it at the time if it bothered her?' İkmen asked. 'She was with İzzet Melik, they could have both followed it up at the concierge's desk.'

'But Sergeant Melik doesn't remember Ersoy and that time and—'

'So what? If Ayşe had expressed her fears to him, he would have backed her up,' İkmen said. 'He's a good officer and he loves her. He would have done whatever she wanted.'

'What are you getting at, Çetin?'

He shrugged. 'Simple. She's still got feelings for Süleyman. She came back to the hotel on the off chance of seeing him.'

'Oh, I don't—'

'Call me cynical if you must, but since we're talking about love, Ayşe Farsakoğlu's abiding love for Mehmet Süleyman can't be ignored.'

'But she's marrying İzzet Melik!'

'Then perhaps she shouldn't,' İkmen said. 'In fact, she shouldn't, and somebody needs to tell her that.'

Arto glanced at him sideways. 'Oh, and I wonder who that will be.'

İkmen didn't say a word.

Arto Sarkissian got up from the bed after several moments of silence and he said, 'But for now, just rest and try to get your blood pressure on speaking terms with normal.' Then he left.

Chapter 26

'You know, greed has become my favourite vice,' Muhammed Ersoy said. 'It used to be lust but now I definitely favour greed. It's such fun.'

They just looked at him. All three had had the pleasure of Mr Ersoy's company ten years before. It was a long time to be in prison. But he hadn't changed a bit. İkmen had always believed in the superiority of incarceration over the death penalty, but he found, to his horror, that in this case maybe prison had been the wrong route to take. In the last twenty-four hours this man had, by proxy, killed and maimed, terrified and enslaved simply for his own amusement. He'd also, albeit indirectly, put İkmen in hospital which he had since left against his doctor's advice. His ribs were raw and sore and it hurt to breathe. But he was glad he was in Silivri staring at Ersoy who, in spite of everything, was still not a free man.

Ersoy looked at Süleyman and smiled. 'Well, you've aged quite well, young Süleyman,' he said. He'd called him 'young' Süleyman a decade ago in reference to the fact that he had been to school with Mehmet's older brother, Murad Süleyman. 'Still popular with the ladies, are you? With the boys too?' His eyes flashed with mischief. Openly bisexual, Ersoy had shamelessly flirted with Süleyman on numerous occasions.

Commissioner Ardıç looked down at the list of names Ersoy had given them of people whom he had recruited, both inside and outside Silivri, to take part in what he called his 'Pera Palas event'. He'd done it willingly and he'd even had a smile on his face. He'd enjoyed the live feed he'd received from the cameraman in the Pera Palas and was in an extremely good mood.

'Don't you worry, Mr Ersoy,' the commissioner began, 'that when some of these people inevitably join you here in Silivri Prison, they will take some sort of revenge upon you? Apart from anything else, we've names of prison staff here and we all know what they can be like.'

'No.'

'You promised them money, which they will not now get,' the commissioner continued. 'They're not going to feel too happy about that, I should imagine. I wouldn't.'

'And who was going to pay these people all this money anyway?' İkmen asked. He coughed. 'You're in prison.'

'Oh, my cousin.'

'Kemal Aslanlı, originally from İskender, sir,' İkmen told Ardıç. 'He is Mr Ersoy's closest living relative and so when Mr Ersoy was incarcerated he took over his fortune and his affairs.'

'Which still belong to me,' Ersoy said.

'Not really, but it is clear that you somehow managed to manipulate Mr Aslanlı into believing that,' Ardiç said. 'What did you do, Ersoy? Convince him that your alleged reconnection with Islam I heard about had made you a better person?'

Kemal Aslanlı was a cousin from Ersoy's mother's side of the family. Little more than lower middle-class grunts from the eastern city of İskender, the Aslanlıs – with the exception of Ersoy's late mother – were an unsophisticated group of people of whom Kemal was typical.

Ersoy smiled. 'Maybe.'

'Did Mr Aslanlı know why you wanted him to pay what comes to several million lire to these people you employed to kill and torment others?' Süleyman asked.

'No.' He shook his head and smiled again. 'Kemal is a bit retarded, to be truthful, young Süleyman. He does what I tell him – or rather what those who I trust tell him.'

'And how do you do that?' Ardıç asked. 'Mr Aslanlı is not a regular visitor to the Silivri. And if, as you say, the man is a little lacking . . .'

'Oh, you'll find that most of my business is conducted through a company that is owned by my old friend Yiannis Istefanopoulos. I invested much of my fortune in it some years ago and I encouraged Kemal to continue to do so. It's called—'

'Fener Maritime Sigorta,' Ardıç said. Then he smiled. 'Clever.'

'Persistent,' Ardıç said. He looked down at the list of names Ersoy had given him again. 'So, Mr Ersoy, tell us all about Mr Istefanopoulos and your legendary golden samovar. How do you know Mr Istefanopoulos?'

'Oh, he is in love with me,' Ersoy said simply. 'Has been for years.'

İkmen looked up at the ceiling in despair. Ersoy's entire life had been punctuated by people who loved him – none of whom he gave a damn about. He had no idea what love was.

'One thing I've never been hard up for in all my years in jail is visitors,' Ersoy said.

'Something, it seems to me, that you've mostly bribed your way to achieving.'

'Oh, yes. Yes I have. But Yiannis was a good friend from many years ago and, as I say, he loves me.'

'But you're not getting out of prison any time soon,' Süleyman said. 'What was in it for him?'

'Beyond the occasional conjugal visit?' This time his smile was pure reptile and it made the three other men in the interview room recoil. 'Gentlemen, apart from the enormous fun that I personally derived from the Pera Palas event, I was also careful to arrange that the principal movers in it got something that they each wanted very badly. Greed, you see. It was a marvellous incentive. Yiannis, more than anything else in the world, wanted to see a man called Haluk Mert dead.'

İzzet Melik had called in sick, or rather too tired to work. Süleyman had been fine about that. İzzet had been up all night and needed to get some sleep sometime. He'd made a brief statement about the part he had played in the Pera Palas events – not that he'd done a huge amount. İzzet had been involved more as a spectator than a participant. Ayşe Farsakoğlu had been far more involved and still had a lot of paperwork to do. İkmen, her boss, who should still have been in hospital, was currently with Ardıç and Süleyman, interviewing the man who had been behind the events of the previous night, Muhammed Ersoy. Just saying his name in her head made her visibly shudder.

'Cold, Sergeant?' Nar Sözen finished up the glass of tea Ayşe had got for her and then sank back into what was İkmen's office chair. She'd come in to give her witness statement which she was about halfway through.

Ignoring her question about the temperature in the office, Ayşe asked Nar, 'The woman you were allocated to guard duty with in the ballroom, the one who made observations about people's clothes, did you recognise her at all?'

'Through her mask?'

'Were her eyes familiar to you? Her voice?'

Nar thought for a moment and then said, 'No.'

Two women had been involved in taking over the Pera Palas alongside the other masked gunmen. One of them had been the prison reformer, Aysel Ökte. Now she was dead.

'Some of them tried to get out by changing their clothes with the hostages, didn't they?'

'Yes.' Aysel Ökte had been one of them. She'd been wearing a very fetching silk kimono when she died.

Then Nar, ever curious about people's private lives and prone to going off at tangents, leaned forward and said, 'Is it *really* true that you're going to marry Sergeant Melik?'

Ayşe looked down at the floor. 'Yes.'

'Are you sure?'

'Am I sure about the fact that I'm marring Sergeant Melik? Or am I sure that I want to marry him?'

'Are you sure you've not lost your mind!' Nar said. Then she went off, flailing her arms in the air and becoming highly agitated. 'Sergeant, Melik is a maganda. What's a pretty woman like you doing with a maganda? It's ridiculous! He won't make you happy, you know.

He'll have you scrubbing the filthy armpits of his shirts, spending hours on end making your own mantı, subjecting you to his arthritic mother whose swollen feet you'll have to—'

'Sergeant Melik doesn't have a mother any more!' Ayşe interjected. What Nar had been saying was bringing tears to her eyes. 'And anyway he isn't like that,' she said. 'He isn't how he . . . how he looks. Sergeant Melik is actually a very fine and sensitive man.'

'But without Inspector Süleyman's nice arse.'

'Nar!'

The transsexual laughed. In spite of her recent ordeal, she had quickly reverted to her usual irreverent self. 'Well, what do you want me to say, Sergeant?' she said. 'I speak as I find. I go along with what I see and I see Melik as a maganda and find him obnoxious. I think that you can do better, but what do I know? I'm a woman with a penis, so I'm not exactly an expert on marriage.'

'Nar, did you recognise any of the other masked individuals, either by sight or sound, who took over the Pera Palas last night?' Ayşe said, trying to return Nar to her statement.

'Er . . . no . . . Don't think so.'

'And when you told Lale Aktar who you were in the Pera Palas toilets, did you get any inkling at all that she might be working with the gunmen?'

'Like?'

'I don't know,' Ayşe said. 'Did you pick up any hostility when you told her who you were?'

'She was a bit pissed off when I first went into the toilets with her,' Nar said. 'But then, once I'd told her what I was going to do, I'd say her attitude towards me softened. I suppose she was duping me, wasn't she?'

'Yes. But then that's nothing to feel bad about, Nar,' Ayşe said. 'Mrs Aktar duped almost everybody. The Special Forces officer who replaced you is dead because of her.'

The rest of the interview took another hour. Then Nar left to go back to her transsexual sisters and no doubt eventually a night on the prowl for men who enjoyed the slightly outré side of life. She had to make up for the previous night's complete lack of action and money.

Alone, Ayşe Farsakoğlu considered what Nar had said about İzzet Melik. There had been a time when she'd seen him in the same way that Nar did. Every time he'd come near her, she'd cringed. But as well as changing considerably over the years, the more she'd learned about İzzet – like his love of all things Italian – the more she'd come to like him. He was, in addition, a gentle and considerate lover. It was true that he did not make her flesh catch fire with desire. But then she wasn't exactly a young, flawless nubile herself any more. And besides, flaming desire wasn't always a good thing. She'd had that and it had only ever brought her pain.

She hadn't spoken to İzzet since they'd both left the Pera Palas just after 8 a.m. Now it was midday and he'd probably be in bed. And anyway she didn't want to call him, not until he'd calmed down somewhat. He had, after all, read her very accurately the previous evening. Seeing Süleyman in a tuxedo had been her real motive all along. But that didn't mean that she wanted to be with him. She certainly didn't want to be his wife. But would İzzet understand that?

In order to make herself feel a little better, Ayşe rang their wedding venue, the Emperor Alexis Hotel, and asked to speak to the manager, Fevzi Bey. She asked him how preparations for her upcoming wedding were coming along. Fevzi Bey paused for quite a long time before he told her that İzzet Bey had called only just two hours before to cancel the whole event.

'Haluk Mert was a ghastly little nouveau riche who cheated Yiannis out of what still remained of his old Phanar money back in the early nineteen nineties,' Muhammed Ersoy said. 'As a friend and sometime lover, I helped Yiannis start Fener Maritime Sigorta just prior to the deaths of my brother and my dear Avram.'

'You killed them.'

He merely smiled at Süleyman and then continued.

'When I first learned that the old Pera Palas Hotel was going to be renovated I wondered how I might have some fun there. One gets so bored in prison!' He looked at Süleyman again. 'I played in the Pera Palas as a child, you see, as I think you did, didn't you, young Süleyman?'

The whole 'young Süleyman' thing was beginning to *really* grate now, but Ardıç and İkmen as well as Mehmet Süleyman himself knew that there was no point in asking Ersoy to stop.

'Yes,' Süleyman answered shortly.

'My father used to bring me along when he met with Jews in the bar – for business – and my nanny would always complain that when I got home my hair smelt of cigars. Happy days.'

'So why try and trash the place?' İkmen asked. All the 'old Ottoman' nostalgia stuff made him want to heave.

Ersoy shrugged. 'Why not? It isn't the same Pera Palas today as it was when I was a child. But if you really want to blame anyone for the damage to the Pera Palas you'd have to point the finger at Burak Fisekçi.'

'Dr Krikor Sarkissian's assistant?'

'I met him with the lovely – here I'm being ironic – Aysel Ökte one day at the beginning of two thousand and nine,' he said. 'Such a nice man.'

'He's dead,' İkmen said baldly.

'Is he?' Muhammed Ersoy furrowed his brow for a moment and then said, 'Oh, well. It was Burak who told me that Dr Krikor was planning some sort of fund-raiser in the Pera Palas as soon as the hotel reopened. He told me that the great and the good from all over the city were going to be invited and it just struck me how similar it was going to be to that event you came to at my palace, Inspector İkmen, when I presented my golden samovar to Krikor. I decided then and there that I'd really like to see you with that samovar again. But I had a problem because it was in Russia by that time.'

'We know that Yiannis Istefanopoulos bought it,' Ardıç said.

'Yes, I asked him to do that,' Ersoy said. 'At the time I wasn't sure how I was going to make my plan to have fun in the Pera Palas work but I promised Yiannis that I'd have Mert killed somehow if he got the samovar for me.'

'So you could "see me with the samovar"? Why?' İkmen asked.

'The money shot of course!' Ersoy said. 'My samovar was so much a part of the whole adventure last time we met, Inspector, it had to be present too. You'd say who you thought had killed that silly boy Söner and hopefully get it wrong. But whether you got it wrong or not, Nurettin would kill you – he'd shoot you while you held the samovar. And in Agatha Christie's old room too! A murder to be savoured! And Nurettin would have killed you too, young Süleyman, as well as Avram's uncle – he never liked me – the Sarkissians and Mrs Aktar.'

'Mrs Aktar? I thought she was on your side.'

'She is.'

'She thinks she's in love with you,' Süleyman said.

'Does she?' Ersoy shook his head and laughed. 'Silly girl! Pretty in a peasanty sort of a way, I suppose, and useful of course. But there was never any future in our relationship, was there?'

'I don't suppose you told her that,' İkmen said.

'I imagine you wish you'd let me die all those years ago when you had the chance,' Ersoy said.

İkmen didn't respond.

Ersoy laughed again. 'I may be many things, but I'm not stupid,' he said. 'Lale wanted to please me and so I let her. As a crime fiction writer she fitted in very well with my design for the evening. A mystery writer in the midst of a real-life murder! A Shakespearean play within a play featuring Ottoman brothers, Armenian lovers and even an Italian. Remember that when the mother of my little brother heard he might be dead she committed suicide in Italy? Just like the mother of the "young prince". It's the details that mean so much, isn't it? But Lale? What can one say? She was greedy for my cock, the little tart. Maybe she'll learn something from the experience. Good Muslim girls don't put out.'

'You really are a classic psychopath, aren't you, Ersoy?' Süleyman said.

'And you really are a man who was once married to a psychiatrist,' Ersoy replied. 'You just can't make your marriages last, can you?'

'Stick to the point, Ersoy,' Ardıç said coldly.

'I am sticking to the point. Everything is about greed,' Ersoy said. 'Love, marriage, consumerism, work, play, everything. Everyone who was part of my plan was brought into it via greed. Not my fault, theirs. It was marvellous. You know, even in my wildest imaginings I never dreamed that there were so many people out in the world just like me. Lale wanted me – greed; Yiannis wanted Haluk Mert dead – greed; Burak wanted to kill that awful boy who had forced Ceyda Ümit to have sex with him—'

'How did he know about that?' İkmen asked.

Ersoy shrugged. 'How should I know? Maybe she told him. She and her actor boyfriend were greedy for success. That dried-up old maid Aysel Ökte was greedy for a life of crime and adventure which she achieved using the pretext of being oh so worried about prisoners. I gave her her moment just like I gave Raşit Demir the example of perfect psychopathic behaviour he had always wanted to write a paper about.'

Ardıç looked down at the list of names that Ersoy had given him again and said, 'So what about Mr Akdeniz?'

'Nurettin, my leading man, I met in Silivri,' he said. 'I left it up to him to pick his crew.'

'So you don't know who he engaged?'

'I was just the money,' Ersoy said. 'They would each get ten thousand lire for taking part and Nurettin would get to keep the samovar. I think Raşit Demir coveted it but I never liked him so that wasn't going to happen. I told Nurettin specifically to employ only scum. The dispossessed, the mindlessly violent, that avaricious day concierge at the hotel, religious fanatics. They're expendable and they don't cost too much. They'll also do as they're told and the pious ones will happily die for the privilege of killing those who like a drink.'

'So you had no contact with the Bowstrings acting troupe?'

'Beyond telling Burak to get them to change their silly original name – so left wing – and making a few little tweaks, again via Burak, to their plot, no.' Then he leaned forward and said to Süleyman, 'Did you like all the Ottoman characters? The way the plot revolved around two brothers of good family? Did you like the name Bowstrings? I put them all in, you know, just for you.'

'Did you?'

'Yes.' He puckered his lips up and blew a very ostentatious kiss. 'But then again, no, I actually did it for my own amusement.'

Çetin İkmen had been thinking. 'But what about Dr Demir, Mr Istefanopoulos and Miss Ökte? Why pretend to shoot them? What was the point?'

'They all wanted to join in,' Ersoy said.

'They wanted to join your group of masked gunmen?'

'Yes.'

'But what about when it was all over? People had seen them die. How were they ever going to . . .' And then he stopped and looked into Muhammed Ersoy's eyes which were, as ever, smiling. A thought so terrible had crawled into his head he couldn't give voice to it.

'What people?' Ersoy said.

'What . . .'

'What people?' he repeated. 'Honestly, Çetin, you don't think I'd have been able to get any of these people on board if I'd given them the slightest notion that any of you would survive, do you?'

'What, you mean the ordinary guests and . . .'

'Oh, when I say all of you, I mean all of you,' Ersoy said. 'Even that little girl Burak Fisekçi was so keen on. I would have had Nurettin shoot her and Burak too if he raised any sort of objection. Not that he knew that. He thought I was going to give him money so that he could run away with her. Ridiculous. But it is a shame it didn't happen the way I had ideally envisaged. But then I was always prepared for the fact that it might not. I don't actually mind either way.'

And everyone in that room knew that he meant every word.

Chapter 27

Ceyda never wanted to leave Alp's side again. She clung to him so hard her knuckles were white. Her mother brought tea and cakes and asked Ayşe Farsakoğlu if she'd like an ashtray. Ayşe said that she would. It wasn't going to be easy interviewing Ceyda Ümit and Alp İlhan, they'd been through such a lot. And Ayşe had her own feelings to deal with too. İzzet had called off their wedding and she was mentally in fragments.

Luckily Ceyda opened the proceedings with, 'Burak Bey wanted to kidnap me.' Her eyes teared up. She said, 'I trusted him! I told Burak Bey things I didn't feel I could tell anyone else.'

Ayşe had already been told by İkmen that Burak Fisekçi had killed Söner Erkan and why.

'You should have come to me,' Alp said to her. 'Why did you tell Burak Bey about what you'd done with Söner?'

'He'd always been like the kindest uncle one could imagine to me,' Ceyda said. 'I could tell him anything. And I had to tell someone or I would have gone mad!'

'If you'd told me what Söner had done to you I would have dealt with him. If I'd known he was threatening you using me and my career, I would have told him to go to hell and take his parents' money with him.'

It was nice to see how much in love they were. A lot of younger, educated men like Alp didn't see women as objects or insist on virginity so much any more, which Ayşe felt had to be a good thing. But it also made her want to weep. İzzet, for all his gentleness, couldn't even forgive her a crime of the mind. But then maybe a crime of the mind was more insidious. And although she didn't think about Mehmet Süleyman all the time, she thought about him every day. She looked at him whenever she could and there were fantasies too. There were, and always had been, a lot of fantasies.

'You say, Ceyda, that Burak Fisekçi wanted to kidnap you,' Ayşe said.

'Yes.' The girl swallowed hard. 'I didn't know until all the shooting started.'

'When the Special Forces officers broke into the hotel?'

'One of the gunmen had made me take off my clothes and so I was just in my underwear,' she said. 'Burak Bey and I were tied together by our hands. But then he managed to get free. My hands were free too but I didn't know what to do. Then when the shooting started I knew I had to get away. I pulled the wire they'd tied my ankles together with off and then suddenly there was Burak Bey.'

'He came to—'

'Rescue me, yes,' she said. 'We ran upstairs. I didn't know why at the time, I just held on to Burak Bey's hands as hard as I could but then we met Inspector İkmen.'

Ayşe, writing in her notebook, said, 'And what happened then, Ceyda?'

The girl put a hand up to her head and she said, 'Then he just threw the inspector over that banister and into that hole in the middle of the hotel.'

'The void above the Kubbeli Saloon?'

'I guess.' She looked at Alp and he nodded at her. 'I couldn't believe that he did that. I didn't understand why.'

'Do you know why now, Ceyda?' Ayşe asked.

The girl shook her head as if she still couldn't quite believe what had happened and then she said, 'He was with them, the gunmen.'

'Why was he with them?' Ayşe knew but she had to get this from Ceyda.

'Because he wanted to kill Söner. He thought he was doing it for me. That I'd be pleased in some way. I was just horrified.' She shook her head again. 'And then he wanted to take me away. Said that we were meant to be together and he tried to kiss me. It was horrible.'

Ceyda had been Burak Fisekçi's prize, his reward for helping Muhammed Ersoy put his terrible plan into operation – but only in Burak's head. From what İkmen had told Ayşe, it seemed that Ersoy's gunmen had been given orders to kill all the hostages, including Ceyda. Had Burak Fisekçi tried to save her, he would almost certainly have been killed too.

'It was terrible when the Special Forces officer killed Burak Bey.' Ceyda's eyes teared up again. 'I will never get it out of my mind! But I knew that it had to be that way. That other policeman was trying to reason with him, but he just wouldn't let me go. He put a knife to my neck.' Alp drew her close and kissed her hair. 'You know, I think he wanted us to be together so much he was prepared to kill me!'

Fanaticism was like that. Mehmet Süleyman had, apparently, tried to reason with Burak Fisekçi, but he had failed. Once, ten years before, he had failed to reason with Muhammed Ersoy too. Ayşe remembered it well. When she'd heard the shot that had wounded Ersoy, she imagined that it was Süleyman and that he had been killed. She'd almost died of horror.

Ceyda Ümit brought her back to the present. 'Is it true, Sergeant,' she asked, 'that a criminal in prison was behind what happened last night?'

'Yes,' Ayşe said. 'It's true.'

'But how can that be?' Ceyda said. 'Prisoners are

surely stopped from doing anything much because they're in prison. Aren't they?'

'Most of the time, yes,' Ayşe said. 'But Ceyda, this is a very particular prisoner. He's very clever and he has access to a lot of money. Put those two together and a lot of things that are normally impossible become possible.'

She remembered Muhammed's cousin, Kemal. She'd met him once out at Silivri. She'd just been leaving while he was arriving to see her 'best love'. They'd had sex, she and Muhammed Ersoy. The guards had given them a room with a clean bed in it and then they'd dirtied everything. He liked to perform anal sex on her and she had no objection. She would have let him kill her and eat her flesh if that was what he had wanted. The heat that came off him was so intense – it was such a contrast to her husband, Faruk. When she spoke to Çetin İkmen and Mehmet Süleyman, it was in a very matter-of-fact way.

'I started going to Silivri Prison with Aysel Ökte,' Lale said. 'She knows – knew Krikor Sarkissian.'

'Who is a friend to your husband, Faruk Aktar?'

'Yes.'

'Why didn't you go and visit your own father in, where is it, Kayseri jail?' İkmen asked. 'If you were so interested in prison reform? If you wanted closure of some sort?'

She changed the subject immediately. 'Are you going to arrest Muhammed's cousin?' she asked.

'I take it your father is a subject that you don't want to talk about,' İkmen said. It was late, almost 5 p.m., and he still hadn't been home – he was still wearing his tuxedo, underneath which his ribs were bandaged up and hurt like hell – but he'd made the time to find out about Lale Aktar's father. 'Convicted of murder,' he said. 'Your sister. He raped her, made her beg forgiveness of him for losing her virginity and then he killed her.' He looked down at the paperwork on the table in front of him. The words on it looked a little fuzzy around the edges, he was on a lot of codeine, but he ignored this. 'We know that he made your sister beg for forgiveness because we have testimony from a witness,' İkmen continued. Then he looked up at her. 'You, Mrs Aktar.'

She put her head down. 'I wasn't there when he killed her . . .'

'And he didn't rape you at any time, according to your statement,' İkmen said. 'Mrs Aktar, I am truly puzzled as to how you could do the right thing and alert the police about your own father when you were just a child and then get involved with someone like Muhammed Ersoy. What were all those books you wrote about murder and revenge in Turkish villages if not your own rage at the helplessness of women and the injustice inherent in that? Ersoy used you, just as surely as the

346

evil men in your books use and abuse their women, just like your father.'

'He never wanted me, you know,' Lale Aktar said calmly. 'It was always Refika.' She actually looked hurt.

Süleyman said, 'Are you telling us that you wanted your father to have sex with you?'

She looked up at him sharply. 'No! Of course not! That's disgusting! But she always got all the attention because she was pretty. I was buck-toothed and fat and nobody ever wanted me. Do you know what it's like to live in a small village knowing that no one will ever want to marry you, knowing that you will never be touched?' She shook her head. 'He wanted her so badly, it made me sick! He deserved everything he got!'

'But Refika didn't,' İkmen said. 'She was innocent.'

Lale Aktar ignored him. 'And then when I did marry, it was to an old man like a eunuch.'

'Your choice. And he turned you into a literary super-star and a very beautiful woman,' Süleyman said.

She smiled at him.

İkmen, still thinking about Lale Aktar's father, said, 'So your books do not so much point out the iniquities of patriarchal village life as allow you to take revenge upon men who found you repulsive. Am I right?'

Lale Aktar didn't answer. Less calm and more animated now, she used her eyes to flirt with both İkmen and Süleyman. İkmen recognised this technique from his childhood. Girls in the Cappadocian village where his father's sister had lived with her husband had behaved like that. Çetin and his brother Halil, as city boys, had been prime targets for their shy attentions when they had gone to Cappadocia for their holidays. But that had been back in the 1960s.

'So why Ersoy?' İkmen said. Both he and Süleyman directly flouted the law on smoking in enclosed public spaces and lit cigarettes. Neither of them had slept for over twenty-four hours, it was smoke or die. 'If you wanted to have an affair, you could have had almost any man you wanted.'

'I wanted him,' she said.

'Why?'

'Because he wanted me.'

'Mr Ersoy knows how to manipulate people,' İkmen said.

'He didn't manipulate me.'

'You don't think so?'

'No.'

İkmen put the paperwork concerning Lale Aktar's father to one side and picked up the transcript of Muhammed Ersoy's first interview conducted by himself, Ardıç and Süleyman. 'Would you like me to read what Mr Ersoy said about you or do you want to read it for yourself?' he asked her.

She smiled. 'It's going to be negative,' she said,

'because you made it up yourselves. Why would I want to read it?'

'He said you were, and I quote, "greedy" and you "deserved everything you got",' İkmen said. 'He never loved you. He used you.'

'He made love to me.'

'He fucked you,' İkmen said. 'Plain and simple.'

She shrugged.

'If you had ever taken the time to actually explore Mr Ersoy's background you would know that he has only ever loved one person in his entire life,' İkmen said. 'And that is himself. Even the "great love" of his life, Avram Avedykian, was only ever just one of his romantic adventures. He wasn't faithful to him, he made him an accessory in the murder of his brother and then he killed him.'

'I know what he did.'

They both just stared at her.

'He's the most beautiful man in the world and he wanted me,' she said. 'He paid a lot of money, to guards, to other prisoners, to get time to be alone with me.'

'In order to satisfy his own sexual needs.'

'Of course,' she said. 'But he didn't want any of the other women who visited the prison. Not Aysel Ökte. He wanted me.'

İkmen ignored the reference to the prison reformer who had always been the physical epitome of the frigid spinster at home with her parents. He said, 'But tell me, Mrs Aktar, was sex with a killer, however exotic that might be, worth the deaths of eleven people plus the wounding of twenty-five more, not to mention the trauma suffered by everyone involved? This is apart from the physical damage to the Pera Palas Hotel, of course, which is not inconsiderable. Is your validation of yourself as a woman "worthy" of a very handsome and charming man worth all that?'

She didn't even hesitate. 'Yes,' she said. 'It is.'

Çetin İkmen breathed in deeply. 'Well, then I pity you, Mrs Aktar,' he said. 'Truly. You had a husband, albeit not a perfect one, a fantastic career, money, fame and beauty, and you threw it all away on a psychopath. I don't think even now you realise how evil he is.'

'Oh, I know he's evil,' she said. 'But then what am I? You know Burak Fisekçi had to get Söner Erkan somewhere private so that he could kill him. When I was given Agatha Christie's room that was just so *right*. For me. I love Agatha Christie – although all that rubbish about her ghost wandering about is just, well, rubbish. But Söner, Burak discovered, wasn't a fan and so he needed another reason to come to my room.'

'You tempted him.'

'I flattered him,' she said. 'I knew from Burak what he was and what he liked and I offered it to him. When he came to our table to do his Ottoman prince act, I made sure he knew that I was interested in him.'

'How?'

'I put my hand on his crotch under the table. I think my leg may have brushed against yours as I leaned over towards him, Inspector Süleyman. Later I told him to come to my room. He was young and wanted a fuck. It was so easy. The first time Burak stabbed him I was lying on top of him on the bed. Then he struggled and I had to hold him down while Burak finished the job. I sat on his chest with my feet either side of his shoulders. As he died I lay down in his hot blood, I felt it against my face and my breasts. It made Burak angry. He was such an ugly troll! He stabbed the boy after he died just out of spite.'

'That was how you got blood on your shoes,' Süleyman said. 'When you sat on Söner Erkan's chest.'

'I imagine so, yes,' she said. 'But it didn't bother me at all.'

'The blood on your shoes?'

'No, the fact that Burak killed that silly boy. Burak was a little nervous afterwards but I felt nothing. Just like I felt nothing when I told one of Nurettin's men about the spy who had come into our midst, the one he killed. Maybe I was a bit excited but that was only because I was doing it for my lover.'

'Ersoy.'

'You can say what you like about Muhammed but he and I are actually very similar,' she said with a smile. 'Good fucking works both ways, Inspector, and what we had was good fucking. I'd sell my soul to the Devil for that.'

'Which is exactly what you did,' İkmen said.

The man who had been the leader of Muhammed Ersoy's gunmen, Nurettin Akdeniz, died that night. As Arto Sarkissian had suspected, his spleen had been ruptured and, in spite of surgical intervention, he did not survive. Çetin İkmen heard about his death just before he was finally due to go home. And so in spite of the fact that his wife Fatma was waiting for him with food, drink and a warm bed, he had a young constable drive him back to Silivri.

Nurettin Akdeniz had been popular with his fellow prisoners when he'd been in Silivri. Convicted of the murder of a love rival twelve years before, he'd been a hard but bright man, who had commanded a lot of respect. His death was not going to be well received.

Çetin İkmen walked into Muhammed Ersoy's cell and sat down on the criminal's bed. A guard stood nervously at the door, watching as İkmen, his head pounding with tiredness, his chest aching, shook Ersoy awake. For one apparently deeply asleep he woke easily and completely. He even smiled.

İkmen came straight to the point. 'I thought you should know that Nurettin Akdeniz has died,' he said.

'Has he?' Ersoy knitted his brows for a moment and then said, 'Ah, well. Kind of you to let me know.'

'I thought you might want to review your personal security measures in light of Mr Akdeniz's death,' İkmen said.

'Why?'

'Because he was popular here. Because some people might want to take revenge on you for his death.'

He shrugged. 'You people killed Nurettin, not me.' He sat up in bed and stretched his arms. 'What time is it?'

'I have no idea,' İkmen replied. 'But what I do know, Mr Ersoy, is that your life here in Silivri will not be as comfortable as it once was from now on.'

Ersoy laughed. 'You mean you're going to give me more than one full life sentence? Chain me to the floor?' He leaned forward and sneered into İkmen's face. 'I've got a lot of money.'

'No, your cousin Kemal has,' İkmen said.

'Kemal, me, it's all the same . . .'

İkmen shifted a little on the bed and said, 'Your money was channelled to you from your cousin via Mr Yiannis Istefanopoulos's company, Fener Maritime Sigorta. Your cousin, an innocent man, will continue to put funds into that business on your behalf but they will not come to you.'

'What?'

'Mr Istefanopoulos is currently in custody for his part in your little murder mystery event,' İkmen said. 'If nothing else, he apparently colluded in the murder of Haluk Mert, and when he was apprehended he had just put down a loaded Kalashnikov rifle. I don't know, as yet, who will take over from Mr Istefanopoulos as head of Fener Maritime Sigorta, but whoever does, they will not be passing any money on to you.'

'You think?'

'I *know*,' İkmen said.

Muhammed Ersoy looked at him, laughed, but then stopped abruptly and his face fell. It was as if he had remembered something unpleasant all of a sudden, something that had just ruined his night. But then he regained his composure and said, 'Oh, well, I really should sleep now and so should you, Inspector.'

Chapter 28

Three Months Later

Ersu Bey checked and then double-checked every shining piece of cutlery on every exquisitely dressed table in the ballroom with a fanatic's eye. Although he was himself a guest at the event that was going to be held at the Pera Palas that evening, he was also the maître d' of İstanbul's most famous hotel. Perfection mattered.

Everyone who had survived the horrors of 12 December was coming, as well as the hotel directorate and the craftsmen and builders responsible for repairing the damage that Muhammed Ersoy's gunmen had done to the building. It was going to be a celebration as well as, for many, a laying of ghosts.

The hotel itself had lost a member of staff in the person of the day concierge. He had colluded with the gunmen and, far from being 10,000 lire better off, was now having an apparently very tough time in Silivri

Prison. Only the man who had delivered the golden samovar to the concierge was still unaccounted for. He had come from Yeniköy where Muhammed Ersoy's palace was located and where the then owner of the samovar Mr Yiannis Istefanopoulos had lived. But nobody knew who he was – or rather, nobody would say who he was. He had come out of the December drizzle with a golden samovar in his hands, left it for Mr Burak Fisekçi and then vanished.

Ersu Bey went down into the kitchens and asked his staff to line up so that he could inspect them – like soldiers. Military habits died hard. Men like him had always been and always would be there to make sure that things ran smoothly – even if, these days, he did occasionally have the odd alcoholic drink with a woman who was actually a man.

The guests could have absolutely anything they wanted from the bar and so Nar Sözen had champagne. Dressed from head to foot in light gold silk, she found that champagne really complemented her outfit. It was odd and not altogether comfortable being back in the Pera Palas, even if she did sometimes see Ersu Bey from time to time. But then Nar was not alone in feeling apprehensive. All the guests were drinking but conversation was muted and, so far, the sound of laughter was rare. Across the other side of the bar, she saw Ayşe

Farsakoğlu standing on her own, nursing a glass of red wine. Nar strutted over to her in her latest pair of fake Jimmy Choos.

Ayşe Farsakoğlu smiled. 'Hello, Nar.'

'Sergeant.' Nar snapped a military salute and just for a moment she looked like Semih Sözen, the man she had once been. She moved in closer. 'How are you?'

'I'm fine.' She smiled.

She wasn't. She was supposed to be a married woman now and, rumour had it, there was another sadness in Ayşe's life too. Nar, unconstrained by society's usual niceties – namely tact – had to ask. 'Is it true about İkmen?' she said. 'Is he—'

'Nar, whatever you may have heard about Inspector İkmen will be confirmed or denied by him,' Ayşe said. 'I'm not saying a word.'

'Oh.'

The sergeant looked pale but when Inspector Süleyman came into the bar, Nar noticed that she coloured up just a little. Could it be that the rumours about the two of them were true? Had Sergeant Melik really stopped his marriage to Ayşe Farsakoğlu because she was still in love with Süleyman? Ah, well, if that was true, it had to be for the best, Nar thought.

Outside the bar, in the warm early spring air, Çetin İkmen stood with Krikor and Arto Sarkissian. Since the events of 12 December, Krikor had started smoking again – after an almost ten-year hiatus. He wasn't happy about it but İkmen at least was grateful for the company.

Arto, who most definitely didn't approve, said to İkmen, 'How's the blood pressure?'

'Back to normal,' İkmen said.

'I do hope that you're not lying to me, Çetin,' Arto said.

'Oh, do give it a rest, Arto!' his brother said. 'Çetin told you he's OK, so he's OK. Leave him alone!'

When Hovsep Pars had died three days after the Pera Palas incident, Krikor had taken his passing harder than anyone else. With no relatives left to mourn for him, the old man's funeral had been a small affair; it had been attended by the Sarkissians, a few disparate members of the Armenian community, Çetin İkmen and Mehmet Süleyman. Krikor felt that it had been a sorry end to a life that had had far more than its fair share of tragedy. And then, on top of that, Krikor had discovered that his clinic was the sole beneficiary of Hovsep's will. Such generosity had first reduced Krikor to tears and then into a breakdown. In spite of a short holiday with Caroun to Morocco, he was still far from feeling like himself. Now he just snapped, whenever, wherever.

Arto took a moment to compose himself after his brother's outburst and then he said to İkmen, 'Are you going to tell people tonight, Çetin, about—'

'No.' İkmen shook his head. 'Tonight is about all of us, not just me. We survived.'

'In a world where wealth can enable killers to reach outside jails to kill again and again?' Krikor said bitterly. 'Should we be grateful for that?' He stubbed his cigarette out on the ground and then lit up another.

Çetin İkmen drank his beer, smoked and kept his counsel. Quite how Krikor was going to deal with this evening, he didn't know. Even with Caroun at his side, he was still really fragile.

'Is Sergeant Melik coming this evening?' Arto asked after a pause.

'Sadly not,' İkmen said. 'He . . . had to go to İzmir to see his family . . .'

'Is it true that he's considering transferring back to his home city?'

'He's considering it, yes,' İkmen said. But he knew that wasn't strictly true. İzzet had already made his decision. After 12 December, he had first cancelled his wedding to Ayşe Farsakoğlu and then requested a transfer back to İzmir. At first Mehmet Süleyman had been loath to accede to such a request from a good officer like İzzet. That was until İkmen had explained to him just why the Melik/Farsakoğlu wedding had been cancelled. They'd talked long and drunkenly into one dark night back in early January about it, with Süleyman insisting that he needed to speak to İzzet man to man.

He didn't have any designs on Ayşe Farsakoğlu and had not encouraged her fixation upon him in any way. This was not strictly true and İkmen knew it. But it had still taken a lot of time and patience to convince Süleyman to keep his mouth shut. The damage, albeit to a large extent just in İzzet's head, had already been done. Now it was better that he went back to İzmir.

'Have you had a look at tonight's menu?' Arto said. There was nothing more to be said about İzzet Melik and Ayşe Farsakoğlu. None of them could do anything about that situation now.

'I know two things about it,' Çetin İkmen said. 'Firstly, it is completely different from the menu we had on my birthday. And, gentlemen, didn't I always tell you that the twelfth of December was an ill-starred date?'

Neither of the Sarkissian brothers reacted.

'Secondly,' İkmen said, 'in honour of the late great Agatha Christie, for dessert we are to have a typically English cream tea with scones, jam and cream. I expect it will be a very smart and fashionable version of the cream tea but . . .' He frowned. 'You know, from what I've read about her, Agatha Christie was rather a nice woman. She was a lifelong non-drinker and non-smoker, which is a little dull in my opinion, but she was ill used by her first husband and had something of a breakdown in the nineteen twenties.'

'When she disappeared,' Arto said.

'Yes. The maître d' Ersu Bey was telling me earlier that some people still believe that the answer to Agatha's mysterious disappearance lies somewhere secreted in room four eleven.'

'What, even after the refit?' Krikor shrugged. 'Unlikely. Years ago they had some woman who claimed to speak with the dead go into that room and hold a séance, but it was all nonsense. Anyway, Agatha Christie's dead now and so what does it matter?'

Çetin İkmen found the new, acerbic Krikor Sarkissian hard to take sometimes and so he distracted himself by looking down over the rooftops of Şişane towards the Golden Horn. It was almost the middle of March and the city was beginning to crawl out of its winter coat of fog, smoke and mud. There was even a slight floral smell on the air which hinted at spring and yet another new start for İstanbul.

'But Krikor,' İkmen said, 'that room is a mysterious place. Somehow, at some point, a golden samovar was secreted in there but I didn't see it.'

'Those gunmen took it in and just put it in a cupboard,' Krikor said.

'I know that.' İkmen laughed. 'But I like the mystery bit of it all too, even if it is just a myth.'

'Well, you're a witch's child and so you would,' Arto Sarkissian said.

* * *

'Will Lale Aktar ever get out of prison, Inspector?' Ceyda Ümit asked Mehmet Süleyman. They were seated together at a table that also included Ceyda's boyfriend Alp, Deniz who had played the American Sarah in the murder mystery performance, Commissioner Ardıç, and one of the original guests, a lady called Fatima.

'She may do but she'll be old,' Süleyman replied. 'She's shown no remorse, Miss Ümit. Judges don't like that.'

'Doesn't she care about her husband? Her family? Her career?'

'Apparently not,' he said.

'I heard that her books are selling more quickly than ever,' Alp said.

'That,' Süleyman replied, 'is sadly the nature of fame, or should I say infamy. Indirectly the offender is rewarded.' Then he looked at his watch for what Ardıç noted was about the fifth time since they'd all sat down to eat.

'Do you have to be somewhere, Inspector?' he asked.

'No, sir.' Süleyman smiled.

Ardıç looked at him from underneath untidy, craggy brows and then pointed his knife at his plate and said, 'This sea bass is excellent. Not an easy fish to get right, sea bass.'

'No.'

They all carried on eating in silence. Music, Chopin,

played gently in the background and there was of course the sound of people talking at other tables which was occasionally punctuated by laughter. This came mainly from Special Forces Commander İpek, for whom the 12 December operation had been just one more job. In the past he and his men had stared down al Qaeda and the PKK, as well as several of İstanbul's more punitive criminal gangs. He'd moved on.

The waiting staff came and cleared away the plates from the fish course and Süleyman excused himself from the table. Ardıç, shaking his head, said nothing but he was annoyed that Süleyman seemed to have better things to do. Then he noticed that İkmen was leaving his table too and he reasoned that they were probably going outside to smoke.

Plates cleared, Ardıç discreetly loosened the cummerbund round his middle and looked at the menu to see what the meat course was going to be. Beef. That was good. He wasn't as partial to beef as he was to lamb or veal but it would do; besides, the wines that had been chosen to accompany each course were making whatever was presented go down very well indeed. They were truly outstanding.

'Ladies and gentlemen, may I please have your attention?'

That was, if Ardıç was not mistaken, Süleyman's voice yelling across the ballroom. He looked up and saw Süleyman standing by the entrance from the Kubbeli Saloon into the ballroom with İkmen and another, younger man he vaguely recognised.

'Ladies and gentlemen, please!'

The talking stopped and everyone looked in his direction.

'Ladies and gentlemen, we have a guest,' Süleyman continued. 'Someone who was not among our number when we all suffered here in this hotel on the twelfth of December. But we welcome him anyway. His name is Mr Kemal Aslanlı.'

He stood aside so that everyone could see a shy-looking man in his mid-thirties carrying a large sports bag. Muhammed Ersoy's cousin. Nobody said a word. But then nobody, including Ardıç, could believe what they were seeing. Although cleared of any involvement in Ersoy's plan to murder as many people as he could in the Pera Palas Hotel three months before, just having a member of the family in the same room was causing some people discomfort. How could İkmen and Süleyman be so stupid?

'Good evening,' Kemal Aslanlı said.

Nobody responded.

But he persisted in his slightly rough, countrified voice. 'I've got something here,' he said and put the sports bag down on to the floor and shoved both hands into it.

Several people gasped. But others looked at the smiles on the faces of İkmen and Süleyman and took them as signals that everything that was happening was really OK. Kemal Aslanlı took something large covered in a white cloth out of the bag and walked over towards the table where the Sarkissians were seated. He looked at Krikor.

'Sir, my family want you to have this,' he said. 'For your clinic. It is our way of telling you how much we are not like my cousin Muhammed. You will want to sell it to raise funds and that is fine with us.'

He pulled the white cloth off to reveal the fabulous Ersoy golden samovar.

Not everyone got drunk but Nar Sözen didn't let that hold her back. Mixing champagne with rakı gave her, she found, the courage to dance with an assortment of men who really didn't want to dance at all – especially not with her. But she was big enough not to be easily pushed away and one of her victims was even Mehmet Süleyman. Eventually, however, even Nar was too tired to go on and so she sat down next to Çetin İkmen in the bar.

Alone, he was quiet and thoughtful. Krikor Sarkissian had taken the presentation of the samovar by Kemal Aslanlı well, but it had been a very emotional evening for all of them and he was tired. In reality he probably didn't need someone like Nar swaying drunkenly about on the seat next to his but he smiled at her anyway and said, 'Have you had a good evening?'

'A celebration of survival and courage!' Nar said, quoting what the event had been billed as on her invitation. Then she leaned in closer still to İkmen and said, 'You know, you should get that old cousin of yours out, that girl over in Beyazıt.'

She meant Samsun.

'She's bereaved,' İkmen said. 'But, yes, you're right.'

'Out with people of her own kind,' Nar said. 'Not on the game at her time of life or—'

'No.'

'So do it, İkmen,' she said. 'Get Samsun over here to Beyoğlu and I'll show her a good time. You know I will!'

He looked up into Nar's eyes which were surrounded by smudged mascara and said, 'Yes. You're a good girl.'

'I am!' Nar took a swig from her glass of champagne and then she lowered her voice and said, 'Inspector, is it true that you're going to retire?'

İkmen thought for a moment and then looked around to check that nobody he knew well was listening.

'Because if you do retire, this city will be in trouble,' Nar said. 'I mean, you are this city, aren't you, İkmen? You and İstanbul, İstanbul and you, you're like . . .'

'Nar . . .' She was right, in a way, and he began to

feel his eyes sting a little with tears as he thought about it.

'Yes?'

Now it was İkmen's turn to lower his voice. 'Tell no one, but yes, I am retiring,' he said. 'Although not until the end of this year. I will be sixty.'

Nar, who hadn't really believed the rumour when she'd first heard it, just sat with her mouth open. Çetin İkmen himself wondered, not for the first time, and quite apart from the issue of his age, why he was doing it.

Epilogue

Muhammed Ersoy shared the champagne his guest had brought him with the guest and with the guard who had been bribed to allow this meeting to take place. Çetin İkmen, Mehmet Süleyman and that fat man Ardıç could rant on forevermore about the effective punishment of the rich but Muhammed had always found ways around the system and he always would.

The man in front of him, Adnan someone or other, raised his glass and said, 'On behalf of my employer, Mr Ersoy, to you.'

'Thank you.' Muhammed Ersoy batted his eyelids slightly flirtatiously and said, 'And how is Kostas? Has he had any trouble with the police?'

'In relation to Fener Maritime Sigorta? No,' Adnan said.

'Good.'

'But it is only one of Mr Istefanopoulos's companies.'

'Yes. The one you work for is . . .'

'Antalya Holdings. Import, export.'

'Of course.' Ersoy looked at the guard and then clicked his fingers at him to signal that he should put his champagne glass down and go.

The guard went.

Muhammed Ersoy leaned in towards the man sitting opposite him and said, 'I trust that Kostas is . . .'

'Grateful that he was given the opportunity to take over his brother's company, yes,' Adnan said. 'Also very pleased that your cousin Mr Aslanlı is continuing to support the business.'

'Well, why should he not?' Muhammed Ersoy said. 'Kostas is not his brother Yiannis, is he?'

'No, sir. Mr Kostas is looking forward to working in your mutual interests enormously.'

'Please tell him that I am too.'

They both drank from their glasses again and then, at around one in the morning, Adnan left.

Later as he lay back down on his really rather comfortable bed after his nice hot shower, Muhammed Ersoy pondered on how easy it had been for Kostas Istefanopoulos to take the samovar from his brother's house in Yeniköy and bring it to the Pera Palas Hotel on the night of 12 December. He'd made himself look shabby, he was from out of town anyway, and when he'd returned to Yeniköy that night he had picked up his car and then driven all the way back to his home town of Antalya. Well, he hadn't wanted to be anywhere near İstanbul when either Nurettin shot his brother or Yiannis got arrested, did he?

Insurance. Not for nothing had Muhammed Ersoy set Yiannis Istefanopoulos up in that business. It was something he knew a lot about.

When he closed his eyes and went to sleep, Muhammed Ersoy did so in a cocoon of complete contentment.

Glossary

Akbil – İstanbul city travel pass

Arabesk – popular Turkish music heavily influenced by Arab forms

Bayram – religious festival. Refers in this context to Kurban Bayram, otherwise known as the Feast of the Sacrifice

Bey – 'Mr' as in 'Çetin Bey'. This is an Ottoman form used before Turks adopted surnames in 1923 – used only with the first name

Efendi – an Ottoman title equivalent to prince or noble

Hamam – Turkish bath

Hanım – 'Mrs' or 'Miss', female version of 'Bey'

Hanımefendi – female equivalent of 'Efendi'

Klezmer – Askenazi Jewish dance band

Lycée – high school

Samovar – metal water heater, usually for tea

Acknowledgements

It would not have been possible for me to write this book without the wonderful assistance provided to me by the staff and management of the fabulous Pera Palas Hotel, İstanbul. Nothing was too much trouble and all my questions were answered and my requests acceded to. Thanks go particularly to Pinar Timer, Esin Sungur and Asli Bilgin. Other heroes and heroines who helped me so much with this book are Pat Yale, Saffet Emre Tonguc, Elsie and Lutfu Alan, Ruth Lockwood, Jeyda Yelkalan, Earl Starkey, Trici Venola, Julia, Alp and everyone who visited me at the Pera Palas. Thanks are also due to my agent, Juliet Burton and to my editor at Headline, Martin Fletcher who was, and remains, so enthusiastic about this series

Now you can buy any of these other **Barbara Nadel** titles
from your bookshop or *direct from the publisher*.